D1572150

PRAISE FOR *THE LIONESS OF LEIDEN*

"*The Lioness of Leiden* is more than just historical fiction; it is filled with suspense, intrigue, and even steamy romance. The Nazi-occupied Netherlands is swarming with killers, collaborators, and Dutch resisters in Robert Loewen's action-packed page-turner. Brave men and braver women risk their lives in a struggle for freedom and survival. I couldn't put it down."

—RICK REIFF, Pulitzer Prize-winning journalist

"Robert Loewen's *The Lioness of Leiden* is a fast-paced and often harrowing story of a group of young people risking all in the Dutch resistance. More than simply a gripping tale, it will serve as a stark reminder of the meaning of genuine courage—and that there are timeless principles worth dying for. What might be most amazing is that it is based on stories the author heard from his own mother-in-law—the inspiration for the book's central character."

—HARRY STEIN, originator of Ethics, the much-loved column in *Esquire*; author of *The Girl Watchers Club;* and co-author of *Eichmann in My Hands*

"'Hetty Steenhuis had never smuggled hand grenades before.' Inspired by actual events and real people, Robert Loewen hooks readers from the first page and delivers a plot filled with so many twists and turns, it's a nail-biter. This engaging story shows women's strength, bravery, hardships, sorrows, and extraordinary friendships. A must read!"

—LYDIE DENIER, French American actor, producer, and director

A NOVEL

The

LIONESS
of LEIDEN

ROBERT LOEWEN

GREENLEAF
BOOK GROUP PRESS

Published by Greenleaf Book Group Press
Austin, Texas
www.gbgpress.com

Distributed by Greenleaf Book Group

For ordering information or special discounts for bulk purchases, please contact Greenleaf Book Group at PO Box 91869, Austin, TX 78709, 512.891.6100.

Design and composition by Greenleaf Book Group
Cover design by Greenleaf Book Group
Cover Images: ©iStockphoto/George Marks,
©Shutterstock/remik44992, ©Shutterstock/Ivan Cholakov,
©Shutterstock/Massonstock, ©Shutterstock/Everett Collection, and
©Shutterstock/Hein Nouwens

Publisher's Cataloging-in-Publication data is available.

Print ISBN: 979-8-88645-022-4

eBook ISBN: 979-8-88645-023-1

To offset the number of trees consumed in the printing of our books, Greenleaf donates a portion of the proceeds from each printing to the Arbor Day Foundation. Greenleaf Book Group has replaced over 50,000 trees since 2007.

Printed in the United States of America on acid-free paper
23 24 25 26 27 28   10 9 8 7 6 5 4 3 2 1
First Edition

To my wife and best friend, Jacinta,
who loved her mother.

PROLOGUE

HETTY STEENHUIS HAD NEVER SMUGGLED hand grenades before.

She scanned the nine passengers standing on the platform in the cavernous station for any hint that a Nazi operative might be among them. They appeared to be ordinary Dutch people, nervous and distracted after four years of German occupation, waiting innocently for Tram No. 1 to Delft. It was October, a cold month in the Netherlands, and her fellow passengers raised their collars against the morning chill as a brisk wind whipped through The Hague from the North Sea. Hetty took in a deep breath of the icy air to help her stay awake. She had stayed up most of the night practicing lifting her heavy suitcase; it had to appear natural, so as not to give away its explosive contents.

Despite her fatigue, Hetty was committed to her mission. She was about to board the tram when two German soldiers whisked by, armed with submachine guns. Hetty stopped breathing and let the soldiers pass. It took every bit of fortitude in her ninety-seven-pound frame to appear unfazed by their presence. If she collapsed or gasped from lack of air, then all eyes would be on her. She had come too far to lose everything now.

By October 1944 the Allied armies had advanced from their Normandy beachhead, offering hope of rescue to the war-weary Dutch, but instead of giving up, the Germans had only worked harder to catch people like her. Hetty exhaled slowly when the soldiers walked by without a second glance, smoking their cigarettes as they patrolled the tram's loading area. When the other passengers began to stir, Hetty picked up her suitcase and moved closer to the boarding point to assure a good seat.

CHAPTER 1

KARL DEBOER STOOD NEXT TO the tracks at Rotterdam terminal, waiting anxiously for the train to arrive. His penetrating blue eyes were framed by his long, dark hair and full beard, making him appear more like a Visigoth from the fifth century than the university student that he was. Of average height, Karl had a strong build after years of making bicycles at his uncle's factory. "The train's not due for another hour," said Uncle Jef, putting a hand on his nephew's back. "Let's go inside the waiting room and relax."

"I can't relax," said Karl, pacing in circles. "The entire time we were training this week, Hetty was all I thought about. I can't believe I made such a mess of things."

Karl studied the train schedule on the wall of the terminal. It was May 10, 1940, only three weeks since he and Hetty had celebrated her twentieth birthday together.

Karl had met Hetty seven months ago at a pub near the university in Leiden, where she was having a beer with his roommate, Brecht.

Karl was smitten immediately. Feisty and confident, she was unlike any woman he'd met. But she was Brecht's girlfriend, so he tried to let the moment pass.

Thinking about the occasion now, Karl was surprised that he had been attracted less by her physical allure—though she was not lacking in that department—than by her quick wit and laughing eyes, coupled with his sense that she was not someone who could be pushed around. He knew Hetty was taken, but he saw no harm in having a three-way chat with Brecht and his girlfriend. He ordered another round of beer and tried to start a conversation.

But before he could say a word, Hetty started in. "Brecht told me you're a communist," Hetty said, smiling in that bantering style he later learned to love.

"I've been to a few of their meetings," he replied cautiously, watching her expression closely for a sign whether this had ruined his chances with her.

"Don't communists believe that 'the history of all hitherto existing society is the history of class struggles'?" she asked.

Hetty was quoting from Marx's *Manifesto*, but Karl admitted he had no idea what she was talking about.

"Ha," Brecht guffawed. "I told you she's smart, Karl."

Hetty ignored Brecht's compliment, instead zeroing in on Karl. "Don't you believe in class struggle, Mr. DeBoer?"

"I never gave it any thought," Karl replied, still flummoxed by the effect this young woman had on him. "All I know is that the communists are the only ones preparing to organize a resistance when Hitler comes."

The next thing Karl knew, Hetty invited herself to attend a meeting of the communists. He was thrilled that this fascinating young woman, who had challenged him with such grace and charm, wanted to spend more time with him. She wanted to know about the communists because the German Reich had just invaded Poland, she said, and she had no confidence that Hitler would abide by the neutrality agreement he had signed with the Netherlands.

Brecht sensed the mutual attraction between Karl and Hetty and was not happy about it—and rightfully so. By the time Karl and Hetty attended their first communist meeting, she had broken up with Brecht. Feeling the inevitable pressure of impending war to make every moment count and to live authentically, Karl and Hetty shared their first kiss after the second meeting, standing at the Leiden station while Hetty waited for her train home to The Hague.

Because Karl was most comfortable wearing work clothes—his regular attire—at his uncle's factory, he stood out at Leiden University, where most young men wore slacks and blazers. His long hair and beard were different too, but they helped him blend in when he attended local meetings of the communists. Hetty remained curiously attracted by the notion that Karl had grown up in a working-class household, even after he told her he was the heir to his uncle's lucrative bicycle factory. His kind smile, natural humility, and ready sense of humor were not, she assured him, something she usually associated with people who had money, and her parents knew a lot of them.

"Whatever is going on between you and your girlfriend," said Uncle Jef gently, bringing Karl's mind back to the train platform, "you can set things right as soon as you get back to Leiden."

Suddenly a policeman scurried urgently along the platform.

"Attack! We're under attack!" he shouted to the waiting passengers. "The Germans have attacked Holland!"

Uncle Jef stopped the policeman as he ran by.

"Are you sure?"

"I just heard it on the two-way," said the policeman, out of breath. "German paratroopers are in The Hague!"

"C'mon, Karl," said Uncle Jef, pulling his nephew by the arm. "No more drills. This is the real thing."

Karl lingered for a moment to gaze down the track. Knowing Hetty would have to wait, he heaved a sigh and ran to catch up with his uncle.

In the woods outside of Rotterdam, Karl and Uncle Jef scanned the skies for trouble. Suddenly a German fighter flew low over the trees, its machine guns blazing. Bullets exploded into the dirt inches from their shallow entrenchments as both men dove headfirst into foxholes on either side of their anti-aircraft gun.

Karl buried his face in the soft dirt, the blood pumping fast through his veins. No one had tried to kill him before. For an instant he was consumed by a sense of calm, which surprised him. Then fear grabbed him like a tiger attacking its prey. He lay frozen in place, afraid to move, when Jef jerked him to his feet, gasping for breath.

"C'mon, boy," Jef barked. "That Nazi fighter will loop back around, and we need to be ready."

The ground rumbled as a cluster of German heavy bombers flew overhead to drop their deadly payloads on the city of Rotterdam.

Breathing hard, Jef shook the dirt from his hair. "That must have been the slowest plane in the Luftwaffe."

Karl, relieved to still be alive, rinsed the dust from his mouth with water from his canteen.

His uncle took a swig from the canteen and added, "Any faster, and it would have killed us both."

Karl nodded somberly as he scanned the sky for encroaching threats. Then he crawled to their anti-aircraft weapon, an Oerlikon 20 mm cannon, where his uncle was already preparing the big gun for battle.

Karl had been nineteen, a few months before he met Hetty at Leiden, when Uncle Jef brought him to his first meeting of the air volunteers, an organization funded by local industry for the air defense of their region. Now, his training was being tested by the attacking Luftwaffe. War was far worse than he'd imagined. At least during training, he could take breaks and start over if he made a mistake. On the battlefield there was no time to catch your breath—and no second chances.

Emboldened by the enemy fire, Jef adjusted the gun's sights to prepare for the return of the low-flying fighter. "Let's see if we can kill *him* next time."

Karl turned his head toward the sky to witness another group of heavy bombers. Explosions boomed in the distance as smoke rose from the center of the city.

"Do you think anyone can rescue Rotterdam from those beasts?" he asked.

Jef shook his head gloomily, while sliding sideways on his knees to make room for his nephew to operate the weapon.

"Our army has held for four days—longer than anyone expected. But now that the Reich has sworn to destroy our cities one by one, I'm afraid the politicians will surrender. They don't have the stomach for it."

"No matter what they decide in The Hague, we can't last much longer out here." Karl pointed to the open box of ammunition that they had been using. "These will go fast." Then he tapped an unopened box of ammunition and added, "We have another box, but that's it."

"We wasted too much ammunition shooting at the heavy bombers," Jeff replied, locking the feeder belt to prepare their gun for action. "We should have known that this gun wouldn't be effective against planes flying that high."

"I wish we could reach the military command for orders," said Karl.

Jef shook his head grimly. "The two-way is dead. We're on our own. Should we leave?"

"Not yet." Karl grabbed the twin handles of the cannon to balance the muzzle on its swivel, just as they'd practiced. "That fighter will come back." Seated behind the big gun, he pointed the weapon toward the sky, searching for his target.

The German fighter suddenly reappeared, executing a slow left banking maneuver to square up into its attack path. Karl tried to control his fear as the vintage fighter came in for the kill. He gripped both handles of the cannon tightly and squeezed the trigger, but the tracers went wide when the German dipped his wing at the last minute. The maneuver spoiled the German's flight path, and it flew past them close to the ground with a deafening roar.

Hurrying to swivel the gun for the next pass, Karl touched the white-hot muzzle with the back of his hand.

"Shit," he yelled as he leapt back, grabbing his right hand. The smell of seared flesh and gunpowder filled the air.

The German plane hung in the sky as it turned its nose toward them for another run. Karl jerked the gun's muzzle toward the fighter, his injured hand on fire as he tried to keep a steady grip on his weapon. The fighter leveled off, pointing its twin guns directly at them. Then Karl pressed the trigger.

Whop. Whop. Whop.

Three rounds penetrated the plane's engine. But the German fighter kept coming, its guns ablaze, while flames leapt from its damaged motor.

Bullets pounded the dirt in front of them, stinging Karl's face with flying pebbles. He ducked involuntarily and his hands slipped from the gun. Quickly, he grabbed the twin handles of the weapon and resumed firing, hurling more hot lead into the plane's engine until the feeder belt was empty.

"Fuck." Karl slammed his fist into the dirt.

Suddenly the fighter exploded, breaking up in a fiery ball.

The smell of gunpowder hung heavy in the air when Karl released his grip on the weapon. He had never killed anyone before, but he felt nothing for the pilot who had just tried to kill him. "She did OK, right, Uncle?"

Karl admired the anti-aircraft gun as if it were his own child.

"Good enough," said Jef, whose triumphant smile turned to shame when he realized his trousers were soaked with his own urine.

"Nothing to be ashamed of," said Karl, patting his uncle on the shoulder. "I've never been so scared in my life. I would still be whimpering in the dirt if you hadn't pulled me up."

Jef looked down as he opened the last box of ammunition to reload the Oerlikon 20. "Another plane will be here any second," he said.

Still reeling from the last round of fire, Karl looked over at his uncle and said, "When our ammunition is gone, we won't stand a chance."

Jef nodded, knowing his nephew was right.

Dismayed by the inexorable procession of Luftwaffe bombers flying toward Rotterdam, Karl allowed despair to creep in as he thought of friends in the city.

"I can only imagine how terrible it must be for the workers at our factory."

Then his despair shifted to his girlfriend. Wishing he'd had time for another conversation with Hetty, Karl wondered whether the invading army had reached Leiden yet. He started to remove his sweater—the blue one with a red stripe that Hetty had knitted for him—when suddenly the shriek of another fighter made him dive into position. Karl pressed the trigger of his gun, sending tracers into the cockpit of the attacking German. He tried to wipe the dust off his face with his sleeve, but his sweater, wet from perspiration, only made it dirtier.

The attacking aircraft swerved and flew away. The noise was deafening.

"Maybe you shot the pilot," Jef shouted, trying to make himself heard as the fighter plane distanced itself from them.

"I'm just glad he left." Karl patted his weapon, taking care not to touch the hot barrel again. "We're out of ammunition."

Karl glanced at a pile of animal excrement, covered with flies, a few feet from where his face had been buried in the dirt. Back at home Karl had killed dozens of flies with a swatter, but today he was the one who struggled to survive while the carefree flies happily planted their eggs in manure, under no immediate threat. He reflected that he and the flies were, in their own way, each doing what was necessary for their species to survive.

"Let's get out of here," said Jef, glancing up at the Luftwaffe heavy bombers. "Without ammunition, we have no chance against another attack."

"What about our workers?" asked Karl, while dusting himself off.

"They'll have to fend for themselves." Jef grimaced.

"Let's go to the factory," Karl countered. "Maybe we can help."

"The last I heard before the two-way died is that the Dutch army is barely holding at the Nieuwe Maas River," said Jef, referring to the main waterway outside Rotterdam. "We can't know when the Germans will break through."

"I still think we should risk it," Karl argued. "We might be able to save some of them."

Jef stared at the expanding plume of smoke over Rotterdam. "There won't even be a factory by the time we get there."

Following his uncle's gaze toward the smoke that eclipsed the late-afternoon sun, Karl nodded as he broke down the firing mechanism on the big gun and scattered its parts in the forest. Despite his desire to save others, Karl knew Uncle Jef was right. They didn't have time. He hopped into the passenger side of Jef's truck, which they had hidden beneath some shade trees. "We got lucky," said Karl, patting the truck affection-ately. "Not a scratch on her."

Karl wrapped a rag around his burnt hand. "Home to Friesland? Is that still your plan?"

Jef nodded while he shifted gears and worked the clutch to navigate the winding dirt road that would take them to the main highway.

Karl was impressed by his uncle's choice. Both had been born in Friesland, a northern province of the Netherlands, where people spoke their own unique language. Karl was a child when they moved to Rotterdam, but Uncle Jef still had friends in Friesland who would help them. Jef had reasoned that the Germans would have their hands full administering the more populous, Dutch-speaking provinces of the Netherlands, making the north country a good place to hide.

Karl was grateful that his uncle had kept a blanket in the truck, which he quickly wrapped around himself as the outside temperature dropped rapidly with the setting sun. The landscape on either side turned to shad-ows as they sped through farm country. For now, they were safe.

"There's nothing worse than not knowing where someone you love has gone," Karl reflected, his eyes locked on the dark road ahead.

They had just entered a hilly area where clumps of trees cast shadows across the narrow highway when Uncle Jef glanced over at his nephew. "I know. It's going to be a while until you see Hetty again."

Karl nodded despondently. "The last time I saw her, we had a fight," he said, staring out the window. "She wanted me to stay with her, but I couldn't miss air volunteer training."

"You did the right thing to keep your oath to the volunteers."

"Did I?" Karl stared silently at the road ahead. "What happens when we get to Friesland? Can I send her a note from there?"

Uncle Jef shook his head. "Can you imagine the risk my friends are taking to hide us? If your note gets intercepted, all of us are done."

"Actually, I already left a note," Karl whispered.

"You what?" His uncle's voice rose in anger.

"I gave Brecht a note for Hetty in case I don't return."

"That was stupid." Uncle Jef shook his head incredulously but kept his eyes on the winding road. "You can't trust a jealous man!"

"Brecht's over that," said Karl, recalling the hours of conversation Hetty had with Brecht after they broke up. "She persisted until all three of us agreed to be friends again."

"Still, it was reckless of you to—"

Suddenly two bullets slammed through the windshield. The truck's brakes squealed, and it swerved to the left, crashing through underbrush as it left the road. Uncle Jef's blood sprayed on the windshield as the truck plunged down a steep embankment. Karl's head crashed into the windshield, knocking him out.

The German ambush team scrambled from its hiding place. They crossed the road and peered into the black void where the truck was last seen. All six soldiers leaped over the road's edge down the embankment into the dark woods, guns ready.

CHAPTER 2

Hᴇᴛᴛʏ sʜᴜᴅᴅᴇʀᴇᴅ ᴡʜᴇɴ ᴀ sǫᴜᴀᴅ of German soldiers marched past them near the university center in Leiden. "I can't get used to seeing them here, Mimi. They're like unwelcome guests at a party."

"Unwelcome guests with guns," Mimi whispered, staring warily at a German's submachine gun.

"Don't stare." Hetty tugged at her friend to accompany her to the opposite side of the street. Trying to blend in, they walked into a small café to distract themselves from the looming threat.

Before the invasion, Leiden had been a quaint medieval university town shared by students, tourists, and small businesses. When the Germans arrived two weeks ago, residents stayed home, wondering how their new overseers would treat them. But the shops had reopened on this sunny June afternoon, and people seemed eager to come outside. While the Germans kept their distance, everyone tread carefully in their menacing presence.

"They say classes will resume next week so that we can finish final exams," said Hetty listlessly as she sipped her coffee. "I don't know how I feel about it."

Hetty was known for her winning smile, which came in handy for a young woman attending Leiden University, where the other students were mostly men. But today she wasn't smiling. Her hazel eyes missed nothing as she sized up the armed German policemen outside the café.

"I'm excited for things to get back to normal," said Mimi, taking a bite of her cookie.

"How can anything be normal while the Germans are here?" Hetty asked rhetorically.

Mimi shrugged off Hetty's pessimism and admired the people walking by on the street. "Maybe the French will force the Germans out of Holland."

"We'll see," said Hetty cautiously. "I heard the war is not going well for the Allies."

"Any news about Karl?" asked Mimi as she sipped her tea.

Hetty shook her head with a frown. "Nothing."

As they were enjoying their beverages, three young men entered the café and turned adoring eyes toward Mimi, whose short, dark hair framed a perfect face with high cheekbones and green eyes that flashed when she was excited. Hetty laughed, despite her own troubles.

"Boys are like puppies around you, Mimi."

"They like you too," said Mimi, allowing a slight smile to acknowledge the attention. "I saw one of them staring at you."

Hetty shrugged, having long ago acknowledged her friend's exceptional allure. But she knew there was more to admire about Mimi than her petite beauty. For one thing, she had a gift for keeping Hetty's spirits up.

"I blew it, Mimi," said Hetty, hanging her head. "My last night with Karl was magical until I let my temper ruin it."

"You keep saying that." Mimi took her friend's hand. "What actually happened?"

"I suppose I can tell you now."

Hetty looked around at the people in the café to see if anyone was paying them any attention. Satisfied they were of no interest to the patrons, she whispered, "Karl is in the air volunteers."

"Seriously?" Mimi's interest piqued. "They're heroes."

Hetty sighed.

"I just hope it doesn't get him killed," said Hetty glumly. "I wanted him to quit. We were falling in love, and I worried about what might happen to him. I talked him into meeting my family for dinner instead of going to Rotterdam for air volunteer training with his uncle."

"It's a big step to ask your boyfriend to meet your parents," said Mimi.

"That's what I thought," said Hetty.

She reflected on the night when Karl had arrived at her family's home in The Hague. Her whole family was already in the dining room, the table elegantly set with an embroidered tablecloth, unique Delftware plates, and fresh tulips, which had become a passion in Holland even though the cup-shaped flower originated in Turkey. Hetty's mother, Henriette, showed Karl the insignia of the governor of Sulawesi on the back of her plate. Hetty smiled at the memory of her mother's pride when she explained to Karl that Hetty's grandfather had been governor of the Dutch colony in the East Indies when Henriette was a little girl.

The first course was cold eel, a family favorite. Just before the family began to eat, Hetty made her announcement. "Karl has made a special sacrifice to be here tonight. He has important business in Rotterdam, but I asked him to come here instead."

Karl had told her that his involvement in the air volunteers was a secret, so she did not mention his reason for going to Rotterdam. She then turned toward Karl, who was seated next to her.

"Thank you for giving up Rotterdam to meet my family, Karl."

Hetty clutched Karl's hand with both of hers. "It means everything."

Karl fidgeted and took a sip of water. Hetty noticed his hand was shaky as he pulled it away.

"What is it?"

Karl glanced at each of Hetty's parents, then at her brother, Jan, before settling his eyes on Hetty. "The last train to Rotterdam leaves in two hours. I told my uncle I'd be on it."

Hetty's jaw fell. *What?*

"But, I thought you were . . ."

"If I could stay, I would."

Wishing to avoid an argument, Hetty's mother redirected the conversation to subjects that were both cordial and interesting—but not controversial. Still, Hetty was furious every time Karl checked his watch. He seemed more interested in not missing his train than being with her.

Hetty's father, Willem, was unusually cordial during the dinner, which was not his nature. The fact that Willem obviously liked Karl would have made it a perfect evening for Hetty—had Karl not ruined it with his decision to go to Rotterdam. "Some dessert, Karl?" he asked politely after the plates from the main course had been cleared.

"Sorry, but my train leaves in fifteen minutes," said Karl, folding his napkin. "I should go."

While Hetty walked him to the train station a few blocks away, she clutched Karl's arm in the cold night air, snuggling her cheek against his shoulder as she was determined to make the best of a bad situation.

"Let's not fight, Karl. When will I see you again?"

"Air volunteer training is scheduled for five days," he said. "Then I'll come right back to you. I love you, Hetty."

This made Hetty smile. "I'll be in Leiden." She squeezed his arm. "Counting the days."

When they arrived at the train station, Hetty held his hand on the platform. Then she kissed him, a warm, deep kiss that made his legs buckle.

When they came up for air, she blurted: "Stay in my room with me tonight," pressing his hand against her breasts.

"Do you need this chair?"

Startled by the unexpected interruption of her thoughts, Hetty looked up at a young woman, presumably a student, standing next to one of the vacant chairs at their table.

"No, please, it's yours," Hetty told her.

She waited for the woman to leave before she resumed her story. Looking at her friend she confessed: "It was my first time, Mimi. I was determined to keep him off that train."

Mimi smiled, glancing at the men who eyed her earlier. "No man would turn that down—especially one who's in love."

"He came to my bedroom later that night . . ."

"And?"

Closing her eyes, Hetty took herself back to that moment when she was awakened by a soft whisper in her ear. Karl had climbed the gigantic wisteria vine below her second-floor bedroom and entered through the window.

"You came!" she exulted. "I thought you took the train to Rotterdam."

"You're more important," he replied with the crooked smile she liked so much.

"In that case—"

Hetty grabbed his cold cheeks between the palms of her warm hands and kissed Karl on the mouth. His lips were ice cold, but they parted sweetly to a warm interior.

"You gave up Rotterdam for me. That's all that matters," Hetty said as she unbuttoned his trousers.

Mimi's cheeks were flushed as she paid for their beverages. "Why would you regret any of that?" she demanded as she guided her friend out the door of the café. A passing pedestrian almost bumped into them on the crowded sidewalk as they glanced across the street at the ever-present German soldiers.

"That's not the part I regret. The lovemaking was so romantic, Mimi," said Hetty, taking her friend's arm as they drifted toward the side streets where the shops were still closed. "Karl told me over and over that he loved me. But early the next morning, he was packing to leave."

Hetty recalled the early light of dawn creeping into her bedroom as she nestled comfortably under a pile of quilts. When she turned to her side, she noticed Karl was already getting dressed.

"The first train to Rotterdam leaves at 6 a.m.," he announced matter-of-factly, checking his watch. "I have to leave in ten minutes, or I'll miss it."

She leveled an icy stare at him. "You're still going?"

Hetty reached into her pocket and pulled out an embroidered handkerchief. Mimi pulled her friend close as Hetty dabbed her eyes.

"I lost my temper," said Hetty, shaking her head at the memory. "I accused him of pretending to give up Rotterdam just to get me into bed, which I knew wasn't true."

"That must have hurt him," said Mimi.

"I regret it so much, Mimi," said Hetty as she gazed across the wide waterway. "Karl tried to kiss me goodbye, but I shoved him away. Five days later, the Germans invaded. I would give anything for five minutes to tell him I'm sorry for what I said—and that I love him."

"We'll keep searching together," said Mimi, putting a hand on her friend's back. "Then you can make up properly."

Hetty looked down, consumed with guilt. Mimi asked, "What about Brecht? Maybe he knows where Karl is."

Hetty shook her head as they continued walking. "I had the same idea, but Brecht is nowhere to be found." Taking Mimi's arm, she added, "I've been to their flat a dozen times since the invasion, but Brecht has disappeared."

"I'm sure he'll turn up," said Mimi. "Do you know anyone who might have a contact in Rotterdam? If someone has started a resistance, maybe a network would be forming to share that sort of information."

"I've heard of no one even rumored to be involved," said Hetty. "I wouldn't even know where to begin."

The sun disappeared behind the clouds, creating interesting shadows in the alleys. Hetty felt a sudden chill and started walking faster.

"What about your communist friends?"

"I can't find them," said Hetty. "If they are forming a resistance, they have kept the secret well."

Suddenly two German policemen appeared on the opposite side of the street. Mimi tightened her grip on Hetty's arm and changed the subject.

The Germans fixed their gaze on the two young women as Hetty and Mimi walked past them toward the shopping district.

"I don't think they overheard us," Hetty whispered, glancing back.

Mimi laughed. "They're not suspicious, just interested."

"You shouldn't make jokes about them."

"I'm not. I just know boys," Mimi smiled.

As if on cue, a young man with curly red hair bounded up to them. "Hetty. I'm glad you're safe."

Hetty hugged the man and turned to Mimi who raised a brow.

"This is Joeri. He studies law with me."

Joeri, a skinny, freckled youth with a baritone voice, shook Mimi's hand.

"Have you heard?" said Joeri with a downcast expression. "France just surrendered."

Mimi clutched Hetty's arm. "Oh no."

"More bad news," said Hetty, watching a change of the guard at a German checkpoint. "Who's going to stop Hitler now?"

"It's pretty depressing," said Joeri, shaking his head before turning toward the square. "Come with me. There's a big crowd. Maybe there will be more news about France."

As she and Mimi approached, Joeri joined some friends to their right. The crowd obstructed Hetty's view even though she stood on her tiptoes. "I've never seen so many people gathered in one place in this town."

Mimi, barely five feet tall, tapped a tall man on the shoulder and gave him a radiant smile. "Do you mind if we stand in front of you?"

The man smiled back, then turned to give them room to move in front of him.

A pavilion with covered sidewalks lined three sides of the square. The crowd stood in the open end. A uniformed group of German police chatted among themselves.

"Why do they wear green uniforms?" Mimi asked the man behind her.

"They're Orpo, short for *Ordnungspolizei* in German," said the man, speaking in Dutch with a Polish accent. "Their green uniforms supposedly identify them as the national police of Germany, but the Nazis use them to oppress occupied people."

The Germans roughly escorted two handcuffed men into the square.

"I know those men," Hetty whispered urgently to Mimi. "That's Hugo and Maurice."

"Who?"

"Communist leaders," she whispered. "They're friends of mine."

An Orpo officer moved to the center of the square with a swagger and raised both hands to quiet the crowd.

"I am Orpo Lieutenant Gerald Hess."

"I have seen this officer, Hess, in Vienna," whispered a man standing next to Hetty and Mimi. "He was with the brownshirts during *Kristallnacht*."

"What's that?" whispered Mimi.

"The Night of Broken Glass," said the man. "A terrible night when the Nazis brutalized Jews in the street. I can't believe they made that guy an Orpo police officer. He's a thug."

"He's pretty young to be an officer," Mimi observed.

"Hush!" said an Orpo policeman waving his baton threateningly.

"Orpo maintains order in occupied territories," Hess continued.

The crowd murmured as people who spoke German translated for the others. "Is Holland an occupied country?" one man near Hetty asked his neighbor.

"We've been occupied since the surrender," the neighbor scoffed.

"Quiet!" Another Orpo policeman confronted the men who'd been talking. One of the men quickly lowered his eyes, but the other stared defiantly at the policeman, which earned him a baton jab to the gut.

"But you should not worry," said Lieutenant Hess, holding up a hand to quiet the crowd. "The Dutch and German peoples are Aryan brothers and sisters."

The crowd murmured.

"You will be treated well as long as you obey our laws."

Several people in the crowd spoke at once. "Maybe they'll treat us fairly," said one woman, who was standing near Hetty and Mimi.

"Nonsense," said the man next to her. "We're *prisoners* of the Germans, not their *brothers*."

Hess turned back to the crowd. "This is a clean slate for the Dutch people; make no trouble for the Reich, and you will barely notice that we are here."

Then Hess turned to the prisoners, who glared back at him defiantly.

"These men are communists, organizing resistance against the Reich," Hess announced in a commanding voice.

The crowd gasped when guards stepped from the shadows, brandishing whips. Hugo and Maurice glanced nervously toward each other, showing their fear for an instant before resuming their defiant expressions.

"This is what happens to resisters," said Hess.

The guards stripped the shirts off the prisoners as onlookers fidgeted uneasily. Some covered their eyes with their hands, but most were unable to take their eyes off the spectacle that was unfolding.

Hess spat his next words: "Thirty lashes."

A low moan erupted from the crowd, reflecting its collective dismay.

Whack!

The whip cracked like the snap of a tree branch. Hugo screamed when the lash tore off a piece of his skin.

Whack!

Hetty turned away when the second lash dug into Maurice.

"Eyes forward," ordered an Orpo policeman, who'd been lurking nearby.

"They won't survive thirty lashes," whispered Hetty, clutching frantically at Mimi's sleeve. "Maurice has a family."

Suddenly Hetty bolted toward the center of the square, but Mimi grabbed her. "*Stop*," she hissed. "They'll arrest you."

Taller than Mimi by half a foot, Hetty would have broken free had she not tripped. Both girls went down in a heap. Then they were looking up into the face of an Orpo policeman.

"Is there a problem here, ladies?" The large Orpo policeman feigned politeness, speaking Dutch with a heavy accent while he hovered over them menacingly.

"No problem," said Mimi. "Just a disagreement over an old boyfriend."

"Take your domestic squabbles inside from now on." The German stared at them coldly for a moment before turning his attention to others in the crowd.

Lying on the ground, Mimi shuddered at the close call as she clutched her friend's arm, relieved that they had only been warned. Hetty's reaction was rage, not relief, as tears sprang into her eyes at the incessant crack of the whip. Mimi and Hetty stood up, helping each other brush the dirt from their clothing.

A middle-aged woman in a flowered dress was crying softly as she tried to walk away, but an Orpo policeman intercepted her.

"Go back," he hollered in her face. "You must watch."

The crowd pressed forward, but a squad of Orpo police intervened with batons. One man went down bleeding when an Orpo policeman clubbed him.

The lashes rained down on Hugo and Maurice, whose screams had fallen silent as their bodies went limp. At last, the whips stopped. Hetty held Mimi tightly, her breathing erratic.

"Is it over?" Mimi buried her face in Hetty's shoulder.

"I don't think so," Hetty whispered, her eyes fixated on Hess, who grabbed a whip from one of his men and cracked it in the air before turning to the limp bodies.

Hess's whip exploded against Maurice's back, where there was no skin left to give. Hetty was surprised by the rage in Hess's eyes. This was personal for him. Perhaps repaying something that happened to him as a child, she thought. Maurice uttered a dull groan. Then Hess turned to Hugo, who had opened his eyes in time to see what happened to Maurice.

The whip rang out again.

When Hess had finished, two Orpo policemen were assigned to lift each man. Hanging onto the policemen's shoulders, Maurice tried to walk but could not. Hugo was unconscious. Their feet dragged on the ground as the policemen hauled them from the square.

"Let's get out of here," whispered Mimi as the crowd broke up. "There's nothing we can do for your friends."

The two women made their way gloomily down the sidewalk.

"Wait for me," called Joeri, sprinting toward them.

Just as he reached them, Hetty leaned toward some bushes outside a palatial home and vomited ferociously. Balancing herself, hands on her knees, she took several quick heavy breaths.

Mimi rubbed her hand softly on her friend's back until her breathing had calmed. Then she grabbed Hetty's right elbow with a glance toward the Orpo police in the square. "We can't stay here."

Joeri grabbed the other elbow, helping her to exit the main street. Eventually they arrived at a quiet park next to a church and took advantage of a public water pump. Hetty and Mimi sat down on a bench under a massive chestnut tree.

Hetty stared vacantly across the lawn.

Joeri shifted from one foot to the other, still unsettled over what they had just witnessed. "Do you two have a radio?" he said at last, trying to distract his friends.

"The Nazis are confiscating radios," said Mimi, "but we hid ours."

"The Queen is giving a speech tonight on the BBC. Maybe she'll have some ideas about what to do."

"Didn't she flee to England?" asked Hetty, with a bitter smirk. "What does she know about living in an occupied country?"

"She had no choice," Mimi replied. "I'm glad she's safe."

"Are you?" asked Hetty sarcastically. "Isn't it enough that she emasculated our lions—our fighting spirit?"

"What are you talking about?" asked Joeri.

"Don't you know that for centuries the lions on our national seal had prominent phalluses?" Hetty was incredulous that her friends were not aware of this history. "Early in her reign, our queen chopped them off. Now she's put her emasculated lions into an island cage called England."

"What else could she have done?" asked Mimi, defending her sovereign. "The Nazis surely would have killed her if she'd stayed."

"She could have gone into hiding to lead the resistance," Hetty replied. "Just imagine how many would have rallied to her colors had she stood to fight alongside her people. Now our people are demoralized, and there is no resistance in sight."

"Isn't the Queen too old to lead the resistance?" asked Mimi.

"She's only sixty," Hetty replied. "Besides, the Crown Prince is still young and vigorous—and very popular."

"So who will lead?" asked Joeri, placing a hand on Hetty's shoulder. "You?"

"There's only one Royal Family," said Hetty, shrugging off her friend's suggestion. "Let's find out who is organizing the resistance in the Queen's absence."

"You should try harder to find your communist contacts," said Mimi. "Maybe they can help."

"Maurice and Hugo *were* my contacts," said Hetty.

Reiner Evers's spacious corner office was located on the second floor of the Civil Service Building in the heart of The Hague. From one window, the number two man at the Tax and Revenue Bureau had a view of the tallest building in The Hague, where Hetty's father, Willem Steenhuis, rented his law offices across the street. Though his civil service salary was modest, Reiner lived like a rich man at work. Sumptuous red leather chairs were located on a highly polished mahogany floor adorned with two elegant Persian rugs, and a full bar featuring expensive imported whiskey.

Reiner sipped his whiskey before leaning forward in the burnished red chair. "I have something to tell you in confidence, my friend."

A short man in his mid-forties with lots of hair and rimless spectacles, Reiner was the sort of drinking buddy that Willem valued—someone with insider information who didn't mind sharing it with his friends.

Willem went to the bar and poured himself a second glass of Reiner's whiskey. Then he sat down heavily in the plush leather chair next to Reiner.

"You can trust me."

On the surface, Willem seemed driven by his own self-regard, but in reality, his behaviors were best explained by the lack of it. His relationship with Hetty had been tense ever since Willem cut her allowance in half to persuade her to pursue a more ladylike curriculum than her chosen field of law. A lawyer himself, Willem had never met a female advocate for whom he had any regard. A pale man whose thick moustache flickered when he was asked a troublesome question, Willem had a foghorn voice that always sounded like he was bluffing at cards.

"I've been asked to take the top job at tax and revenue." Reiner produced a letter from his pocket.

Willem smiled enthusiastically while he read the letter of appointment. "Congratulations. There must be a raise in this for you."

Reiner nodded with a self-satisfied grin. "I'm just proud to perform this service for my country."

Reiner took the letter from Willem and placed it on his desk.

"It must remain our secret for now."

"Why the secrecy?" asked Willem. "This is news you should be proud of."

Reiner lowered his voice to a whisper. "You know my boss, Quinten?"

"I remember him," Willem nodded. "He was falling-down drunk at your Christmas party last year."

Reiner nodded at the memory.

"He did something stupid. The Germans are letting him retire quietly."

"Quentin is still a young man, nowhere close to retirement," Willem grimaced. "He must have done something terrible for him to lose his job."

"It's not public yet, but the Germans are going to require Jews to register with the government," said Reiner. "The Germans want our agency's tax records to identify them."

"And Quinten refused?" asked Willem. "That *was* stupid."

"Quinten said that in other occupied countries, registration led to harsher measures like deporting Jews to camps."

"Is that true?" Willem finished his drink.

"Does it matter?"

Reiner held up the whiskey bottle, which had been on the table next to his chair. Willem offered his empty glass for a refill.

As Reiner poured whiskey into Willem's glass, he added, "I'm not about to lose my job to protect Jews."

Willem thought for a moment about what Hetty would have said about that remark. It would have been an unpleasant conversation, for sure.

"You have my support, as always, Reiner. But some people will call you a collaborator for helping the Germans."

"If I don't do it," said Reiner, opening the door to show his friend out, "they'll appoint someone worse than me."

Willem paused with a quizzical expression. "When will registration of Jews begin?"

Reiner glanced around the room before replying in an icy calm voice, "Sooner than you might think."

CHAPTER 3

WEARING A WHITE PLEATED SKIRT that swayed when she walked, Mimi hurried past two men in suits, who cast admiring glances in her direction. The sunshine was welcome on this summer day in Leiden. A member of the declining Dutch aristocracy, Mimi took care to shield her family history from others. She wanted to fit in, and aristocrats, even declining members, were not popular.

Suddenly a familiar face from her past made her smile.

"Gerhardt! What are you doing here?"

A tall, muscular man in his late twenties with wavy dark hair glanced up, a warm smile replacing the surprise on his face. Mimi took a quick breath as they embraced.

"I'm visiting my Aunt Esther," said Gerhardt, holding her tightly.

Mimi inhaled the familiar scent of the soap he used. The sidewalk was crowded as students passed, some alone and others chattering in groups, getting ready for the university to reopen.

"I'm not a child anymore. Tell me what you're *really* doing here." Mimi gave Gerhardt an exasperated look.

He allowed his eyes to inspect her from head to toe. "Not a child, for sure." His face stretched into a broad smile. "You've grown into a beautiful woman, just as I predicted when you were ten."

Mimi guided Gerhardt to a quiet alley used by merchants for deliveries. "You've never liked your Aunt Esther. Why aren't you in England with the Crown Prince?" Mimi whispered, glancing around to confirm that they were alone. "I was relieved when I heard the Queen and her son had made it to London, but I assumed their bodyguards went with them. Aren't you still a bodyguard?"

"I am," said Gerhardt, speaking quietly. "But I can't tell you why I'm here. It's government business."

"What government?" Mimi put a hand on her hip. "The Nazis run things now, or hadn't you heard? I don't like guessing games."

"Same feisty Mimi," said Gerhardt, shaking his head. "The Royal Court wasn't the same after you left." He brushed a stray hair from her cheek with his fingertips. "Why haven't we seen you?"

"Papa was the one who was popular at court." She smiled at the memory. "He and the Crown Prince really enjoyed their whiskey."

"And everything else the bartender served," Gerhardt chuckled. "But I had the best assignment of my life when they visited the pubs."

"Babysitting me was your best assignment?" Mimi raised her eyebrows skeptically. "That's pathetic." Then she kissed his cheek. "I had such a crush on you."

"It wasn't exactly unrequited," he confessed, placing his fingertips on his cheek where she'd kissed him. "But you were too young—"

Mimi opened her green eyes wide and took his hand with a fetching smile. "I'm not too young now."

They practically ran to Aunt Esther's cottage, giggling and holding hands. A small white cottage with blue trim, his aunt's home fit perfectly into the tightly packed residential neighborhood where shopkeepers and household help lived. The cottage was located a fair distance from the university center, so they were out of breath by the time Gerhardt produced a key at the front door.

As soon as the door closed behind them, they grabbed each other, locking lips with desire that had been bottled up for years. When Gerhardt removed his shirt, she smiled lustfully, allowing her fingertips to glide lightly across his muscled stomach.

"Oh my. Bodyguards stay in shape, don't they?"

"Some of us do." He kissed her while he unbuttoned her blouse.

"When will your aunt return?" whispered Mimi breathlessly as she removed her bra, letting it fall to the hardwood floor.

Thunderstruck, Gerhardt stood motionless for a moment, admiring her beauty. "We have time," he said at last, cupping her breast while his tongue explored the inside of her mouth. "Are you sure you want to do this?" he asked when they came up for air.

"Mm-hmm." Mimi nodded as she allowed him to lead her into his bedroom.

Mimi was beside herself with joy as Gerhardt's kisses on her neck sent electric chills down her spine. Even though Mimi was old enough now to welcome him willingly inside her—she'd had other lovers, after all—she was aroused beyond belief by the sense that this was forbidden love.

"It's not every day that a girl has sex with her babysitter," Mimi teased when they had finished.

Exhausted by their lovemaking, Gerhardt lay on the bed, breathing hard. Mimi pressed her body against him, her fingers floating along his bicep.

"Why didn't you visit the Royal Court after your father died?" asked Gerhardt, lighting a cigarette after he caught his breath. "We missed you . . . I missed you."

Mimi frowned. "My father left us in bad shape financially."

"I had no idea," said Gerhardt.

"Papa spent all our money on gambling and booze," said Mimi with a flare of anger that threatened the romantic mood. "Before he died, he was even talking about marrying me off to a rich family."

"But your *mother's* family owned the castle, right?" Gerhardt tried to draw her close, but she shrugged him away with a distracted wave of her hand.

"Mother had to sell the castle to cover Papa's debts," said Mimi. "The government owns it now, and mother makes her living as a docent for tourists. She still sends me a monthly allowance, but she makes sacrifices even for that." Eager to change the subject, she began running her fingers through his wavy hair. "When will I see you again?"

"I'll be in Leiden for a while," said Gerhardt, kissing her forehead.

Mimi furrowed her eyebrows. "Ah. That *secret* assignment again. Is it dangerous?"

Gerhardt kissed her on the lips. "It's still a secret."

"But it affects *us*." She allowed her hand to rest softly on his manhood. "You have to tell me."

Gerhardt closed his eyes and exhaled slowly. "I'm so glad I found you." He gasped when her hand moved purposefully. "And I *really* like what you're doing right now. But my work here is still a secret."

"Maybe you can help my friend Hetty," said Mimi, moving her hand to his shoulder.

"Who's Hetty?"

"My roommate." Mimi propped her head on her hand. "Her boyfriend, Karl, went missing during the invasion. Do you know anyone who can help find out what happened to him?"

"Maybe." His fingers touched the stubble on his chin. "How does Hetty feel about the Germans?"

"Hates them," said Mimi firmly. "The Orpo police whipped two of her friends within an inch of their lives."

"Do you think she'd be interested in joining the resistance?" asked Gerhardt. "They might be able to track down what happened to Karl."

"Resistance?" Mimi was suddenly alert. "What do you know about that?"

"I know they're looking for young women to carry messages," said Gerhardt, playing with Mimi's hair. "We need both of you if you're interested."

"You're the organizer." Mimi's eyes grew wide at her epiphany. "*That's* your big secret! Why didn't you just tell me?"

"I didn't say anything at first because I don't want to expose you to danger, but the situation is dire, and we need more people. Even if you and Hetty volunteer, I'll only have four members of the Leiden resistance," said Gerhardt.

"Ah, so that's why there's no evidence of resistance in Leiden," Mimi observed. "There isn't any."

"I don't know why I'm having so much trouble finding volunteers in Leiden," said Gerhardt, shaking his head worriedly. "The Amsterdam resistance has been far more successful. They've promised to help us here."

"I'll ask Hetty," said Mimi, toying with the hair on his chest. "But count me out of the resistance. I want to lead a normal life."

Gerhardt pulled Mimi closer and stroked her hair. "Things will never be normal as long as the Germans are here."

Mimi studied him with a quizzical expression.

"Please. The Nazis will never suspect a courier as pretty as you."

Mimi rolled on top of Gerhardt to straddle him with a playful grin. "Do you really think I'm pretty?"

On a cold, dark night in farm country north of Leiden, Kees helped two men drag a tree across a narrow dirt road. Then they waited.

"Quiet. They'll be here any minute," Kees whispered.

"We're ready," whispered Robbe from the other side of the road, his back to a vast cornfield. A local farmer in his late thirties, Robbe chambered a bullet in his World War I vintage rifle and slid the bolt forward. His neighbor Pauwel, hiding a few feet away, did the same. "Make sure to thank the Amsterdam resistance for these rifles, Kees."

"The leaders in Amsterdam taught me that no one should have to face the enemy unarmed," Kees replied.

At twenty-seven, Kees had been satisfied with his life working as a clerk for a greengrocer, but when the Germans invaded, he got mad. A boxer by avocation, he wanted to punch every German he saw.

"Why punch them in broad daylight and get arrested, when you can do much more damage by attacking them from the shadows?" Kees's best friend Menno argued. Menno had been an early member of the Amsterdam resistance, and before Kees knew it he had also joined, where he was trained to organize others.

Suddenly Kees froze, alert to the sound of a truck approaching. The Germans came to an abrupt halt when they encountered the tree blocking the road. The driver emerged, shining a flashlight on the tree that blocked the truck's path, a pistol in his holster. He didn't see Kees hiding behind a bush three feet away. Another German soldier stepped out of the truck from the passenger side, rifle pointed toward the darkness.

Bang! Bang!

Robbe and Pauwel opened fire on the soldier, who cried out before slumping to the ground. The driver turned his flashlight on the attackers, his eyes wide. Kees, who had remained in the shadows, fired his pistol.

"Fuck," yelled the German, dropping his flashlight. Holding his right arm, the driver fled into the cornfield.

Pauwel started to give chase.

"Don't bother," said Kees. "It's too dark to find him in there." Kees was surprised when Pauwel returned from the field without a word, wondering why these men would follow him so readily when he was only a clerk who checked groceries. But follow him they did, just like the men he had recruited on his previous assignments, each of them affected by Kees's natural leadership and loyalty to the cause.

Kees turned over the body of the German soldier. "One of you is a good shot," said Kees solemnly as he examined the wound. "You hit him square in the chest."

"I wish you'd killed the driver too," said Robbe. "He had a good look at our faces and could bring the legions of hell down on us."

"I'm sorry I put you in danger," Kees said, shaking his head. "Three months of training, and the Amsterdam resistance could never teach me to shoot."

Pauwel sat in the dirt beside the road, clutching his knees against his chest. His body convulsed as he sobbed into his hands.

Robbe sat down next to Pauwel and put an arm around his friend's shoulders. "We've been neighbors for twenty years, old friend, and I don't think I've ever seen you cry."

Pauwel peeked at Robbe, keeping his hands where they were. "It's easy with sheep and pigs, but people? That's different."

"You'll have to get used to it. The Nazis are scum." Robbe stood and patted his rifle affectionately.

"I've never shot anyone either," Kees confessed. "But these are different times."

Kees grabbed the fuel can from the German vehicle and splashed gasoline on the front seat. Then he lifted the canvas that covered the cargo area and poured gas into the back of the truck. Robbe watched as Kees tossed a match into the cab. The flames exploded with a swift *whoosh!*

"The Amsterdam resistance sent me here to get things organized," said Kees. "I'd call this a good start."

Maria sat on a wooden chair outside her house skimming the cream from cow's milk when she saw a plume of dust on the horizon. She swiveled her head to find her father, Robbe, but he was nowhere in sight. *He's probably in the barn.* The chickens clucked around the barnyard, pecking at the grain she'd just scattered.

A life spent working on her family's farm had made Maria strong for a teenager. When her mother died two years ago, Maria had quit school to help her father run the farm. She soon preferred farm life to an academic one, having learned more, she reckoned, from making life or death decisions about crops and livestock than she ever had from reading books.

"Papa, you'd better come out here," she hollered, using her broad-brimmed hat to block the sun while she peered down the road. Swastikas on the approaching vehicles were now plainly visible as they sped through the endless fields of flax.

"As soon as I finish with this last pile of hay," Robbe called from the barn.

Maria could see the faces of the Germans as their vehicles approached the gate. Then she gasped in horror. Was that a human body bouncing behind the German vehicle from a tether tied to its rear bumper?

"Leave the hay for later, Papa," she insisted more urgently.

Just then an officer stepped out of the jeep and dusted off his uniform.

"They're here, Papa. You'd better come now."

"What—"

Robbe stopped short as he emerged from the barn. A German officer, flanked by two soldiers with submachine guns, blocked the entrance.

Robbe's face briefly flashed concern, which was quickly replaced with a welcoming smile. He wiped his dusty hand on his trousers and extended it to the officer.

"What can I do for you?"

The officer sneered at Robbe's outstretched hand. "Where were you last night?"

Robbe's expression became grave. "Here with my daughter." He nodded his head toward Maria. "Why?"

"Take a look," said the officer, gesturing toward the body that Maria had seen attached to the jeep.

Robbe inhaled quickly at the sight of his friend Pauwel, whose mutilated body had obviously been dragged behind the jeep with a rope. Still alive, Pauwel moaned quietly, trying to move but unable to manage it.

"He told us the two of you raided a German supply truck," said the officer. Without waiting for a response, the Nazi stepped back, and the soldiers' guns roared into action, blowing Robbe backward with a fusillade of bullets. His body came to rest next to the barn door, blood saturating the hard-packed dirt.

"No!" Maria screamed. "He didn't do anything! He was with me!"

Tripping over the milk bucket, she rushed to her father. Sobbing, she put her hands on the bullet holes, trying in vain to staunch the blood flow, kissing her father's face repeatedly.

Drenched in blood, Maria tilted her face toward the officer. "You bastard!"

Ignoring her, the officer gestured toward the house and barn. "Burn them," he ordered in a clipped voice before turning on his heel to saunter casually toward his jeep.

A soldier produced a can of gasoline from the truck and splashed it on the house.

Another soldier entered the house and emerged with cash and earrings. "No sense in burning this," he laughed as he shoved the booty into his pockets. Two soldiers lit cigarettes and inhaled casually while they doused the barn with gasoline.

"At least let me get the cow out of the barn," Maria pleaded. She sat in the dirt next to her father's body with a defeated expression.

The soldiers threw their cigarettes on the gasoline-soaked structures, and the fire exploded into a conflagration that engulfed both buildings. Maria used all of her strength to drag Robbe's body away from the oppressive heat while the cow wailed in pain from within. For a while the soldiers watched the flames, smoking fresh cigarettes and chatting casually among themselves.

One of the soldiers pointed his pistol at Maria. "What about her?" he asked, cocking the weapon.

"Let her live," said the officer, climbing into his jeep. "She can tell others what happens to traitors."

CHAPTER 4

BRECHT TOUCHED THE CURFEW PASS in his pocket as he left the Leiden flat that he'd once shared with Karl. It was a moonless night, and with streetlights extinguished for curfew, he could not distinguish objects in the dark shadows.

His thoughts drifted back to a quieter time before the war when he'd met Hetty in Leiden on the path that ran along the New Rhine, a wide canal that connected to the river Rhine before it emptied into the North Sea. His bicycle was broken, and he was surprised when she'd fixed it so easily—a skill her younger brother had taught her. His two months with Hetty were the best of his life, but it ended when he'd stupidly blurted his admiration for Adolph Hitler. By coincidence, that was also the day he introduced her to his roommate Karl. Just as well that Hetty had found someone new, he decided, since his life was now fully committed to the Third Reich. Still, he missed her sweet kisses.

Brecht stopped abruptly when SS Headquarters suddenly loomed before him like a malign demon. This would be his first visit to the converted schoolhouse since the SS had occupied it. A huge swastika hung from the bell tower, which rose in the middle of the two-story structure. Screwing up his courage, Brecht advanced toward the German headquarters. He inhaled sharply when he approached the SS sentry out front and only exhaled when the impeccably uniformed soldier let him pass. As instructed, Brecht climbed the stairs to the office of SS Major Felix Jacek.

Corporal Schultz, a large man with a chiseled chin and brown eyes that darted nervously about the room, ushered Brecht into his boss's office and retreated to the corner.

"Be seated, Mr. Brecht," said Major Jacek with a stern expression. "I am told that you did well during your training in Berlin. Are you ready to serve the Reich in Holland?"

A man in his mid-thirties, Jacek was sensitive about his lack of Aryan features. His dark hair and swarthy complexion made others suspect a Slavic strain in his ancestry. But his fine mind and absolute dedication to national socialism had earned him his rank in the SS, or *Schutzstaffel*. As ranking SS officer in Leiden, Jacek oversaw spies and the Gestapo in his region.

The Major snuffed out a cigarette into an ashtray overflowing with butts. His uniform was crisp and polished with an array of ribbons pinned to his chest. Corporal Schultz emptied Jacek's ashtray into the waste basket, wiping away the cigarette residue with his own kerchief before slipping it back without a sound.

"I have already started helping the Fuhrer, sir," said Brecht nervously in response to Jacek's question.

"Yes," said Jacek with a calculated smile. "Thank you for your information about Karl DeBoer. He won't be an impediment to the Reich anymore."

Brecht's face dropped, his eyes darting from side to side. "Is he dead?" He was fond of his roommate and before now, had not considered the possibility that giving up his name might get him murdered by the Nazis.

Jacek glared at Brecht. "Just follow orders and don't ask questions," he said harshly. "We have also dealt with the communist leaders you identified," Jacek said in a friendlier tone. "They're at Scheveningen Prison, but they won't be sleeping on their backs." Jacek chuckled faintly as he simulated the snap of a whip with his hand. "Excellent work."

Brecht managed a slight smile. He had no love for communists.

"The Dutch call Scheveningen Prison the 'Orange Hotel.'"

"Do they now?" Jacek smirked. "I suppose we should fill it up to honor the Queen's House of Orange. We still don't know who helped her majesty escape to England."

With the *click* of his flip-top lighter, Jacek lit another cigarette. He held the lighter with his fingertips and examined it.

"The Fuhrer himself gave me this lighter when I was promoted." Jacek glanced up at Brecht with a slight smile, reaching across the desk with the lighter.

"What an honor that you met the Fuhrer," said Brecht, turning the lighter over in his fingers to examine the SS symbols embossed on both sides. "Are the SS emblems real gold?"

Jacek chuckled with a friendly nod. "Keep it, Peter," said Jacek. "A gift from me for the excellent work you have done."

No one had called Brecht by his first name since he was a little boy. "D-do you mean it?" he gasped, admiring the lighter. "I'm overwhelmed."

Shy about meeting other children, Brecht's childhood in Amsterdam had been a lonely one. His wealthy parents were heavily committed outside the home—his father with an international business that required extended travel to the colonies, and his mother with her social commitments. To make matters worse, his parents were hard on their hired help, which meant that the housekeepers and governesses assigned to care for him rarely stayed in their jobs long enough to learn his first name. So they called him "Master Brecht" and later just "Brecht." Brecht regarded Hans, the Nazi operative who recruited him to spy for the Reich, as his first real friend. Hetty was his second.

Jacek nodded with a paternal smile, allowing Brecht to use his gift to light a fresh cigarette for him. "Now, Peter, what more do you have for me?"

Brecht produced a neatly folded paper from his pocket on which he had written a numbered list of names. "Here are all the Jews and communists at Leiden University. I marked them 'P' for professor, but that category includes all faculty. 'S' is for student and 'O' for everyone else." Then he added with a self-satisfied expression, "The 'J' and 'C' are self-explanatory."

Jacek thumbed through the list, then glanced up with a penetrating glare that sent a foreboding chill through Brecht's digestive tract. "Are you holding out on us, Peter?"

Brecht shook his head cautiously.

"Our sources say that two women were regulars at the communist meetings. Why haven't you named them?"

"I, uh, didn't actually go to those meetings," Brecht stammered, his heart going cold at the thought that Hetty was one of the women to whom Jacek referred. How could he possibly turn in the girl he still loved?

"I'll tell you what," said Jacek, standing to indicate their meeting was over. "Because you've done so well, I'll give you another chance to get that answer right. Next time, bring the names of those women."

Brecht stood up and nodded. It would be difficult to turn Hetty in. What if he faltered? To avoid arousing suspicion, he shot his arm out, ramrod straight and declared, "Heil Hitler," before turning on his heel and leaving the office.

Corporal Schultz closed the door behind Brecht. "That thing you do with your lighter never gets old, sir," he simpered.

"Do you want one?" Jacek opened his desk drawer. Eight lighters, each identical to the one he had given to Brecht, were lined up neatly in a row.

Hetty's stomach knotted as she climbed the familiar stairs to Karl's flat. She'd lost count of the number of times she'd visited, but it was the only place she knew to look for him. Maybe this time she would find him there.

When she reached the door, her heart leaped into her throat. The muffled sound of a man's voice came from inside. She started to knock, but then she stopped short, her knuckles barely touching the door.

The voice wasn't Karl's. Speaking German, the man responded to someone she couldn't hear, like he was conversing on the telephone—except Karl didn't have one. Could it be a two-way radio, she wondered?

Hetty drew closer to the door, pressing her ear up against it. Abruptly the door swung open, and Hetty tumbled inside, touching the floor with her hand to steady herself.

"What the hell are you doing here?" said Brecht tersely, one hand on the doorknob. He glanced up and down the empty hallway before grabbing her by the arm and dragging her inside.

"Ow!" said Hetty, pulling her arm away. "Don't grab me like that."

Brecht turned the deadbolt.

Clunk.

Then he turned toward Hetty, taking a notebook from her hands. "What's in here?"

"School notes," said Hetty tentatively. "I just came from a lecture on English common law."

Brecht glanced at the notes, then returned the notebook with an embarrassed expression. "I'm, um, really glad to see you Hetty. It's, uh, been so long."

Hetty was relieved to return to an ordinary conversation. Glancing past Brecht into the bedroom, she saw no one. While this must mean that Brecht was the one she heard through the door speaking in German, she did not want to believe that her former boyfriend was an agent of the enemy.

"Just as awkward as ever, I see." Hetty put her hand on Brecht's cheek with a gentle smile, striving to distract Brecht while her mind raced through her options, none of which were particularly attractive. "It's always been your most endearing quality."

Brecht blushed. "Look," he began, "I never stopped having feelings for you."

"That's so sweet," said Hetty, giving him a hug, eager to divert him from the questions she knew he might ask.

Brecht closed his eyes and slowly wrapped his arms around her. He remained silent for a moment, enjoying the scent of her perfume.

"But Hetty," he whispered at last, his grip tightening around her. "I need to know what you heard when you were out in the hall." Brecht's anxious expression revealed the answer he was hoping to get—that Hetty had not heard anything that required action on his part.

An electric current of dread traveled down her spine as Hetty pushed herself out of his embrace. His question seemed to confirm her worst fears about what she had heard.

Desperately, she continued the pretense. "Heard what? I'm looking for Karl. He's missing."

"I haven't seen him," said Brecht. "I still need to know—"

Before he could interrogate her further, Hetty interrupted: "Where have *you* been, Brecht?"

Eager to leave, she took another step back toward the locked door and crossed her arms. "I've been here a dozen times, and you're never home."

Brecht cocked his head to one side, making clear that he knew she had ducked his question. "I've been visiting relatives," said Brecht, using both hands to steady the flame to light a cigarette.

Hetty froze at the sight of Brecht's SS-embossed lighter. If there had been any doubt in her mind, it was gone now. She must escape. With a quivering hand, she reached for the door.

"I really should be going. It was so nice to see you, Brecht. We should have coffee and catch up soon. OK?"

Brecht glanced at his lighter, his eyes fluttering slightly before he returned it to his pocket.

Holding her breath, Hetty unlocked the deadbolt, but Brecht put his hand against the door before she could open it. Her stomach churned as she glanced up at the man she once thought she knew.

"I'll go with you," said Brecht with a thin smile, taking her elbow with a firm grip.

"Oh, I don't want to be a bother," said Hetty, pulling her arm away. "I'm fine on my own. Honest."

"It's no bother," Brecht insisted as they descended the stairs into the street. "These days, it's not safe for a woman to be out alone."

He returned his grip on her elbow and hung on tightly when she tried to pull free. He guided her in the direction of the old schoolhouse, two blocks away. Hetty swallowed hard when she saw the massive Swastika on the tower at the center of the building.

"Hetty! Is that you?" Hetty turned gratefully toward the distraction. Wearing a peasant blouse and plain skirt, Hetty's friend Mieke made her way toward her, waving. The two young women had met on their second day at the university and became fast friends. Hetty smiled with relief.

With kind, intelligent brown eyes, Mieke acknowledged Brecht with a nod and hugged her friend.

"I didn't know you two were back together," said Mieke in a lilting voice, her eyes shifting back and forth between them.

"We're not," Brecht scowled. "Just out for a walk."

Mieke eyed the harsh manner in which Brecht gripped Hetty's elbow before turning toward Hetty in an upbeat tone. "It's been forever since we've caught up."

"Way too long." Hetty returned the hug, chancing a brief glance at Brecht, who glared at her. "What are you doing right now, Mieke?"

"Nothing. We should have coffee," said Mieke enthusiastically.

Hetty took Mieke's arm and gave it a gentle squeeze. "Yes. Let's go!"

"I'll go with you," Brecht offered.

"Oh, you'd just be bored," said Hetty, holding her hand up with a perky smile.

"Girl talk," Mieke explained with a wink before they strolled away arm in arm as Brecht watched, cocking his head to one side with worry lines on his forehead.

Mimi used a key to let herself into their second-floor efficiency flat, which was sparsely furnished with two single beds, a chair, and a desk. With a dazed expression, Hetty sat on her bed beneath a photo of her brother, Jan. The walls were mostly bare, a photo of Mimi's mother and a small mirror being the only other adornments. A small kitchen, bathroom, and a surprisingly large closet completed their modest dwelling.

Mimi locked the front door behind her and tossed her notebook on the table, then gazed at her friend, who stared blankly at the wall. "What's wrong, Hetty? You look like you've seen a ghost."

"Brecht's a spy," Hetty blurted, her voice quivering.

"You think Brecht is collaborating with the Germans?" said Mimi incredulously. "That can't be right. Are you sure?"

Mimi had to raise her voice to offset the noise of an airplane roaring overhead. The Luftwaffe had been making regular sorties over Leiden since the invasion.

"No one but a spy would have a lighter embossed with an SS symbol," said Hetty, sinking into the only chair the two young roommates owned.

"Brecht has an SS lighter?" said Mimi. "I've never seen one. Maybe there's an innocent explanation. Did you ask him?"

"How many Dutch patriots do you know who would own something like that?" said Hetty, pacing the floor. "When I arrived, he was on a two-way radio—speaking German! Brecht knows that I speak German, but during the year that we've known each other, he never tried to speak German with me. And where the hell did he get a two-way radio?"

"I admit it looks bad," said Mimi tentatively, not wanting to believe the evidence.

"I never thought I'd be scared of Brecht, but I am," said Hetty, squeezing her friend's hand. "He was forcing me to go with him to Nazi headquarters when Mieke showed up out of the blue."

"Is Mieke a spy too?" Worry lines deepened on Mimi's forehead.

"No. No. She rescued me," said Hetty, using her sleeve to wipe sweat from her forehead. "It was pure coincidence. I hadn't seen her in weeks, and then all of a sudden, there she was. I was so lucky."

"Where's Mieke now?"

"I sent her home," said Hetty. "She was shaking like a leaf after I told her about Brecht. Arie will take care of her."

Hetty had met Arie and Mieke the day after the couple met each other, and they were already talking about marriage. She knew of no couple better suited for each other.

"What should we do about Brecht?" said Mimi, bringing a near-empty bottle of whiskey and two glasses from their tiny kitchen.

Hetty held up her hand. "None for me."

Mimi arched an eyebrow.

"All right," said Hetty. "A small one . . . I just wish Karl were here."

Mimi poured two glasses and handed one to Hetty. "Still no word?"

Hetty shook her head miserably, coughing when she took her first sip of the strong liquor. "Brecht didn't know where Karl was either."

"He's probably lying," Mimi frowned. "Did Brecht know anything about Karl that he could have told the Nazis?"

Putting her hand on her chin, Hetty puzzled over the question. "Shit," she said with sudden conviction. "Do you think Brecht turned Karl in for attending communist meetings?"

Suddenly Mimi's face turned ashen at an unsettling thought. "Aren't you in danger too? Karl didn't go to those meetings alone."

"I never would have believed it since he still has feelings for me." Hetty narrowed her eyes and paused for a moment. "But you're right. There can be only one reason why Brecht was forcing me toward Nazi headquarters."

"If he hasn't reported you yet, he will. And we need to stop him before he does."

Mimi stood up and took lipstick from her purse.

"Where are you going?" Hetty asked.

Mimi smoothed her lipstick in front of the small mirror. Satisfied with what she saw, she put her lipstick away and walked toward the front door.

"We can't handle this by ourselves."

Brecht leaned into the howling wind that threatened to knock him off his feet. He hadn't slept well for the last three nights. But his encounter with

Hetty helped him see everything more realistically: despite his feelings for her, he must turn her in. Jacek already suspected he was withholding information and would be merciless if he learned that he concealed her identity. And now Hetty was a threat to reveal Brecht's secret life. *I have no choice*, he thought miserably.

As usual, there were no civilians on the street after curfew. But tonight there were no police either. Brecht assumed they'd been driven inside by the raging windstorm.

He had just turned a corner in a place not well lit by streetlamps when two Orpo police confronted him from out of nowhere.

"I have a pass," said Brecht before they asked, shouting to be heard above the wind. He rummaged nervously through his pockets to produce the officially stamped document.

The policeman on the right, a large burly man, glanced at the pass before tossing it on the sidewalk. The wind blew the flimsy paper away instantly.

"I need that," Brecht protested, but the burly policeman hit him with a sharp left fist to the belly. Gasping for air, Brecht tried to invoke the name of Major Jacek, but the words stuck in his throat.

"Come with us," commanded the other policeman in perfect Dutch. Taller than the man who hit him, this blue-eyed policeman had an athletic, wiry presence. The strong wind nearly blew Brecht backward, but the policemen held him upright while forcing him into a dark, isolated alley.

When he could breathe again, Brecht tried to scream, but his voice was swallowed by the howling wind. Suddenly the wiry policeman's baton struck him squarely in the mouth. Brecht fell when a second blow struck his head. As Brecht struggled to his hands and knees, the burly policeman stabbed him from behind—three quick thrusts under the rib cage into his heart.

The wiry policeman scurried to the boulevard and looked right and left. "No one's coming," he said.

He helped the other man lift Brecht's body onto a cart and covered it with a canvas tarp. The bell in the tower over SS headquarters tolled, making both men jump.

"I didn't know those bells still worked."

The wiry man put a cloth sack over Brecht's inert head.

"Gerhardt, you should leave now," said the burly policeman.

He handed Gerhardt a shirt and jacket. Glancing up the alley, Gerhardt removed his police uniform and put it under the tarp with Brecht's body. His eyes focused on a pool of blood on the pavement.

"I suppose there's nothing we can do about that?"

In the dark, he did not notice the lighter with an SS symbol that had fallen from Brecht's pocket.

CHAPTER 5

HETTY AWAKENED TO SOMEONE POUNDING on the door.

"Mimi! Mimi!"

Hetty wrapped her robe around her nightshirt and opened the door just wide enough to peek through when the man on the other side tried to push the door open.

But the chain lock held.

"Please, let me in. I must see Mimi!"

"Wait!" Hetty peered at the man on the other side of the door. "How do you know her?"

"Mimi!" Gerhardt called out past Hetty's shoulder.

"Shh," said Hetty. "Someone will hear you."

Gerhardt lowered his voice. "Please, open up. Hurry."

"Who is it?" Mimi's voice came from the bathroom.

"Me! Gerhardt! Hurry. Let me in!" He was shouting again.

Hetty shot him another look, disapproving of the renewed shouting.

"Gerhardt!" Mimi emerged into the living area, a towel wrapped around herself, still wet from her shower.

Hetty's eyes widened at Mimi's daring appearance while she reluctantly unchained the door. Holding the top of the towel against her with one hand, Mimi walked toward Gerhardt and planted a kiss on his lips. She then turned to a bewildered Hetty.

"Hetty, meet Gerhardt." Mimi turned back to him. "Darling, you need to be nicer to my friends."

"I apologize for my gruff entrance." Gerhardt moved a stray hair off of Mimi's face.

Hetty cleared her throat. "Why the rush?"

"I need to tell you something." Gerhardt didn't take his eyes off Mimi. "I'm going to England."

Mimi dropped her towel momentarily but quickly covered up. "What? When?" Her ears turned red.

"The Crown Prince needs me."

Mimi turned away to conceal her disappointment and headed toward the closet to find something to wear.

Gerhardt followed her and pleaded. "Please understand, Mimi. I don't want to leave you."

Mimi turned around suddenly, pain written all over her face. "Tell them you won't go."

Gerhardt plopped down on one of the beds, unable to meet Mimi's somber gaze.

"You know I have no choice, honey. I swore an oath to the House of Orange."

Both were quiet for a moment before Mimi turned back to the closet.

"The timing's not set yet," Gerhardt continued, raising his voice so that he could be heard from the closet, "but I'll leave as soon as a boat has been arranged to pick me up at Scheveningen Beach."

"I knew it wouldn't last," she said sadly as she returned wearing a bathrobe, the towel wrapped around her head. "I never felt this way about anyone."

"Should I make some tea?" Hetty asked, feeling like an intruder.

Neither Gerhardt nor Mimi responded, their eyes locked in silent communication.

"I love you too," said Gerhardt after Hetty had headed for the small kitchen to busy herself while giving Mimi and her lover some privacy.

Once Hetty was out of the room, Mimi placed her hand softly on his cheek as she sat down next to him. "This all sounds too dangerous."

"No more dangerous than organizing the resistance," said Gerhardt.

Mimi thought about that. "What will happen to the resistance?"

Hetty returned from the kitchen with a tray of tea.

"The Amsterdam resistance is sending a man to replace me."

Mimi and Hetty exchanged worried looks.

"His name is Kees. You'll meet him this afternoon."

Mimi wrinkled her nose. "What if I don't want to meet him?"

"I told Amsterdam leaders that you two were ready to help the resistance in Leiden," said Gerhardt, his eyes tracking Mimi while she removed the towel from her head and went to the mirror to brush her hair.

Watching Gerhardt in the mirror, Mimi frowned. "I said we'd help you, not someone we don't even know."

"Please do this for me, Mimi," said Gerhardt, as he stood to wrap his arms around her. "Our country needs you."

"Where will we meet the Amsterdam guy?" asked Hetty, pouring the tea and taking a sip.

"You'll meet in the park next to the Presbyterian church. Do you know the place?"

Mimi nodded with a look of resignation. "I attended a baptism there once. Won't you be there to introduce us?"

Gerhardt shook his head. "I have a million things to do before I leave."

"How will we know him?" asked Hetty, surveying the street through their window.

"One of you must wear an orange scarf." Gerhardt gestured toward his neck. "Do you have one?"

Hetty reached for a box on the shelf and produced a reddish orange scarf. "Will this do?"

"Perfect," said Gerhard.

"What's he look like?" asked Mimi.

"I haven't met him. But Kees will know your names."

"What about Brecht?" Hetty glanced toward Mimi, who returned to the closet to find some shoes and something more suitable to wear for their meeting with the new leader. "Won't this fellow Kees be reluctant to meet people who are well known to a spy?"

"We neutralized Brecht." Gerhardt set his jaw and narrowed his eyes.

"Does that mean you *killed* him?" Hetty choked on the words.

Gerhardt stared at her. His meaning was crystal clear.

"Couldn't you have taken less drastic measures?" Hetty asked, still unsettled by the news.

"What other measures did you have in mind?" Gerhardt asked as he paced the room. "The resistance doesn't operate any jails."

Mimi emerged wearing a fresh skirt and blouse with matching shoes. "Why should it matter, Hetty? You hate the Germans."

"Brecht wasn't German."

Hetty went to the sink and splashed water on her face.

Mimi studied her friend. "Why are you so upset?"

Hetty lifted her head and dried her face gently with a towel. Before answering she folded the towel and laid it on the sink, trying to compose herself.

"He was the first boy I ever kissed."

"I didn't know." Mimi placed her arm around Hetty's shoulders.

"I know how you feel," said Gerhardt, placing his hand on Hetty's back. Hetty shrugged him off.

Gerhardt stepped away but was determined to finish his point. "You should be more concerned about who will betray us next."

Hetty and Mimi fidgeted nervously on a park bench on a cold gray afternoon. Church bells rang and white oak trees rustled overhead in the strong wind. Looming over the small park was a church big enough to be called a cathedral had it been Roman Catholic. A well-built man and young woman approached them.

"Hetty and Mimi?" Kees smiled in a friendly way.

Touching her orange scarf, Hetty nodded slightly.

"This is Maria, and I'm Kees. Gerhardt sent us."

Maria smiled shyly.

"Gerhardt didn't say anything about a girl," Hetty frowned.

Feeling a chill, Mimi buttoned her coat. "How old are you, Maria?"

Maria clutched Kees's arm. "I'm seventeen."

Hetty eyed her skeptically.

"She's a mystery to me too," Kees shrugged. "But I worked with her father, and he was a patriot."

"Was?" Hetty arched her eyebrow.

"My father was killed because he went on a commando raid for the resistance," Maria explained. "He told me I should find Kees if anything happened to him."

"I was on that raid," Kees added. "Her father was a brave man."

Hetty suddenly became distracted as her eyes focused on the street on the far side of the park.

"Just a minute," she said, walking briskly across the lawn toward a man with long dark hair and a beard.

"Excuse me," she called out to the stranger. "Karl?"

The man kept walking, and Hetty broke into a run.

"Karl," she shouted. "Is it you?"

The man turned around with a puzzled expression. "Who's Karl?"

"Oh." Hetty took a step back. "I'm so sorry. I thought you were . . ."

Disappointed, Hetty turned around and returned to Mimi and the others.

"Who was that?" Mimi asked.

Kees and Maria stared curiously at Hetty. "Karl is my boyfriend," she explained. "He went missing during the invasion. Sometimes my mind plays tricks on me."

Maria grabbed Hetty's hand. "I miss my father too. It doesn't get easier."

"I need to get used to the idea that he's probably not coming back."

Hetty glanced down at her hand resting in Maria's. Though she was a stranger, Hetty took comfort in this gesture. Mimi placed her arm around Hetty and waited a respectful moment before turning her attention to Kees. "So what do we do now?"

"If you know Gerhardt, you know why I'm here," said Kees, glancing in all directions until he was satisfied that no one was listening. "I can't say more in the open. Come to my cottage tomorrow morning at 9:00. Maria will show you where it is."

"Wait. Isn't Maria going with you?" Hetty's eyes narrowed.

Kees shook his head. "She's going to stay with you."

"Our flat is barely big enough for two," Mimi protested.

"You'll have to work it out," said Kees as he turned on his heel to leave.

Hetty and Mimi glanced worriedly at each other, then at Maria, who managed a weak smile.

"Come on then," said Hetty, holding her hand out to the teenager. "I know someone who will lend us a bed—if it fits."

The next morning Hetty, Mimi, and Maria were in the living room of Kees's safe house, a two-bedroom cottage owned by a supporter of the Amsterdam resistance. The unassuming abode was painted white with green trim, much like the other cottages in the quiet Leiden neighborhood. It had almost no front yard, which suited Kees, who planned to be too busy for yard maintenance. There was, however, a raised porch outside the front door, which Kees thought was perfect because it was impossible for an intruder to cross its wooden floor without being heard.

"I need you to become mail carriers for the resistance," said Kees, pacing back and forth in front of his recruits.

The young women looked on nervously.

With a hand gesture, Kees invited Hetty to join Mimi on the sofa. "The Germans won't suspect that a pretty young woman is carrying mail for me."

"That's what Gerhardt told me," Mimi said, brushing her hair back with her fingers.

The shrill whistle of the tea kettle interrupted them, and Maria went to the kitchen.

"Wait a minute," said Hetty as she took her place on the sofa. "Are you just giving us safe and easy jobs because we're women?"

"I won't lie to you," said Kees, lighting a cigarette. "Some resistance leaders have old-fashioned ideas about the assignments they think are suitable for young women. But they are wrong. The work I have in mind for you matters, and it will be neither safe nor easy."

Kees put one leg over the arm of the crowded sofa so that he could sit next to Hetty. "People in hiding from the Germans can't survive without food. Someone needs to bring them ration cards and food. The ones who are leaving Holland also need false papers to travel safely, and everyone needs money. Couriers will provide this support, and that's important work."

"Where will the money come from?" asked Mimi.

"Some of our countrymen have been generous."

"What about us?" asked Maria. "I don't have a dime."

"I have found you a job waiting tables at a local café," said Kees. "That should cover your expenses, Maria, and I am hoping that Hetty and Mimi keep getting their allowances to attend the university."

"My father has been paying the rent on our flat," said Hetty. "If I don't say anything, he probably won't notice that I have two roommates."

"My mother doesn't have much money," said Mimi. "But there's no reason why she would stop sending my allowance."

"I just want to fight the Germans," said Hetty.

"Don't worry about that," Kees replied. "If we help people in hiding, the Nazis will have to use more resources to find them—resources that won't be available for their war with the Allies. I never understood why Germans hate the Jews so much, but they do. And it will give them fits if we help Jews to hide."

"One of my professors might be hiding out." Hetty slid forward to the edge of the sofa. "He's not a Jew, but he was a vocal opponent of the Dutch Nazi Party. He hasn't been seen since the invasion."

"He's probably in hiding," said Kees with a frown. "There are hundreds like your professor, and helping them is the best tool we have available to fight the Nazis."

He turned to Maria. "Today I have a courier assignment to deliver ration cards to a woman who is hiding a Jewish family in her home. Will you do it?"

"I'll do anything to help," said Maria warily.

"I want to help too," said Hetty. "If Hitler hates the Jews, they're my new best friends."

"You'll get your turn," said Kees with a wave of his hand. "But I have a different assignment for you. Day after tomorrow you'll meet a pilot."

"What kind of pilot?" Hetty furrowed her eyebrows.

"I've heard that British pilots who get shot down are on the run," offered Mimi.

"That's right," said Kees. "We're forming a network of people who smuggle them out of the country through France into Spain."

Kees continued: "On Thursday you will make contact at the cinema with a British pilot named Jim and escort him on the bus to a safe house just outside of Leiden."

"I attend a class on Wednesday nights," said Hetty, finishing her tea. "So Thursday will work."

"They're playing *Rembrandt* at the cinema," Maria offered enthusiastically. "It was made before the occupation."

"She's not going there to watch the movie," Kees scolded. "All of you need to stay focused on what's important or you'll be caught."

"Sorry," said Maria timidly. "It's just that I haven't been to the cinema since my father took me before the war."

Kees stared at the floor, remembering with sadness the night when he and Robbe set the German truck on fire. He felt remorse at failing to kill the German driver, who likely had provided the information that led to Pauwel and Robbe's death. It was the last time he saw Maria's father. Returning to the moment, he turned to Hetty. "I don't like giving you such a dangerous assignment for your maiden voyage. But this young pilot has been on the run for three weeks and needs our help."

"Can't you ask someone else to do it?" asked Mimi, placing a protective arm around her friend.

"You three are the first I have recruited to help me in Leiden. Eventually there will be more, but for now, you're all we have."

"Will we know the others?" asked Maria.

"No. I've been trained to organize in cells."

"What's a cell?" asked Maria.

Mimi stood and paced the floor, a nervous habit she had developed as a child to distract herself whenever there was turmoil at home over her father's money problems.

Hetty stepped across the room to Maria and took her hand, this time offering her the comfort Maria had given the day before. "It's a tool to prevent the Germans from arresting others in Kees's network if someone talks," Hetty explained. "I heard about it from the communists at the meetings I attended with Karl."

"That's right," Kees said. "I will organize cells in small groups—like this one. If one member of the cell is captured, she can only identify the other members of the cell, which protects the other volunteers."

"That didn't help my friends Hugo and Maurice," said Hetty.

"That's because Brecht had exposed their cell before the invasion," Kees replied. "You're lucky you weren't swept up in the dragnet, Hetty. Surely Brecht knew you attended those meetings."

"I guess he didn't tell them," Hetty reflected somberly.

"What about you, Kees?" asked Mimi, peering out the front window.

"I'm sort of a go-between," he explained.

"I thought you said we were your only couriers," said Maria, sipping her tea.

"I plan to recruit more courier cells soon," said Kees, "and I will coordinate the assignments for all of you."

"But what if they catch you?" asked Mimi, returning to the sofa. "Aren't you the weak link who knows everyone?"

"I have a cyanide pill for that."

"Take that knife off her neck, Gerhardt!" Maria shrieked, aghast at the scene before her as she entered Kees's cottage the next day.

She had just delivered ration cards for a Jewish family in hiding—her first assignment—and had arrived late for their courier meeting.

Showing surprise at the interruption, Gerhardt lifted the two-edged dagger from Mimi's throat.

"Sorry for the scare," said Mimi with a grin. "We were only pretending. Gerhardt would never hurt me."

"I asked Gerhardt to give us some lessons in hand-to-hand combat before he leaves for England," Kees explained.

"Pay attention," Gerhardt said to Maria. "You never know when you might need these skills." He handed the sharp two-edged knife to Hetty. "This is the commando knife issued to me as a bodyguard for the Crown Prince. Let's practice what we learned, Hetty. Use Mimi as your sparring partner."

Holding the knife in her right hand, Hetty stood face to face with Mimi. When Mimi took a mock swing at her, Hetty ducked under the blow and moved around behind her friend, pulled her head back by the hair, and placed the dagger at her throat.

"That's a good start," said Gerhardt. "But you're too timid. Try to be more aggressive. A real fight will be to the death."

CHAPTER 6

THE MOVIE WAS ALREADY PLAYING when Hetty entered the crowded cinema. She wanted her first assignment to unfold precisely as Kees had instructed. Wrinkling her ticket nervously between her fingers, her eyes darted around the movie house, looking for a man in a hat as Kees had instructed.

Using the light from the screen, she surveyed the crowded audience. But then she began to panic. There were *two* men wearing hats, one in the back and one in the second row near the screen. Which one should she approach?

She took a deep breath and settled into the seat next to the man located in the back.

"Popcorn?" she offered. This was the password Kees had told her to use.

"Don't mind if I do," said the man, removing his hat.

This was not the proper response. Besides, the man's head was completely bald, and Hetty knew immediately that he was too old to be a British pilot.

"Sorry, I have to go," she said, leaving so quickly that the man had no chance to reach for the popcorn. She instantly regretted leaving so abruptly, realizing that her behavior was suspicious. She caught a glimpse of an usher retreating toward the lobby. Had he gone to fetch the police?

She went to the lobby but did not see the usher anywhere. Hetty wondered whether she should go through with her assignment. After all, she hadn't broken any laws yet, and she could easily go out the door and head for home. It took only an instant for her to decide to return to the darkened theater. Pilots are heroes, she knew, and she could not leave one of them alone to fend for himself.

Once again summoning her courage, Hetty sat down next to the man in the second row.

"Popcorn?"

"That's my favorite."

Hetty exhaled with relief. He'd given the correct response. Kees had ordered her to watch the film with Jim and take him on the bus to the safe house. It helped that she spoke Jim's language.

"Have all you want," she whispered in English. "It's not even rationed."

Jim glanced at Hetty before reaching into her bag of popcorn.

"What happens now?" he whispered, glancing up at the screen toward the characters conversing in Dutch.

To avoid arousing suspicion, Hetty took his arm as a girlfriend would.

"Watch the film," she whispered, nuzzling his ear.

"I don't understand a word they are saying."

"Pretend that you do."

Jim glanced at Hetty curiously.

"Laugh when I laugh," she instructed, laying her head on his shoulder.

While Hetty pretended to be calm on the outside, she was actually terrified. One mistake could cost her and Jim their lives. And where was that damn usher?

Hetty detected commotion in the back of the theater. Turning her head, she saw the usher leading two Orpo policemen into the cinema. The usher glanced toward the first man she had approached, then swiveled his head right and left to survey the crowded theater in the darkness. The police scanned the crowd, holding their batons at the ready.

"C'mon," she ordered, grabbing the pilot's arm. "We need to leave."

"Huh?" Jim remained in his chair.

"Right now!" Hetty hissed.

She guided him to a door at the front of the theater to the left of the screen. Good thing they'd sat in the second row, she thought. She opened the door, gesturing for the pilot to go ahead of her.

Just then, one of the Orpo policemen shouted, "Hey, you. Stop."

Hetty closed the door behind her and found herself in an alley. She was familiar with this area because she and Karl had often gone to the movies here.

"This way," she ordered as they took a sharp right turn and then a quick left. She could hear the Orpo police behind them.

Nothing in Hetty's training told her what to do next. She could not risk taking Jim on a bus as planned. She needed to find a hiding place quickly.

"We need to get you off the streets, Jim."

"How do you know my name?" said the pilot, out of breath as he struggled to keep up.

Hetty guided him through a labyrinth of alleys and side streets before emerging on the main street several blocks from the theater. Trying to control her heavy breathing, Hetty looped her arm in Jim's as they endeavored to blend in with the other pedestrians. A young couple kissed and sauntered away, holding hands while an older couple murmured about the movie.

"Where are we going?" Jim's eyes surveyed the street.

"Hush."

Hetty glanced over her shoulder at two Orpo police walking across the street.

"We don't want anyone to hear us speaking English. Put your arm around me."

Jim did as he was told, and Hetty looped her arm around the small of his back.

They turned off the main street into a quiet neighborhood. No lights were on inside when Hetty knocked on the door of a small house. After a long wait, the door cracked open a few inches. A woman peeked out.

"Hetty, what are you doing here?"

"I need you to do me a huge favor, Elke," said Hetty as she shoved Jim through the front door and closed it. "This is Jim. He's a British pilot hiding from the Nazis."

"He has to leave," Elke insisted. "They'll shoot us if they find him here."

"I know you have your reasons for not joining the resistance, Elke," said Hetty, pulling back the curtains a few inches to glance out the front window. "But there's nowhere else I can go. Jim needs to stay off the streets tonight. The town is teeming with Orpo. They're all looking for him."

Elke stared at her skeptically. She was a plump woman about Hetty's age with short brown hair and a no-nonsense demeanor. They had been friends since grammar school.

"Please, Elke, I'm desperate," said Hetty, taking her friend's hand. "Think about his family back home if the Germans shoot him."

"All right," said Elke reluctantly as she checked again out the front window. "Just for tonight. I don't like taking chances like this."

"Thank you, Elke," said Hetty. She turned toward Jim. "I'll come back to fetch you early tomorrow. Then we'll see what's what."

She kissed him on the cheek, allowing her lips to linger briefly before she left Elke's house.

CHAPTER 7

KEES HANDED DOCUMENTS TO MARIA as he entered the girls' flat. "These are your papers. They're forgeries, of course—but good ones."

"Thank goodness," said Maria, reading the papers excitedly. "I've been carrying out assignments for weeks without an ID. I'm lucky no one has stopped me."

"No one has stopped me during any of my assignments either," said Hetty, who sat on her bed knitting. "The only close call I've had was that first time—with the pilot—and I doubt my ID would have saved me if the Nazis had found us."

"Sorry it took so long, Maria. I wanted to make sure these are perfect," Kees explained. "Do I smell cookies?"

"Try some," said Hetty, nodding toward a plate on the table. "Mimi made them with some sugar she brought back from her visit with her mother."

Kees chewed on a cookie while Maria flipped through the documents Kees had given to her.

"What are you knitting, Hetty?" asked Kees, helping himself to another cookie.

"It's a scarf for my brother."

Hetty fumbled her knitting needles before holding up something that looked like a light green scarf, except the rows were askew.

"I suppose I need to rework this last part," she offered. "This is only my second project, and my technique isn't so good. I knitted a sweater for Karl before he disappeared."

"Put me on your list," said Kees, holding the crooked green scarf up for inspection. "It doesn't have to be perfect. All of my sweaters are tattered."

Maria frowned as she placed a finger on one of the documents Kees had given her. "This says that I'm a student."

"That was my idea," said Kees, pleased with himself. "It fits, in case anyone connects you to your roommates."

"I'm not sure I can pretend to be a university student," said Maria, tossing the papers on her bed despairingly. "I never even finished high school."

Suddenly Mimi came through the door, out of breath. "Have you heard about Professor Miejers?"

"He's one of my law professors," said Hetty. "Is he alright?"

Mimi took off her coat and draped it over the back of a chair. "People are saying the Nazis fired Miejers from the Leiden faculty because he's a Jew. Professor Cleveringa isn't happy about it either."

"I have a lecture with Miejers tomorrow at Groot Hall," said Hetty, sitting on the edge of her bed.

"No you don't," said Mimi, taking a bite of one of the cookies she'd made. "Cleveringa's giving Miejers's lecture for him."

"The three of you should go," said Kees excitedly. "This might rally Leiden students to the resistance."

"Can we get back to my problem?" said Maria, pointing to her identification papers. "I'm still confused about what I should say if I'm stopped—about being a student at the university. I've never even attended a class."

"Hetty and Mimi will give you a crash course," said Kees, glancing toward Hetty.

"I've been too busy to attend many classes since I started making courier runs," said Hetty, putting down her knitting. "But I can teach you enough to fool the Germans."

Hetty scrambled to secure three vacant seats toward the back of Groot Hall, then waved across the auditorium at Mimi and Maria, who made their way toward her through the boisterous crowd. Eagerly anticipating Professor Cleveringa's speech, a never-ending stream of students filed in, shedding their coats and sweaters as they transitioned from the cold November air outside to the oppressively warm lecture hall.

Hetty attended most of her classes at Rapenburg Hall, home to the law faculty. The imposing structure rose majestically on a square located where the waterway known as the New Rhine joined its sister, the Old Rhine, before both flowed north to empty into the North Sea. Inside on the first floor was Groot Hall, where Hetty was meeting her friends. A modest auditorium inside the grandiose Rapenburg building, Groot Hall provided the venue for most lectures given by the law faculty.

Maria fought the crowd to claim the seat next to Hetty among the murmuring students, who filled the auditorium to capacity.

"So this is what a lecture hall looks like." Maria caught her breath while she surveyed the large group of students standing in the back. "I wonder what Cleveringa will say."

"Gerhardt was disappointed that more Leiden students haven't volunteered to resist the Nazis," Mimi whispered as she took her seat. "I hope Cleveringa inspires them."

"Shh," said Maria. "Here he comes."

The murmuring crowd suddenly became silent when Cleveringa took his place behind the lectern.

"I stand here before you today," Professor Cleveringa began, "at a time when you expected someone else. Your teacher and mine, Eduard Miejers, was scheduled to give this lecture." He held up a folded piece of paper. "This is a letter he received yesterday from the Department of Education, Arts and Science: 'In the name of the Reich Commissioner of the occupied Dutch Territory concerning non-Aryan government staff and equivalent personnel, I inform you that as of today you've been relieved of your duties as professor at the Leiden University.' *Relieved* of his duties!" Cleveringa repeated for emphasis. "How *dare* they! Professor Meijers is one of the finest scholars I know—and a friend to all of us."

After Cleveringa finished the letter, he excoriated the Nazis for their mistreatment of his colleague for being Jewish. Then he walked off the podium. The auditorium fell silent.

Suddenly a golden baritone voice carried over the crowd. It was Hetty's friend Joeri, the red-headed law student, who started to sing the *Wilhelmus*, the Dutch national anthem. "William of Nassau am I, of Dutch descent; I dedicate undying Faith to this land of mine," he began. The *Wilhelmus* traditionally declared that William was of "German descent," but the crowd began to buzz, even as Joeri continued the uplifting song, when some noticed that he had changed it in defiance of the Germans. The audience paid rapt attention to the pure baritone voice, which sent electric chills up Hetty's spine.

She stood, compelled to rise and sing along. Unlike Joeri, Hetty was cursed with a terrible singing voice, and she could only imagine the off-key sound that was about to interrupt the gorgeous vocal solo—but she *had* to sing. Then Hetty was saved by a miracle, for at the very moment the song left her throat, she was joined by a host of other voices, singing loudly about the Dutch revolt against Philip II of Spain, a revolution that had secured democracy for the Netherlands.

The sound of this makeshift choir prompted everyone to sing, and soon Groot Hall was filled with the joyful sound of passionate voices intoning the patriotic lyrics.

"That voice!" Mimi enthused when they flowed out of Rapenburg Hall with the crowd. "It was so patriotic—and so brave." A young man nearly knocked her over as the crowd squeezed through the narrow exit.

"Now is the perfect time for students to rise up," said Maria, running to catch up with her friends. She inhaled the cool afternoon air.

"Look." Mimi pointed at students holding hand-drawn anti-Nazi signs. "Protests have already started."

"We should protest too," said Maria enthusiastically. "We can recruit volunteers for the resistance."

"Kees said that if there are demonstrations, the only thing we would recruit is a jail sentence," said Hetty shaking her head. "They'll be riddled with German spies."

"I don't care." Maria ran toward the growing crowd of protesters. "It's time to stand up for our country."

"Wait for me," shouted Mimi as she ran after Maria.

"They're out of their minds," Hetty mumbled to herself. Walking slowly toward the demonstrators, she watched someone handing Maria a sign. Suddenly, out of the corner of her eye, Hetty saw German soldiers getting organized behind a building. She broke into a dead run. "Get away from there," she warned, panting when she caught up with her friends. "German soldiers!" She tossed Maria's sign into the street.

All three froze momentarily at the sight of the advancing troops.

"Quickly," said Hetty, taking Maria by the arm. "Follow me. Hurry!"

Most of the crowd had not seen the Germans yet. When the soldiers marched toward the gathering students, panic set in. Because of Hetty's quick action, she and her friends had a head start. This allowed them to enter a café that was still open for business. The waiter was befuddled by their agitated demeanor, unaware of the chaos that had erupted in the square.

Outside, there were screams as the Germans brought down batons on the heads of student protesters. The three women peered anxiously through the window, where Nazi troops were placing demonstrators into waiting trucks. "They're probably taking them to Scheveningen Prison," said Maria. "That's where they've been jailing resisters."

Two young men burst through the entrance of the café, peering out the window after they had shut the door. "Leave," Hetty ordered. "The Nazis will follow you in here."

One of the students glared at her defiantly. Then he sat down at a table. "Waiter," he blustered. "Coffee for my friend and me."

Frustrated, Hetty guided her friends to the kitchen. They had just closed the kitchen door when two soldiers burst through the entry of the café. The students at the table tried to run, spilling their coffee, but the soldiers subdued them quickly, dragging them back into the square.

"Let's get out of here," Hetty whispered, peering from the kitchen door into the empty café. She led her friends out a back door and started down an alley, but two more soldiers stood at the entrance. Reversing course, the girls managed to find a narrow walkway. At the other end, Hetty studied both directions before choosing one and signaling that her friends should follow her.

In their flat, Hetty awakened from a peaceful sleep and smiled happily. "Is that *real* coffee I smell?"

"As real as it gets." Maria smiled as she held out a cup filled to the brim.

Hetty sat up in bed and took a sip. "Ahhh. Where'd you get this?"

"I made friends with a woman on my courier run."

Maria handed a cup of coffee to Mimi. "When I brought her ration cards yesterday, she gave me this coffee."

"This is a welcome gift," said Hetty, closing her eyes to enjoy the rich flavor.

"You two have been so kind to me that I wanted to give you something special."

"Thank you," said Mimi, toasting with her coffee cup.

"There's more," said Maria excitedly as she reached in her purse and handed each of them a ring made from colored yarn that had been intertwined.

"A little girl in hiding, Aliza, made these rings for me, and I want you to have them—friendship rings."

Mimi put the ring on her finger. "Thank you, Maria. I'm glad we're friends."

"I feel like we're sisters," said Hetty, admiring the ring before slipping it on her finger.

Peering out the window, Mimi watched a squad of six Orpo police marching on the street below.

"I'm panicked about all the student arrests after Cleveringa's speech last week," she said. "Do you think they'll come for us?"

"If the Nazis knew who we were, we'd already be in jail," said Hetty, still admiring her friendship ring.

"Will they close the university?" asked Maria.

"Let's ask Kees," said Hetty.

"Speaking of Kees, where's he been the last couple of days?" asked Mimi, closing her eyes to enjoy another sip of coffee.

Maria checked her watch. "He'll be here in ten minutes."

Hetty and Mimi exchanged knowing looks. "Haven't you been out with Kees after curfew quite a few nights lately?" Mimi teased.

"Not that often," said Maria dismissively.

"Exactly how did you know about his plans for today, Maria?" Mimi laughed.

"Are you two *special* friends now?" Hetty teased.

Maria blushed but said nothing as she returned the empty coffee pot to the kitchen. "I had an innocent beer with Kees last night," said Maria when she returned. "He told me that we should expect him at 9:00."

Mimi and Hetty rolled their eyes at each other.

"Having a beer together doesn't make Kees my boyfriend," Maria insisted with mock exasperation for the teasing.

Hetty and Mimi laughed even harder. And soon all three were giggling like schoolgirls.

Suddenly there was a knock at the door. The laughter stopped abruptly.

"It must be Kees," Maria whispered, glancing at her friends for reassurance.

Hetty left the chain lock fastened while she cracked the door open to peek out. Her body relaxed.

"It's him," Hetty said as she unfastened the chain.

"Who did you think it was?" Kees asked sarcastically as he walked in and placed a leather carrying bag on the table.

The three girls fidgeted as Kees strode to the center of the room. He glanced around with a puzzled expression at the bottled-up secret his couriers seemed to share. The three young women suddenly burst into uproarious laughter.

Kees raised his eyes to the ceiling, as if imploring the heavens for strength. "I have news." He held up both hands for quiet. "Cleveringa is in jail. The Nazis took him to Scheveningen Prison last night."

All three faces, laughing and excited only a moment ago, suddenly collapsed.

"That brave man. How unfair," said Maria.

"Do they have room for him?" said Hetty in a snarky tone. "They've already filled the Orange Hotel to capacity with student demonstrators."

"There's more," Kees continued. "The Nazis have closed the university in retaliation for the student demonstrations."

"Closed?" said Mimi, bringing a hand to her cheek. "I was clinging to the idea of getting back to normal."

"I'm glad they closed it!" said Hetty defiantly. "Classes will interfere with my courier work anyway."

"Then you'll have time for your next assignment," said Kees.

Hetty's interest was piqued. While her work for Kees had been risky so far, she was eager to do more.

"I'm sending Maria with you to The Hague to deliver some false papers." He wrote an address on a scrap of paper. "The man who lives here, Pier, smuggles airmen to the Belgian border, and they'll need them. We will stitch the papers into the lining of a satchel that you can stuff with schoolwork. You know the neighborhood well, Hetty. It's near your grandmother's house. I want Maria to learn it too."

"Is there something else, Kees?" asked Mimi. "I feel like you're holding back."

Kees stared at Mimi for a moment before speaking. "Gerhardt left for London last night."

Mimi's coffee cup jiggled as she set it down on the table. "He never said goodbye," she whispered.

"He left you this note." Kees produced a neatly folded piece of paper, and Mimi held it. Hetty could see that her friend was still processing the news of Gerhardt's departure.

Hetty placed her hand on Mimi's shoulder. "We'll all miss him."

As Mimi read the note, Kees reached into his leather bag.

"Oh. That reminds me. Gerhardt left these."

Mimi perked up. Kees held out four daggers and handed three of them around. "A commando knife for each of us. Just like the one Gerhardt used in our training."

Hetty ran her thumb delicately along the blade and whistled. "That's a keen blade."

Kees tested the blade of his dagger by slicing a piece of paper with little effort. "Both edges are equally sharp, so you can slit someone's throat with either side."

"Slit someone's throat?" Maria asked as she examined her dagger. "Do you think you could kill someone, Hetty?"

Hetty continued to run her thumb across the smooth blade. "I hope we don't have to find out."

CHAPTER 8

"Do you mind if I ask you something personal, Hetty?"

Maria was vigilant for Orpo police—who frequently stopped and questioned pedestrians at random—as they walked through one of The Hague's upscale residential neighborhoods in the early evening.

"Anything."

"In all the time I've known you, I haven't seen you with a man." Maria hurried to keep pace with Hetty. "Are you waiting for Karl?"

"Pay attention to every turn that we make," said Hetty, leading the way down a deserted alley. "Kees wants you to do this assignment solo next time."

"I'm watching." Maria turned her head right and left. "But you promised to answer my question."

Hetty walked in silence for a moment. As Maria took mental notes of their path, Hetty decided it couldn't hurt to reveal her little tryst.

"I slept with a British pilot during my first assignment."

"That was months ago," Maria laughed with surprise as she hit Hetty with a barrage of questions: "Why didn't I know about it? What's his name? Are you still seeing him?"

Hetty smiled and gave Maria a sideways hug. "Sorry I kept mum about it. It always takes me some time before I trust someone completely."

Maria stared back, her eyes pleading for the rest of the story. "Is he the one you met at the cinema? I remember now that Kees said his name was Jim."

As they crossed the street, Hetty nodded, "That's right. When the Orpo chased us out of the theater, I had to keep him off the street. So I left him overnight with a friend who has no connection to the resistance. That was pretty risky, but it worked out."

"So when did you two get together?"

"When I went to fetch him the next morning, my friend had left for work, and one thing led to another. It was no big deal. Really."

"Do you feel guilty? I mean, what if Karl comes back?"

"If I believed deep down that Karl was coming back, I would have waited for him," said Hetty, stopping to glance around the edge of a building. "And I'll keep hoping for a miracle until someone proves to me that I need to give up. But I could die tomorrow, so . . ."

Finding the road empty, Hetty stepped around the corner. "So I have no regrets about what happened. And no, I haven't seen him since. With any luck, he's back in England."

Maria nodded, taking everything in. "I've never slept with anyone," Maria whispered, afraid someone would overhear her big secret.

"Don't lie, Maria." Hetty glanced at her friend skeptically. "We both know you're sleeping with Kees."

"I am not," Maria blushed. "Not yet anyway."

Hetty pointed down a cross-street. "My grandmother, Oma Betje, lives down there. That's where we'll sleep tonight."

As they continued down the block toward their assignment, Hetty probed further, "Don't you like him?"

"Of course. I like Kees, and we flirt a lot," Maria smiled shyly, "but he's so much older."

"And he has a crooked nose," said Hetty with a laugh.

"I actually like his boxer's nose," said Maria, sharing the laugh.

"Of course you do," said Hetty. "You're in love with him."

Maria stared at the pavement. "You think so? I mean, is it that obvious? Do you think he knows too?"

"You didn't ask for my advice, but here it is," said Hetty putting an arm around her friend's shoulder. "If you like him, don't wait around. Age doesn't matter. Kees has a dangerous job. So do you. As far as I'm concerned, you're perfect for each other."

"I'm not sure how to start with him," said Maria, trying to concentrate on the turns Hetty took as they zigzagged through the neighborhood.

"Just let him know how you feel. He'll do the rest."

"It's nice to have a friend I can talk to about—" Suddenly Maria froze. Two Orpo policemen stood at the end of the block facing the other direction.

"Hide!" Hetty commanded, shoving Maria hard into some shrubs.

"Herr policeman," Hetty called out in German as she advanced with a smile on her face and a swing to her hips. "What a fine evening we are having." She glanced to her right. Maria had disappeared. Thank goodness.

All business, the German policeman thrust his hand out as he closed the distance between them. "Papers, please."

Heart racing, Hetty produced her identification card. The other policeman stood a few paces away, watching the street.

The German studied the leather bag hanging on Hetty's shoulder. "Where are you going?"

A streetlight illuminated the German's face. He was about Hetty's age, tall and clean shaven. Trying to remain calm, Hetty smiled as she wondered if Maria had escaped.

Two pedestrians walked by on a cross street. The other policeman followed them, leaving Hetty with her lone interrogator.

"I'm on my way to visit my grandmother," said Hetty. She tried smiling again, but the policeman didn't seem to notice.

The German gazed at her satchel with a slight lift of his head. "What's in the bag?"

Hetty handed it over. "Schoolwork," she said.

The German raised an eyebrow as he hefted the briefcase in one hand, the other resting on his pistol. Hetty knew that with a careful inspection, the policeman would feel the false papers under the lining.

"I'm told the university might reopen any day." Hetty opened her hazel eyes wide and gave him her prettiest smile.

"Who told you that?" the German scoffed without a hint of interest in her flirting. When he started to unzip her handbag, Hetty swallowed involuntarily.

Suddenly Maria's voice rang out from a distance. "Hey, you! Kraut!"

The German policeman turned toward the voice. Maria flashed into view, running hard two blocks away. Close behind her was the other Orpo policeman, giving chase.

Hetty's interrogator dropped her handbag and joined the pursuit. Snatching her bag from the sidewalk, Hetty ducked around the corner into a nearby alley. She leaned against a brick wall, hands on her knees, and took slow, deep breaths. She felt the lining of her briefcase to confirm that the false papers were still inside. Then she hurried down the street to deliver them, hoping Maria had managed to get away.

Hetty glanced over her shoulder as she approached the address Kees had given her. She scanned the area hoping to see Maria, but the street was empty.

"Don't knock; just walk in," Kees had instructed. Holding her breath, Hetty turned the knob to the front door.

As she locked the door behind her, she found herself alone in a well-appointed living room illuminated by a single lamp. Three glasses half-filled with whiskey sat on a table at the edge of the room.

"Paris."

Hetty's eyes searched the room but could not see the source of the voice.

"Bruges," she replied, her voice quivering.

As though a magic puzzle box had opened, two women and a man appeared from three doors.

"I'm Pier Arden." The man held out his hand. He was tall, in his early twenties, with red-blond hair, blue eyes, and a boyish smile.

"Hetty." She shook Pier's hand, looking over the two women standing next to him.

"Isn't it a bit reckless telling me your last name?"

"I trust you," said Pier nonchalantly.

"I hope you won't mind if I only use my first name," said Hetty.

"Of course. That's protocol," said Pier as he placed his arms around the two women. "These are my aunts, Rini and Thyrza." Both women were short, in their mid-forties, with straight, graying hair that hung straight to their shoulders. Rini wore glasses.

Hetty tossed her leather bag on the sofa and plopped down in a straight-back chair next to the table where she'd seen the whiskey. Her hands wobbled as she filled one of the glasses to the top and drank it down.

Pier's awkwardness was immediately apparent to Hetty. *He must know how unsettling it is when he stares at a girl's breasts*, she thought. Still, she admired his courage; this wasn't the first time he had escorted pilots to the Belgian border, Kees had said.

Rini put her hand on Hetty's shoulder. "Are you all right, dear?"

"I'm worried about my friend," said Hetty as she eyed the half-empty whiskey bottle. "She was running for her life the last time I saw her."

"Shall we go out and search for her?" asked Rini. "We know this neighborhood."

"It's after curfew," said Pier. "Four people wandering in the dark are sure to get caught."

"You're right." Hetty nodded grimly. "If they haven't caught her, she's already on her way back to Leiden anyway."

"You shouldn't go outside either, dear." Thyrza spoke in a kind, self-assured voice.

"It kills me to sit here doing nothing," Hetty frowned. "My friend just saved my life."

"Do you want to sleep here tonight?" suggested Aunt Thyrza.

"No," said Hetty, glancing cautiously at Pier, who smiled awkwardly. "I have somewhere else to stay."

Then she rose abruptly, knocking her chair backward, and grabbed her leather bag. She used Gerhardt's double-edged dagger to slit the lining of her handbag. Reaching inside, she located official-looking papers, which she handed to Pier. "These are for your pilots."

"Thank you," said Pier, still gazing at Hetty with admiring eyes.

"Are they here now?" asked Hetty, trying to ignore his obvious interest. "Can I meet them?"

"Unfortunately, no. We rendezvous tomorrow." Pier gazed at the dagger in Hetty's hand. "That's a fine weapon you have there. May I see it?" He balanced the blade on his fingertips. "Ever kill anyone with this?"

"You might be the first if you keep looking at me that way," Hetty retorted as she retrieved the dagger.

"You should reconsider my aunt's offer to stay the night," said Pier, glancing at the whiskey bottle. "We'd have fun finishing that whiskey."

"My friend is out there all alone, running from the Germans because of me," said Hetty tersely. "How can you think about having fun?"

"There's never a good time for fun since the Germans arrived," said Pier. He took her hand, but she pulled away.

"My nephew didn't mean to offend," said Rini, placing her arm around Hetty's shoulders. "He's actually a good guy. Smuggling human cargo can be a lonely business."

"Don't embarrass me, Aunt Rini," said Pier, forcing a laugh. "Besides, Hetty's not interested."

Hetty stared at him for a long moment. "You're right. I'm not," she said, opening the door to check for Germans before stepping outside. Pier handed her a note, which she stuffed into her pocket. Then she kept to the shadows as she hurried toward Oma Betje's house.

"It's a miracle." Maria flung herself into Hetty's arms as she entered their flat the next day. "I was so worried about you."

"You're the miracle," said Hetty as the two friends embraced. "I thought they'd catch you for sure."

"We waited up all night for you," Mimi called from the kitchen, where she was washing dishes.

"I slept at Oma Betje's." Hetty continued hugging Maria tightly. "You should have seen how brave Maria was. She saved my life."

"You were the brave one, Hetty." Maria hugged her again. Then she turned toward Mimi. "She threw me behind some bushes, then faced the Germans alone. I couldn't believe when she tried to flirt with the policeman."

"Flirt?" asked Mimi, laughing at the thought. "Did it work?"

"Not at all," said Hetty. "He would have found the papers if Maria hadn't distracted him. How did you get away, Maria?"

"I got lucky," said Maria, taking Hetty's hand as they sat down together. "When I yelled at the policeman, I thought I could easily out-run him because he was two blocks away," Maria began. "I was wrong; that guy could run really fast."

"But here you are," said Hetty, squeezing Maria's arm.

"He almost had me, but he tripped over a pail that someone had left on the sidewalk."

Maria clapped her hands together sharply to simulate the sound of his fall.

"The other guy came around a corner and tripped over his friend. I lost them on the zigzag streets you made me memorize."

"You sidetracked them just in time," said Hetty, smiling broadly. "They would have found the cargo if not for you."

"What about our assignment?" asked Maria. "Did you deliver the papers?"

Hetty nodded. "I met three nice people, a guy named Pier and his two aunts. They wanted to search for you."

"They wouldn't have found me," said Maria. "I was long gone."

"Tell us about the guy you met," said Mimi with a knowing glance. "Pier?"

"Well," said Hetty with a sparkle in her eyes, "he has a nice smile. His aunts were practically forcing us together."

"Is he a prospect?" asked Maria excitedly.

"He was interested all right," said Hetty with a big smile. "I told him flat out he had no chance. But he wouldn't take no for an answer."

"Which means you must have said yes," said Mimi excitedly. "Tell us."

"As I was about to leave," said Hetty, "he passed me a note that said he was coming to Leiden on business, and he asked me to meet him for a drink."

"What did you say?" said Maria, clapping her hands.

"I didn't say no." Hetty laughed and shifted in her chair. "I went back to his house this morning to give him my answer."

"You naughty girl," said Mimi with a laugh. "What happened to that shy girl I met at university who had never kissed a boy?"

"That girl doesn't exist anymore—not since the Germans invaded," said Hetty. Then she winked at Maria. "What about *your* love life?"

"I'm planning to do something about that tonight," said Maria in a shy voice.

"What aren't you two telling me?" said Mimi, shifting her gaze back and forth between her friends.

"It's great to be alive," said Maria, flipping her hair back exuberantly with both hands.

CHAPTER 9

WITH THE IMPOSITION OF REGISTRATION laws, things grew worse for Jews in Holland. When Kees was visited by Menno, a member of the Amsterdam resistance, the three couriers learned that conditions had become intolerable there, sending even more Jews into hiding. Knowing they were fortunate to have escaped just in time on their last assignment, Hetty and Maria were more than willing to listen to someone else's stories about encounters with the Germans, dreadful as they were. Sipping whiskey in Kees's living room, the three couriers listened intently to Menno's account.

"I watched the Nazis drag Jewish citizens from their homes," said Menno from his seat on the sofa. "These are human beings—mostly Dutch citizens like us—and the Germans treated them like livestock."

"Why do you think the Nazis decided to act now?" asked Hetty, leaning against the wall. "Ever since the invasion, they've been moving slower on their Jewish program in Holland than in other occupied countries. I know they did that for propaganda, but why abandon that policy now?"

"Maybe it was always their plan to move against Jews after we had become accustomed to the occupation. It also might have something to do with the huge migration of Jews into the Netherlands," said Menno. "They're trying to escape German persecution. The numbers are noticeable in Amsterdam."

"It sounds so cruel," said Maria, bringing rubbing alcohol and bandages to tend to Menno's wounds.

"At first, the Amsterdam Jews were arrested as hostages," said Menno, grimacing at the memory. "One member of the Dutch Nazi Party was killed in the street, and they rounded up four hundred Jews—all young men—as hostages. Can you believe it?"

Maria winced as she dabbed the wounds on Menno's face with alcohol. "How did you get these?"

"We fought back," said Menno, grimacing in pain when the alcohol penetrated a deep cut on his forehead. "The Dutch in Amsterdam shut down the whole city with a general strike."

"Did it work?" asked Hetty, running a hand through her thick, curly hair, cut short just above the shoulders.

"Not really," said Menno, jerking his head back sharply from Maria's touch. "The Germans deported the hostages to a work camp. I don't know whether that was the result of our strike or if it was their plan all along."

"I've heard about the strike," said Mimi, leaning forward from her seat on the sofa. "They're calling it the *Februaristaking*. Those people are heroes."

"The heroes are the leaders," said Menno, pushing Maria's hand away when she tried to bandage some fresh abrasions. "My wounds are nothing compared to what happened to them. They're all dead."

"Menno is a wanted man," said Kees, turning toward the others. "He's going to stay with me for a few days until he finds a better hiding place."

"Doesn't that jeopardize the whole Leiden operation?" said Mimi with alarm.

"Where do you suggest he stay?" Kees asked sarcastically. "Menno's been my best friend since we were eight years old."

"I suppose you have no choice," said Mimi grudgingly as she stared at the wall. "Still, I don't like taking unnecessary risks."

"Things will get worse," Maria observed as she finished her work on Menno's wounds. "The Amsterdam deportations will drive more Jews into hiding, and they'll need our help."

A short, bald man in his fifties squinted at Hetty through a small opening in the door of a rundown row house in The Hague. "What do you want?" he demanded. Hetty stepped back. The man smelled as if he hadn't bathed in a week.

"Kees sent me."

Hetty wondered if she had the right address. The Germans had deported Jews by the thousands during the weeks since Menno told them about Amsterdam, causing a scramble that sometimes confused the growing resistance about where people were hiding.

The disheveled man pulled her into the house by the wrist, closing the door quickly behind her. Hetty could barely make out two people, a man and a woman, huddled side-by-side in the corner of the dark room. As unkempt as the bald man had been, the two people before her were clean and well dressed. Both had dark, straight hair with deep-set, hollow dark eyes that reflected both pain and exhaustion. They clung to each other, watching Hetty cautiously. A clang of pots and pans from a nearby kitchen told Hetty that the bald man had left the room.

"I'm Daniel and this is Hanna," the well-dressed man said in German.

"We're from Prague," said Daniel. "We owned a dry-cleaning business there. But the Nazis took it from us."

"You don't deserve to be treated like that," said Hetty as her eyes adjusted to the darkness.

"We're not the only ones," said Daniel. "When Jewish persecutions started in Germany and Eastern Europe, lots of Jews migrated to Holland. We all thought it was a safe haven, but the Germans got here first. Now we're on the run again."

When Hetty's eyes finally adjusted to the dark, she saw they were alone in what seemed to be someone's poorly kept living room. A threadbare sofa and chairs covered in dusty cracked leather occupied most of the floor space. At one end was a brick fireplace. "How did you get here?" asked Hetty.

"We booked rail passage to Amsterdam on the black market in Prague," said Daniel, pacing the floor. "It cost a king's ransom. That was two years ago. We've been hidden by strangers ever since, never long in the same place."

Hetty sneezed as she took in the dusty surroundings.

"Today, my wife and I leave for England," Daniel continued. Hetty studied the two small suitcases resting on the floor at their feet.

"That's a long journey," said Hetty.

"A dangerous one too," he nodded grimly. "That's why we're leaving our son here."

"Your son?" From overhead, a floorboard creaked. Hetty pulled her dagger from her purse. "Who else is here?" Her head turned toward the ceiling.

Daniel eyed the dagger and stiffened. "My son isn't here." Daniel's voice quivered. "That noise is probably the bald man who let you in."

Hetty returned the dagger to her purse without unsheathing it.

"My little boy needs your help," Daniel explained, staring at her purse as if he could still see the knife.

"What can I do?" asked Hetty.

"We have arranged for him to hide in plain sight with a gentile family." Daniel placed his arm around Hanna. "That's where he is now."

"How could you leave your child?" Hetty blurted the words before thinking.

Hanna started to cry.

"These are desperate times," Daniel explained, putting his hand on his wife's shoulder. "We had no choice."

"I'm sorry," said Hetty, studying her hands, "I have no right to judge you. Please tell me what you need."

"Yacov is only four. The gentile family won't keep him unless you deliver this money."

Daniel retrieved a package from behind a loose brick in the fireplace and handed it to Hetty. The package was filled with cash.

Hetty started to speak but could not. "How will you find him when you return from England?" she asked on the second try.

"We'll figure that out if we survive," said Daniel with worry lines on his forehead.

Hanna started trembling from head to toe. "No!" she choked out, as she buried her face in her husband's chest. "We can't leave our boy."

Daniel put his arms around Hanna's shoulders and whispered something to her in Yiddish. Hanna nodded but continued to whimper quietly.

"Please, take the money to this address." He handed Hetty a slip of paper. "You must hurry. If they don't have the payment by four o'clock, they'll put Yacov out in the street."

Hanna stood and faced Daniel. "I can't leave my baby." She'd stopped crying, but the agony on her face was worse. "We must take him with us."

Daniel reached out to touch her, but Hanna slapped his hand away and went to a corner of the room. Her husband went to her and stroked her back. "We agreed to this, my love. There is no other way."

Hanna placed her arms around him and muffled her moaning with his shirt. "I can't live without him," she murmured. She allowed Daniel to lead her to the sofa, where she sat back down.

Hetty examined the slip of paper and checked her watch. Then she cleared her throat and said in a raspy voice, "I know this neighborhood. I can get there in plenty of time."

Daniel exhaled with relief. Hanna's anxious eyes did not leave her husband.

"But this is not a nice neighborhood," Hetty continued, tapping her finger on the paper Daniel had given her. "Respectable families don't live there."

Daniel put both hands on his wife's cheeks and gazed into her eyes. Hanna nodded almost imperceptibly. Then he kissed her forehead and turned to Hetty. "Please go before she changes her mind."

Hetty saw a pair of eyes watching her from beneath the threadbare drapes at the address Daniel had given her. She reached into her purse and touched the money she carried. The drapes dropped, and the door opened. A fleshy man in his late thirties, two inches taller than Hetty, stood in the doorway with a hostile expression. "Is Gunnar around?" she asked, trying to sound casual even though her heart was racing.

The man rubbed his hand through his long greasy hair. "No one named Gunnar lives here." Hetty knew there was no Gunnar; she'd made up the name to get things started.

"Maybe he just used that name with me," said Hetty nonchalantly, as though people lying to her was an everyday occurrence. "He owes me some money on account of some tricks I did for him, if you know what I'm talking about."

A big, fleshy smile crossed the man's face. "My roommate Tom might fit that description," he offered, and Hetty gave him a relaxed smile. "He's not here. Do you want to come in and wait for him?"

"Fine with me," said Hetty, patting the man's thick arm while she squeezed past him through the doorway. Hetty knew this was dangerous, but she had to know whether Yacov was inside.

"What's your name?"

"They call me Ad. How about a pint?"

"Sure thing," said Hetty, folding her arms so that Ad wouldn't see her hands tremble. "Gunnar—I mean Tom—told me you boys have a kid here."

Hetty tried to sound casual as she surveyed the room. To her right was a closed door—to a bedroom, she guessed. Ad kept smiling, but his face became alert, suddenly on guard. "Why do you want to know about the boy?"

"Tom said there's money in it," said Hetty in a breezy voice.

Ad's smile disappeared. "No one knows 'bout that." His face turned red in anger. "*No one.*"

Fighting off her fear, Hetty looped her hand through Ad's elbow and nuzzled his flabby bicep. "I told you, Tom and I are close." She resisted the urge to recoil from Ad's body odor.

Ad grabbed Hetty by the hair and kissed her, ramming his tongue into her mouth. Then he laughed. "*Ha. Ha.* Are you and Tom *that* close?"

Hetty sputtered, spitting out Ad's saliva as she stepped away, rubbing her arm, which had been bruised by Ad's strong grip. *How did I end up alone with this stinking brute?* "Where's my pint?" she asked with a forced smile.

A crafty grin spread across Ad's face. "Coming right up."

He waddled into the dirty kitchen. As soon as the door closed behind him, Hetty tiptoed to the closed door she'd seen earlier. It was locked. She produced a nail file from her purse. Ad was humming in the kitchen when she picked the lock—*click*—a trick she'd learned from her brother.

Her mouth dry and heart pounding, she opened the door a crack. A small boy with dark hair and big brown eyes sat on the floor with one hand tied to the bedpost. When he started to speak, Hetty shushed him with a finger to her lips. "I'm a friend of your parents," she whispered in German, hoping the Czech boy would understand. "I will get you out of here."

Hetty's eyes fixated on a gun resting on the table outside the bedroom door. How had she missed that? She reached for the weapon, but it slipped through her fingers, clattering to the table with a loud *thunk*. Footsteps from the kitchen told her Ad was about to appear, so Hetty quickly closed the bedroom door as she touched the gun lightly to steady it. She turned a smiling face toward Ad, who entered the living room holding two bottles of ale.

"So when will Tom get back?" Hetty took a sip of her ale. She grimaced at the putrid flavor and nearly spat it out, but she swallowed it to wash away the oniony drool that Ad's tongue had left behind.

"He went on an errand," said Ad, taking Hetty's bottle and placing both on a nearby table. "Won't be back for a couple hours. So there's plenty of time for you and me to have a little fun."

Before Hetty knew what had happened, Ad clutched her forcefully, pawed her breast and rubbed himself against her pelvis.

Hetty's heart raced with fear as she struggled in vain against him. She remembered Gerhardt's words: "It will be a fight to the death." Seeing no better option, she used the move he'd taught her, ducking her head under Ad's armpit and sliding around behind him, fumbling for her knife.

"You bitch!" Ad shouted as he rammed his elbow into her stomach, leaving her struggling for air. Hetty grabbed his hair the way Gerhardt had taught her, but she lacked the breath she needed to yank his head back. Gasping, she clutched his hair with both hands, but Ad shoved her to the floor with a mighty howl. Staring up from the floor at his bright red face, Hetty unsheathed the killing knife. *Shhhick!* Ad, standing above her, hesitated for a split second. When his eyes flickered toward the gun on the table, with the apparent intent to use it, Hetty lashed out at his feet, cutting his Achilles tendon.

"You fucking cunt!" Ad screamed in pain as he collapsed to the floor, clutching his ruined ankle. With both of them on the floor, Ad tried to grab Hetty by the throat, but she scuttled out of the way.

She found her footing and leaped around him as he clutched the air in a vain attempt to grab her. Kneeling behind him, Hetty grabbed a mass of his greasy hair and pulled it back with all of her strength, pressing the knife against his neck.

"*Be aggressive,*" Gerhardt had urged her during their training. So she pressed the knife down hard on his throat. Beads of blood appeared where Hetty held the knife's sharp edge.

"Keep your hands off me, you filthy bastard," said Hetty in a voice that she did not recognize. Breathing hard from exertion, her knife hand shook, increasing the size of the laceration on Ad's throat. A rivulet of blood trickled down his fleshy neck. "And who the hell holds a little kid prisoner anyway?"

"All right. All right, bitch," Ad cried out through his pain. "I wasn't going to hurt the kid."

Copious amounts of blood covered the floor from Ad's ankle wound. Hetty forced the fleshy man to lean against the wall cross-legged.

"Take off your belt," Hetty ordered while continuing her dual assault on his hair and throat.

"Make me." Ad lunged to grab her.

Without thinking, Hetty stabbed him hard in the forearm, making him recoil, his hand pressed against the wound to staunch the consider-able flow of blood.

"Holy fuck!" Ad's eyes widened when he removed his hand to exam-ine the knife wound. "Take it easy, bitch," he whimpered as he unfastened his belt and held it out for inspection.

"Now strap it around your ankles!" Hetty held the knife menacingly in his face. "Cinch it up tight," she ordered. "It will help with the bleeding."

He had stopped defying her. When he had finished, the belt held his ankles tightly together, serving double duty as both a shackle to limit his movement and a tourniquet to staunch the flow of blood from the wound.

Hetty put her face next to his. "I'm taking the boy, and you won't follow, understand?"

"You'll pay for this." Ad glared at her with menacing rage.

Hetty went into the bedroom and cut Yacov's restraint, carrying him to the sofa in the living room before she picked up the gun. Then she pointed the pistol at Ad's face and cocked it.

"Don't shoot," he begged with a shudder.

She uncocked the pistol and put it in her bag. "I'm saving my first murder for a Nazi, not some big, dumb Dutchman with bad breath," she declared. "But I will *fucking kill you* if you try to follow us," she hissed, surprised that she meant it.

Once outside, Hetty put the boy sidesaddle on the frame of her bicy-cle. "Hold the handlebar, Yacov," she said in German, guiding his hands. "Tightly," she said, wrapping her hand around his. "OK. Here we go." She pedaled hard through the seedy neighborhood. "Everything will be all right," she said, wondering if it was true.

Her confidence grew as she put distance behind her. "Did you learn how to ride like this when you lived in Prague, Yacov?"

"How do you know my name?" the boy asked in German.

Hetty rode onto the sidewalk of the narrow street to dodge an over-sized truck coming from the opposite direction. "I know your parents," she said as she tossed the gun into some bushes.

Yacov lifted his questioning eyes back toward Hetty. "Won't we need that?"

"The Germans would be cross if they caught me with it," she explained as she continued to pedal.

Hetty and Yacov turned the corner, and the house where she had met Yacov's parents came into view. She hoped that Daniel and Hanna had not left yet.

Hetty pushed the back door open with her foot. Nothing but dark-ness. She fetched the knife from her bag and unsheathed it while she pushed Yacov into a closet near the entrance to keep him safe. Feeling her way down a dim hallway, Hetty came upon a doorway. Slowly, she peered inside but couldn't see anything in the dark.

Suddenly someone grabbed her hard by the arm. In an instant, she ducked to avoid a blow that she just managed to escape and thrust her knife in the direction of her assailant.

Then she froze—a knife was pressed against her ribs.

"Wait. Hetty. Stop."

Hetty's eyes widened in the dark. "Kees?" Then she wrapped her arms around his neck. "I've never been so glad to see a friend in all my life." She sobbed uncontrollably. "I had to use my killing knife."

"You killed someone?" Kees said with surprise.

"No, just threatened him," she replied, clutching Kees's arm and gulping air to control her crying. "I've never done anything like that."

A child's voice rang out in German. "Help me."

Kees swiveled toward the sound, but Hetty just smiled. "Yacov, you can come out now."

The doorknob on the closet began to shake and rattle. Hetty opened it, and Yacov threw his arms around her legs. "I thought you'd left me," he cried desperately in German, clinging tightly.

"Is this Yacov?" asked Kees.

Hetty nodded as she hugged the little boy.

"What's he doing here? Your only job was to deliver money."

"Some bad people had him, so I took him," she said with a defiant stare. She handed him Daniel's money and added, "Here. You'd better keep this."

"I just helped his parents connect with the Dutch-Paris network. Hopefully, they can find their way to England."

"They're not here?" Hetty rubbed the back of her neck while she glanced around wildly. "We must find them. They think he's living safely with a gentile family."

"Daniel and Hanna are at the station," said Kees, guiding Hetty and Yacov urgently toward the front door. "Their train leaves in ten minutes."

"Don't be afraid, my brave little man." Hetty took Yacov's hand and led him quickly from the house. "We need to hurry."

Hetty put Yacov on her handlebars again and pedaled as fast as she could. Finally, ahead, smoke billowed from the stack of the steam engine. "Thank God. It hasn't left yet," murmured Hetty as she pedaled toward the giant iron engine. But the train began to leave the station, slowly at first, then picking up speed.

She pedaled alongside the train, peering into the windows.

"There's your father!" she screamed, breathing hard and pumping furiously alongside the train with Yacov holding the handlebars. Hetty yelled for Daniel to look at her, but her voice was drowned out by the locomotive. Daniel, facing away from the window, never saw them. Then the train pulled away.

CHAPTER 10

THREE WEEKS PASSED BEFORE HETTY had the opportunity to make a courier run to the farm where Yacov was hiding. When she arrived at the front gate, a skinny teenager extended her hand.

"Hi, I'm Rachel. Welcome to the farm." The girl swept her long dark hair away from her face.

"Hetty."

"Kees told us you were coming." Wearing a sweater and plain cloth skirt that hung loosely below her knees, Rachel squinted up at the sun, which provided little warmth to the chilly afternoon. "Have you brought something for us?" she asked.

Hetty handed her a package. "There's money in there. Keep it safe."

"Don't worry," said Rachel with a smile. "I know a secure place to put it."

While Rachel put the money away in the farmhouse, Hetty surveyed the property. The buildings at the farm made an idyllic portrait; the large farmhouse, old but majestic, sported fresh white paint and blue eaves. Alongside stood a large barn where a cow mooed. There was a sizeable barnyard with lots of chickens and goats. Next to the house a vegetable garden featured tomatoes, carrots, beans, and herbs. Two more farmhouses were visible in the distance. In between, fields of corn and flax stretched out to the horizon. Hetty stood for a moment, taking it all in before stepping through the gate.

"I came to see Yacov," said Hetty when Rachel returned.

"He's around here somewhere." Rachel waved to a girl with blond hair whom Hetty judged to be about ten years old.

"Angelique, have you seen Yacov?"

"I'll go look for him." Giggly and bouncy, Angelique seemed like a typical ten-year-old, but something in the girl's deep blue eyes and demeanor told Hetty that Angelique was an old soul, mature beyond her years.

"Wait, come here," said Rachel. "Angelique, I'd like you to meet Hetty. She's the one who rescued Yacov."

"Pleased to meet you," said Angelique as she shook Hetty's hand. "I hope you'll stay for supper. Mother and Father are out in the fields, but they will be cross when they return if we don't feed you."

"Are all of the adults out in the fields?" asked Hetty, scanning to the horizon where people working among the corn seemed to be the size of ants.

Angelique nodded. "Most of them. Mothers with babies stay in the farmhouse during the day. My Aunt Sylvie is feeding the livestock in the barnyard, but she'll return to the fields when she's finished." Angelique waved to a woman who was feeding the goats.

"Is it safe to leave the other children alone?" Hetty touched the sharp blade of a plough.

"It's safer for the adults to stay in the fields, where the Germans can't count them," said Rachel. "Too many adults on one farm would be suspicious."

"My parents say these are desperate times," Angelique added. "So each of us must do a little more than is usually expected. Rachel and I watch the young ones while the adults work at the far corners of our property."

"Do your parents own this farm?"

"Angelique and her parents are saints," said Rachel, tousling Angelique's hair. "My parents were deported to the camps not long after the first Amsterdam outrage. You must have heard about the strike."

Rachel walked to the stable, where she studied pebbles that she moved around with the toe of her shoe.

Hetty joined Rachel and put an arm around her. "You must miss your family."

"I'm still figuring out how to live without them," said Rachel, brushing away a tear. "It's really hard."

"The resistance rescued Rachel from school the day her parents were arrested," said Angelique, who had followed Hetty to comfort her friend.

"They brought me here," said Rachel. "Their farm is a safe haven compared to Buchenwald."

"Buchenwald?"

"It's a prison camp in Germany—near Weimar," said Rachel, furrowing her eyebrows. "We think that's where the Germans took my parents. I don't even know if they're alive or dead."

"I hate those bastards more every day," said Hetty, giving Rachel a hug.

"When the Nazis made us wear the yellow star, my father said it was only the beginning." Rachel stared into the cornfield. "Turns out he was right."

Hetty surveyed the horizon uneasily. "How many are hiding here besides you and Yacov?"

"My parents are hiding eleven Jews in plain sight," said Angelique proudly. "Two joined us last week."

Hetty's eyes tracked Aunt Sylvie, still feeding the goats. A little boy was with her, scattering food for the chickens.

Angelique followed her gaze. "That little boy, Isaac, is one of the people in hiding. No one except people on this farm would know that he's not related to Aunt Sylvie, so they work together. That's how he hides in plain sight."

"All of us work for our supper," Rachel explained.

"Even Yacov has chores," said Angelique, turning to leave. "I'll go find him for you."

"Come with me, Hetty," said Rachel, watching Angelique disappear around the corner of the barn. "I'll show you the farm."

Suddenly Rachel stopped and focused on a child running toward them. The boy, about eight years old, was out of breath when he whispered something in Rachel's ear.

"OK, Peter," said Rachel, using her hand to shade her eyes while she gazed up the road. "Tell the others to go to the shelter."

"Is there trouble?" asked Hetty.

"I'm afraid the Germans are about to pay us a visit," said Rachel, glancing nervously toward the horizon where she saw a cloud of dust from the approaching vehicles. "Peter and Angelique will help distract the Nazis."

"How do you know they're Germans?" asked Hetty, her gaze following Rachel's.

"The children tell us. They play up the road there," said Rachel, pointing. "If they see Germans, they run a relay across the fields to warn us."

A column of military vehicles with German markings came into view.

"Now do you believe me?" Rachel nodded toward the convoy of jeeps, trucks, and armored personnel carriers. She took Hetty's elbow. "I'll show you where to hide."

"What about Yacov?" Hetty protested.

"He's right here," said Angelique, holding Yacov's hand.

"Oh, Yacov," said Hetty as she hugged the boy tightly. "I'm so glad you are all right."

"None of you will be all right if you don't hide," said Angelique, staring at the approaching convoy. "Follow Rachel," she told Hetty. "There's room for you in the shelter."

"What about you, Angelique?" Hetty asked as Rachel led her by the wrist.

"Don't worry about me. I'm trained for this," said Angelique, practicing her confident smile. "My parents left me in charge."

Hetty and Yacov followed Rachel into the cornfield. They shoved the thick leaves of the tall stalks of corn aside until they came upon a tree branch, which Rachel used as a lever to lift a thick layer of sod. This revealed a deep hole, where people, mostly children, were already packed like sardines. Everyone scrunched and scooted to make room for Hetty, Rachel, and Yacov, who wedged themselves onto benches fashioned from dirt. Hetty gagged at the thick odor of wet soil as Rachel closed the opening.

When Hetty's eyes adjusted to the darkness, she could make out the faces of the others. A woman seated next to Yacov on Hetty's right rocked an infant, but the child fussed, sensing the tension in his mother.

"What will happen when the Germans find the farm empty?" Hetty asked, placing an arm around Yacov.

"It's not empty," whispered Rachel, who had squeezed in on Hetty's left. "Angelique's in charge."

"That poor little girl is out there alone?" Hetty exclaimed while chewing her fingernails.

"Not alone." Rachel turned her head toward the sounds outside. "Peter is with her."

Before Hetty could react to this bit of news, the roar of military vehicles filled the earthen chamber. "Is there a way out of here?" whispered Hetty, her voice unsteady.

Rachel shook her head. "We control what we can. The rest is up to God." She laid her head on Hetty's shoulder and clutched her free hand.

"I wish—"

"*Shhh.*" Rachel put her fingertips on Hetty's mouth. "They're here."

Keeping her breathing shallow to preserve oxygen, Hetty reflected on how she had gotten here. Her assignment to carry money for Daniel and Hanna had sounded simple enough. She could not have guessed that it would lead to the ferocious fight with Ad, followed by her failed dash to reunite Yacov with his parents. But why had she come to this farm? There was only one answer: she cared about Yacov. Hetty squeezed Rachel's hand. And now she cared about this brave girl, whose family had been ripped away from her. They were tethered by their common peril. Hetty knew she would do it all again even if it meant that her life would end in this musty hole.

Eight-year-old Peter's voice floated into the shelter. "Angelique!" he called, just as they had rehearsed.

"I'm busy. What do you want?" said Angelique, pretending she was unaware of the German presence.

"There are soldiers out here," said the boy.

A rooster crowed. Then the squeaky sound of the barn door opening penetrated the subterranean hideout.

"Hello, sir." A milk bucket clanged to the ground. "I didn't realize anyone was here. What can I do for you?" Angelique's voice sounded confident.

"*Waaah!*" Hetty jumped when the baby near her cried out. Quickly, his mother clasped her hand tightly over the infant's mouth.

Please don't smother him, Hetty thought, too afraid to speak.

In the barnyard, the rooster had crowed again about the same moment the baby cried. Everyone in the shelter stopped breathing and glanced anxiously toward the exit, hoping the rooster had covered the sound of the child.

"Where are your parents?" A man, presumably an officer, spoke gruffly in German to Angelique. A translator repeated his question in Dutch.

"They are working in the field." Angelique approached the officer. "But I can answer your questions."

"We have a report that too many people are working some of the farms in this area," the officer declared sharply. "Are you hiding Jews?"

"No Jews here." Angelique shook her head, gesturing toward the horizon. "Everyone is out in the field. My mother and father won't mind if you search our farm."

Hetty was amazed at how calm and mature Angelique's clear voice sounded. This was not the bouncy little girl she'd just met in the barnyard.

There was a long silence. Perspiration poured from the faces of everyone in the hole, trying not to cough as the oxygen level deteriorated.

"No. We have several more farms to investigate," the officer said at last. "But tell your parents we will be watching this place."

Without another word, the Germans sped away.

It seemed like an eternity before Angelique yelled "all clear," and Hetty and the others scrambled out of their earthen prison, inhaling the fresh outdoor air with relish.

"You brave girl." Hetty ran to Angelique and embraced her.

"Next time, they'll bring their dogs," Angelique warned tersely.

"But this time they didn't," said Rachel, placing her arm around the younger girl's shoulders. "And everyone's safe."

"Thank God you're all right," said Hetty, stroking Angelique's golden hair.

"I was running out of things to say to those bastards," said Angelique. She put her hand over her mouth, embarrassed by her coarse language, and they all laughed with relief.

Hetty's companions from the hiding place started to disperse. They had farm work to do. "How strange," Hetty said to Rachel and Angelique. "We shared a moment of agonizing terror together. Now we go on with our lives—as if nothing happened."

"Something happened, for sure," said Rachel, putting a wadded cloth object in Hetty's hand. "I won't forget any of it."

Hetty sat across the table from Kees in a café overlooking the New Rhine. After gazing at the busy canal, she told him about her visit to the farm where Jews hid in plain sight.

"At the meetings I attended with Karl before the war, the communists told stories about the deportation of Jews to terrible camps in Nazi-occupied countries. Yacov and Rachel make it real. They might never see their parents again. I feel so helpless."

"You're not helpless," said Kees, turning his head around to find the waiter. "You risked your life to bring money to that farm, and our donors take a huge risk every time they give us money for people in hiding."

"We need to do more," she said as a fisherman rowing his boat down the middle of the waterway caught her attention.

Kees watched as Hetty put something on the table.

"Rachel gave me this. It's the yellow star the Germans made her wear before she was rescued by the resistance. See? It says 'Jew' right in the middle. Why do the Nazis care so much about who's a Jew?"

"I've seen people wearing them everywhere, by order of the high command," said Kees, turning the vile object over with his fingers. "It's disgusting. But we can't stop it except to help people like Rachel and Yacov when they go into hiding."

"I've heard that non-Jews in Amsterdam are wearing them," said Hetty, pinning it on her blouse, "as an act of solidarity with the Dutch Jews."

"Take that thing off!" Kees ordered tersely. "You'll get arrested. That's what happened when people wore them in Amsterdam."

"So what?" she said defiantly. "Let them arrest me. Why don't you care about Jews, Kees?"

"That's insulting. I care as much as you do," said Kees, exasperated. "If your entire courier cell gets arrested, who will deliver ration cards and money to Jews in hiding? Would you sacrifice that important work for a futile gesture?"

"I hadn't thought about that," said Hetty, removing the despised yellow object. "But we need to do more."

"The resistance is small," said Kees. "We do what we can."

"And leave the rest to God," Hetty said, nodding and putting the yellow star in her purse. "That's what Rachel told me yesterday when we were hiding."

The fisherman on the New Rhine stopped rowing and, using only a fishing line, dropped a baited hook into the water.

"I only have ersatz coffee today," said the waiter apologetically as he placed two cups of the dubious brown liquid in front of his customers. "But at least I have a little milk to go with it."

"We're used to ersatz swill," Hetty laughed. "Milk is a rare treat." She glanced back toward the canal, where the fisherman had caught a fish.

Kees fidgeted uncomfortably. "Are you still seeing Pier?"

"Off and on," said Hetty, stirring milk into her coffee. "We enjoy each other when he's in town, which isn't too often. Why do you ask?"

"No reason," said Kees. "I'm glad you have someone."

"Meaning what?" Hetty was suddenly alert. "You're acting weird, Kees. What aren't you telling me?"

Kees paused to collect his thoughts. "Karl and his uncle were shot to death during the invasion," he said at last, his face twisted with anxiety. "Our resistance friends in Rotterdam just brought the news that police found their bodies on the road leading north out of town."

Hetty's face turned ashen. "Are you sure it's them?"

Kees nodded. "They still had their IDs. The Rotterdam police found them two years ago, but our friends in Amsterdam couldn't find any next of kin to notify."

"Karl and his uncle only had each other," Hetty whispered with a stunned expression. "Now everyone in their family is dead."

Kees sat silently while Hetty closed her eyes and took a deep breath before firing off more questions. "Did the bodies match the ID photos? Did the police say what the men looked like? Did one of them have a beard?"

Kees shook his head. "It's been two years. Maybe there's no one around who remembers those details." He reached into his bag and pulled out a blood-soaked blue sweater with a red stripe. "But they gave me this."

Hetty covered her face with her hands and began to sob. "That's the sweater I gave to Karl. How did you get it?"

Kees reached out for Hetty's hand. "When he couldn't find next of kin, our resistance contact took the sweater home with him and put it in a drawer. Recently, he met a person who knew that Karl had attended Leiden University. It didn't take our colleagues long to find me."

"I had always hoped," said Hetty through her tears, "that somehow . . ."

The fisherman caught another fish, but she wasn't watching.

CHAPTER 11

THERE WAS ONLY ONE PERSON Hetty could talk to about Karl—her brother Jan. So she took the train to The Hague to find him at their parents' home. Four years younger than Hetty, Jan had always been mature beyond his years. There was no one in the world she loved more. They shared everything with each other.

"I made this scarf for you, Jantje," said Hetty. She had repaired the crooked rows on the light green scarf she'd shown to Kees when she first started knitting it. "I've been working on this for a long time. Now that it's finished, I want you to have it."

"Thanks, Sis," Jan grinned, admiring her work. The scarf was lumpy, clearly not the work of a practiced hand, but he tossed it around his neck with a flourish as though it were a work of art. "I'll need this when the weather turns ugly."

Blessed with a flawless complexion, blond hair, and a boyish grin, Jan had always exhibited a playful manner, but Hetty sometimes remarked that this was a disguise for his mature brain. Congenial by nature, Jan adored his mother and sister and was the only family member who tolerated—even enjoyed—outings with their father.

The two of them sat on the floor of the loft above the second floor, constructed to allow light from a skylight in the roof to filter directly past the third floor, through a window in the floor of the loft, and down to the ballroom on the second floor of their sizeable residence. They had discovered the secret hideaway as children when Jan purloined the key from the apron of Sussje, their nanny, who had accompanied the family from Indonesia. It became their own private hiding place where they had shared secrets since childhood. Jan noticed a sadness in his sister he hadn't seen before.

"What's wrong?" he asked her. "You seem preoccupied."

Hetty started to talk, but her throat caught. After a moment, she tried again. "Karl is dead. He was shot during the invasion." Tears welled up in Hetty's eyes. "Oh, Jantje, I didn't know where else to turn."

"You've come to the right place," said Jan, embracing his sister. She clung to him for a long time, making his shirt wet with her tears.

Out of the corner of her eye Hetty saw a slight movement near the door. Instantly the tears stopped, and her face lit up.

"Sherlock! How did you get in here?"

She reached out to pick up the gray-and-white lop-eared rabbit—a present from her father on her sixteenth birthday—snuggling her face against its soft fur.

"You're just what I needed today." She cuddled her rabbit silently, comforted by the affection she shared with her pet.

"You must have suspected, right?" said Jan after a few moments.

"About Karl?" Hetty asked, bringing her thoughts back to the reason for her visit. "It's been two years. I suppose I knew deep inside that he was gone," Hetty said, clutching the rabbit next to her cheek. "But I couldn't give up hoping he'd turn up as a prisoner of war or something."

Jan began humming a tune softly. After a time, his pleasant voice grew louder, filling the corners of the tiny loft.

"What is that song, Jantje? It's so soothing."

"A lullaby that Sussje sang to me as a child. I think of it whenever I'm sad."

"Sussje was a wonderful nanny," said Hetty, soothed by Jan's song. "She still gives me advice."

"Me too," said Jan. "Our childhood wouldn't have been the same without her."

Hetty closed her eyes and leaned on her brother's shoulder. "I haven't seen you in such a long time," she said without opening her eyes. "How are you doing in school?"

"I graduate in six months," Jan said softly.

"Really?" Hetty sat up in surprise, laughing at herself. "I lost track of time. What will you do next year?"

"I hoped to attend Leiden University," said Jan, reaching to stroke the rabbit. "Any chance it will reopen?"

"Unlikely," said Hetty. "The Nazis are still punishing us for the student protests two years ago."

"Wish I'd been part of them," said Jan, gazing with admiration at his sister. "I was too young then, but I'll turn eighteen next month."

Suddenly realizing what was on Jan's mind, Hetty's eyes narrowed. "No, Jantje. You are *not* joining the resistance. It's too dangerous." She put Sherlock on the floor and watched the rabbit hop silently to the corner.

"What would be wrong with it?" Jan argued. "We could fight the Germans together."

"Today I completely lost it when I saw Karl's sweater covered in his blood and riddled with bullet holes," she told her brother, her face contorted as she reached for the green scarf she had just given to him. "I *never* want to go through that again." Her voice broke as she examined the scarf. "I don't even want to think about how terrible it would be if someone brought this to me with your blood on it."

Jan squeezed her hand. "That won't happen."

"You don't get it, Jantje. If the Germans catch you, they'll kill you."

"I'll be old enough to fight when I graduate," he said stubbornly.

"I *forbid* it," said Hetty, her teeth clenched. "I'll find out if you try, and I'll stop you."

Compressing his lips tightly, Jan looked away. Then he squeezed Hetty's hand, and she saw the pure love in his expression—and sorrow at the enormity of what she had lost. "I'll do anything you ask," he said flatly. "But I want you to think about it."

"I'm home, Mimi," Hetty called out as she was opening the door to their flat, her voice unemotional after her unsettling conversation with Jan.

"Look who's back," said Mimi, grabbing her robe, not the least bit embarrassed by her nakedness.

Hetty covered her mouth and quickly turned her head away when she glimpsed Gerhardt lying on the bed without any clothes.

"Hi, Hetty," said Gerhardt, pulling the covers over himself. "I just arrived last night."

"I'm so glad he's here," Mimi giggled, tying her robe as she danced toward the kitchen.

Facing the wall, Hetty handed Gerhardt his pants and waited.

"You can turn around," said Gerhardt after he finished dressing.

"What are you doing here?" asked Hetty, giving him a quick hug.

"A British destroyer dropped me off," he said as he peeked out the window. "I've been working with MI6."

"Gerhardt is helping to organize the Dutch-Paris network," said Mimi, putting a tray of tea on the table.

"Don't we already have an underground railroad through France?" asked Hetty. "I know that Pier still escorts pilots to the Belgian border."

"It's only a loose association of volunteers," said Gerhardt. "But MI6 wants to turn it into a more organized operation. The current network doesn't even have a name. Some are calling it the Dutch-Paris connection, others, like you, call it the underground railroad. It doesn't matter. But it's important that we do a better job of repatriating Allied airmen, who are parachuting into Holland with increasing frequency."

"I helped two Czech Jews who left on the network," said Hetty, sad at the memory of Yacov's tears when they watched Daniel and Hanna speed away on the train. "Can you find out if they made it to England?"

"If they're still alive, they're most likely in a refugee camp in Switzerland," said Gerhardt, yawning as he rubbed the sleep from his eyes. "Too few Jews have made it to England. But I'll ask my sources."

"I'll keep an eye out for them too," said Mimi.

Hetty raised her eyebrows.

"I'm going to join the network in France. It's the best way I know to help Gerhardt," her friend explained.

"Her French *is* perfect," Gerhardt pointed out.

Hetty set her teacup on the table with a sober expression. "Are you abandoning your courier work?"

"Changing responsibilities, not quitting per se," said Mimi, flashing a smile at Gerhardt. "I'll still live with you between assignments, Hetty. But you know how much I love France."

"In peacetime, maybe," Hetty muttered tersely. "But you know nothing about wartime France."

"Hetty's right," said Gerhardt. "The French resistance is riddled with spies. But we take precautions."

"What precautions could possibly protect her against partisan collaborators?"

"The Dutch resistance has collaborators too," said Gerhardt.

"You know that doesn't answer my question," Hetty pressed.

"Stop bickering," Mimi interrupted, putting her arm around Gerhardt's broad shoulders. "I trust Gerhardt. That's the end of it."

"I still don't like it." Hetty set her jaw, arms akimbo.

Mimi changed the subject. "What are you going to do about Pier's visit?"

"I don't know," said Hetty, giving up the argument reluctantly while taking a seat on her bed. "He's been gone for a month this time."

"But he's home now," said Mimi, touching her friend's cheek. "What have we always said about seizing opportunities for romance?"

"Not sure I'm up to it. The news about Karl is still fresh."

"Nothing will get your mind off Karl like a roll in the hay with Pier," said Mimi with a mischievous grin.

"You're incorrigible," said Hetty, smiling in spite of herself. "Anyway, I'm hoping Kees will find someone else to carry a message in my place tomorrow afternoon so that I can spend the day with Pier." Hetty poured three cups of tea from the hot kettle. "Can you do it?"

"You know I can't," said Mimi, nuzzling Gerhardt's shoulder affectionately.

"I'm here only until tomorrow afternoon when I have to leave for Utrecht," Gerhardt explained, kissing Mimi on the forehead.

"I wonder if Maria can do it?"

Awakened by the sun shining through the window of his bedroom the next morning, Kees opened his eyes slowly and smiled.

"Good morning, sleepyhead," said Maria, her naked body sliding toward him under the covers. "Can I sleep here again tonight?"

"I have to go out of town," Kees whispered, kissing her ear. "If I get back before curfew, you can come over."

Maria flashed a radiant smile.

Kees cleared his throat. "I have a favor to ask you."

"Again?" Maria laughed softly as she stroked his face with her finger-tips. "We did it *four times* last night."

"No, not that," he said with a chuckle. "Though I am open to an encore."

Maria tossed a pillow in his face, laughing. "What favor?"

"Can you carry a message to The Hague today?" asked Kees, kissing her lightly on the forehead. "Hetty had agreed to do it, but Pier is in town."

Maria sat up to get dressed. "I want to be with you as much as Hetty wants to be with Pier."

Kees quickly buttoned his shirt while studying Maria. "Hetty just received bad news about Karl."

Maria's furrowed brow reflected her immediate concern.

"The Rotterdam resistance confirmed that he was killed during the invasion. It might be good for her to spend time with Pier."

"Poor Hetty," said Maria, buttoning her blouse. "She deserves a day of romance. You can count on me."

Kees held out a tiny cylinder of tightly rolled paper in the palm of his hand. "This is the encrypted message I want you to deliver." Kees jotted down an address and held it out for Maria to memorize. "Got it?"

Maria nodded, and Kees lit the paper containing the address with his lighter, tossing the flaming note into an empty ashtray. "It's critical that you deliver this message before two o'clock."

Maria glanced at the clock on the wall. "I've got plenty of time."

"But you've never been stopped at a German checkpoint."

Maria's expression turned serious. "Do you think that's likely today?"

"They set one up yesterday on the road to The Hague. I hope it won't be open today, but you need to leave early just in case."

"What if they find the encrypted message?" Worry lines formed on Maria's forehead.

"I'm not concerned about that." Kees reached into her blouse and used two fingers to lodge the paper cylinder under her bra beneath her left breast.

All business, Kees faced her and nodded with a grunt. "Good. Even if they stop you, they'll never find it in there."

CHAPTER 12

IT WAS STILL MORNING WHEN Kees returned to his cottage after having breakfast with Maria at their favorite café. He noticed immediately that a window was open. This was suspect, as he always checked the windows and door whenever he left. Sensing danger, he reached for his dagger as he scanned the living room. Then his eyes settled on a small lump under a blanket on the sofa. Kees relaxed and put the knife back in his pocket.

"Aldon, what the hell are you doing in my house?" he demanded.

Startled awake, Aldon smiled. "You told me I could stay here." He wiped the sleep from his eyes. Pointing at flowers in a vase, Aldon grinned. "Did your girlfriend bring those?"

"That's none of your business." Kees handed some cash to Aldon. "This is for the information you gave me last week. It was useful."

Aldon smiled mischievously. "I'm a good spy for an eight-year-old, huh?"

"You're too cute for your own good," said Kees.

When he'd met Aldon six months ago, the dimple-cheeked boy had been living on his own after his parents were killed by Nazis and already seemed wise to the ways of the world. His ever-present smile charmed everyone—including German soldiers, who had no idea their casual conversations with a child provided valuable information to the resistance. Kees had not named his own child, who had died with his mother during childbirth, but these days he would have been proud to have named his son Aldon.

"You need to knock," Kees lectured. "You know my rule. You can sleep here, but only when Maria's not around."

"I watched her leave with you this morning," said Aldon with a self-satisfied grin. "Where'd you go? You've been gone for two hours."

"Have you been spying on me?" said Kees, exasperated.

"You should be happy to have such a pretty girlfriend," said Aldon cheerfully. "Why don't you introduce us? I'm sure she'd like me."

Kees chewed on some jerky, offering a piece of it to Aldon. "I want you to go out now to scout the checkpoint on the road to The Hague. Let me know when she gets through."

It was a warm day on the road out of Leiden, with clear skies and lots of sunshine—the kind of day Maria loved. A woman with a basket offered to sell her scones, Kees's favorite. She bought two and ate one while she pedaled toward The Hague. She sighed in anticipation of her upcoming evening with Kees. She'd never been in love before.

Maybe I can get real coffee to go with his scone, she thought. She planned ahead for her return from The Hague. It wouldn't be too far out of the way to stop by Sarina's house, the woman who had given her real coffee before. She smiled at the opportunity to visit Aliza, a little Jewish girl in hiding at Sarina's house who had won Maria's heart.

It was 10:00, so there was still plenty of time to deliver the message that was neatly tucked inside her bra. Maria's heart stopped when she saw the German checkpoint ahead. She had passed checkpoints before, but she'd never been stopped. She took a deep breath and pedaled forward, eyes straight ahead.

An Orpo corporal stood in her path. Maria did her best to remain calm when he demanded, "Identification please."

She reached into her bag and produced her papers, wondering if the corporal would know they were fake. The German policeman examined them. "So you're a student?"

Maria nodded.

Hetty had told her to smile, but she was too nervous and looked down to avoid showing her fear.

"The university's closed," said the corporal, trying to decide if there was any reason to be suspicious.

Maria met his gaze. "I'm hoping it will reopen."

She gave the response she had prepared with Hetty—but it was much harder now without her there as a guide. Maria could feel beads of perspiration forming on her forehead.

The Orpo policeman examined the contents of the leather bag that Maria carried on her shoulder. He removed the scone, took a bite, and threw the rest into the brush beside the road.

"Hmm," he said, reaching deep into the bag. He held up her dagger. "Where did you get this?"

"My father gave it to me," said Maria, strangely grieving for the scone she would not be able to give to Kees. "For protection against thieves."

"Where can I find him?"

"You can't; he's dead." She was surprised to hear herself speak with such confidence when her stomach was churning.

The corporal put the knife in his belt. "What courses did you take before the university closed?"

Maria froze. "I, uh—" she stuttered. She had prepared all the responses with Hetty during their practice, but her nerves got the better of her and made her mind go blank.

Without hesitation, the corporal pointed to an area next to the guard shack, which was screened off by bedsheets hanging on clotheslines. As they stepped behind this makeshift screen, the corporal called out, "Lieutenant Hess, permission to do a strip search?"

Orpo Lieutenant Gerald Hess emerged from the guard shack, sipping vodka from a flask. He was dressed more casually than the day he commanded Orpo police to whip communist leaders Hugo and Maurice. Hess seized Maria's dagger from the corporal's belt while he watched his subordinate pat her down. Maria froze when the corporal ran his hand up her skirt but relaxed when he stopped before going past the tops of her thighs. The corporal stepped aside.

Lieutenant Hess gestured toward his chest. "The Lieutenant says I have to search under your blouse."

Maria eyed Hess suspiciously but unfastened the top two buttons. The corporal peered down her bra and then ran his finger under it lightly. He turned to Hess. "All clear, sir."

Kees was right, Maria exulted, relieved that they had not found the encrypted message.

"Wait!" Hess commanded.

A jolt of panic swept through Maria, but her face remained impassive. The corporal took a step backward and stood at attention.

"I will show you the proper way to conduct a search, Corporal."

He turned back to Maria. "Take your blouse off, Fraulein."

His voice was polite, but his eyes conveyed this was an order. Maria's hands shook as she unfastened the last button, but even when it was completely unbuttoned, the blouse hung limply to cover her small breasts. The tiny cylinder remained where Kees had put it.

Hess stepped closer. Maria turned her head away from the sour odor of alcohol on his breath.

"No," he commanded. "Remove it *completely*."

Hess yanked on the blouse violently, ripping the fabric. Blood rose in Maria's cheeks. Hess gave her a condescending smile as he tossed the torn blouse on the ground.

Maria stared at the corporal for help, but his eyes rolled up to the sky behind the Lieutenant's back as if to say that he had no say in this. Then the corporal walked around the corner of the bedsheet to resume his checkpoint duties, washing his hands of the matter.

Hess watched the corporal leave, then clumsily unfastened Maria's bra, watching it fall to the ground. Maria reflexively crossed both arms over her chest, but just as quickly she brought her arms straight down on both sides, hoping the weight of her breast would keep the message in place. It did.

Hess switched to heavily accented Dutch. "Small but better than I expected," he said, leering at her breasts. "What's your name, dear?"

"Maria." Her voice fluttered.

Hess looked her up and down. Then he unsheathed her dagger and held its point an inch from her left eyeball.

Maria closed her eyes tightly.

Hess turned to the side and made two sharp jabs into the air. "Ever use this, Maria?"

"No. Never." Her lips quivered as she stared at the knife.

Hess held the blade under her nose while he stroked the nipple of her left breast with his right index finger.

"Don't!" Maria cried out in Dutch, recoiling reflexively from his touch.

"Come with me!" Hess spat the order in German as he yanked her hard by the left elbow toward the guard shack. Then he froze as his eyes followed a tiny cylinder of paper that fluttered to the ground. "What's this?" He rolled the cylinder between his fingers. "Did you put this under there?" He pointed toward her breast. "What a clever hiding place."

Maria retched, leaving vomit dripping from her chin. In her head, Maria could hear Kees's lecture: "*If you are caught, expect to be tortured. Everyone talks under torture.*"

Hess retrieved her torn blouse and used it to wipe the spittle from her chin, his eyes never leaving hers.

Hess unfolded the small paper. "Corporal, come here." Knifing the small message with Maria's dagger, Hess held the tiny note on the tip of the knife in front of the man's face. "You missed this," he sneered. "What we have here is a member of the infamous resistance carrying some sort of message."

"It's in code, sir," said the corporal, examining the message.

"The Gestapo will be able to make it out, I'm sure," said Hess, his eyes traveling to Maria, who could not disguise her terror.

Hess glanced toward the guard shack a few feet away. "Keep an eye on the checkpoint, Corporal." Hess paused. "While I interrogate this girl inside."

Maria followed him toward the guard shack, her head hanging. But when Hess opened the door, she stopped cold in her tracks.

"No," she said, pushing Hess toward the open door. "You can't make me go in there."

Hess slapped Maria hard across the face and yanked her inside, closing the door and locking it. She staggered to the ground, then rolled over and leaned against the wall, her entire body trembling.

Hess reached in a drawer and found another flask. Slowly, he removed the cap and took a leisurely swallow. "How old are you, Maria?" Hess wiped vodka from his mouth with the back of his hand.

"N-nineteen," she stammered.

"So young." He tried to simulate paternal concern, but her father had never sounded anything like that. "Whoever sent you should be ashamed. Maybe I can help you." Maria's eyes narrowed skeptically. "But we must complete the strip search first," Hess whispered menacingly.

"Where could I hide anything?" said Maria, glancing down at her half-naked body.

"Don't worry," said Hess pacing the floor. "I won't hurt you."

He thought briefly of *Kristallnacht* in Vienna, when he had been a nineteen-year-old brownshirt wielding a club, which he used to beat up a Jewish family. He dispersed three young boys who had just raped a Jewish girl, whom he judged to be about twelve. Hess still regretted that he didn't have a turn with the girl himself.

"Remove your panties," he told Maria. Bullied in grammar school, Hess had learned that there were two kinds of people, predators and prey. *I will never be prey again*, he reminded himself as he watched Maria shudder on the floor, slow to follow his orders.

With lightning quickness, Hess produced a Walther P38 military-issue pistol. He chambered a live round and pointed the gun at Maria's forehead. "Take off your fucking panties, you little twat!"

Frozen with fear, Maria leveraged her back against the wall and did as he demanded.

She closed her eyes. When she opened them, Hess was standing naked and erect just inches from her face. Then he was on her. She cried out in pain as he thrust hard against her dryness. Without concern, Hess finished quickly and zipped up his pants. Maria tried to turn her head away from the disgusting smell of him all over her. She searched for a weapon, but Hess had put the pistol back in its drawer.

Hess put on his pants and took a sip of vodka. Then he used the toe of his right shoe to slide Maria's underwear toward her. "Here, get dressed."

"I can go?" Her incredulous voice was barely audible.

"Of course. I'm not a monster."

Bending over, Maria teetered on her right foot, holding her panties low to the ground so she could slip her left foot through. Then Hess shot her in the back of the head.

Her body collapsed where she had stood, brains and blood splattered everywhere. Satisfied, Hess stuck the Walther in his belt, took a swig from his flask, and straightened his tie.

Paralyzed by shock and fear, with tears streaming down his face, Aldon slowly stepped away from the knot hole in the guard shack where he'd seen everything. Then he turned and ran. Hard. In his haste he tripped over his own feet and fell, skinning a knee and both of his hands. Scrambling to his feet, he glanced over his shoulder. No Germans. Then he ran as fast as he could toward Kees's house.

CHAPTER 13

"You're home early, Hetty." Mimi glanced up from reading a book as her friend entered their flat. The sun was just setting as the summer solstice drew near. "Did you have a nice time with Pier?"

"Pier and I broke up," said Hetty, slumping down glumly on her bed and putting her elbows on her knees.

"You two have been together for a long time," said Mimi, laying her book on the nightstand and folding her hands in her lap. "Do you want to talk about it?"

"A year's not that long, considering how often he was away." Hetty found her knitting bag under her bed and extracted tangled black yarn. "Has Maria come home yet?"

"She's probably with Kees." Mimi picked up her book. "You don't seem too upset about Pier. I hope you at least had some intimacy before you broke it off," she teased.

"Even that was boring." Hetty exhaled loudly as she wrapped the black yarn into a clumsy ball. "I think we were both ready to end it."

Suddenly Kees was at their door. "You need to stop everything you're doing," he said urgently, brushing past Hetty for a quick peek out the window.

"But I have a meeting in two hours," Mimi protested, putting her book back on the night table. "We have a pilot waiting to go to the Belgian border."

"We'll worry about that later."

"Sounds serious," said Hetty who began winding the black yarn again, worry lines forming on her forehead. "What's the emergency?"

Kees paused, struggling to share the news. "The Germans killed Maria."

"Oh no," Hetty whispered, covering her mouth as the ball of yarn fell to the floor. "Where?"

"At a checkpoint on the road to The Hague." Kees took his time scanning the street from the window, then drew the blinds while his jaw clenched tighter.

"That was supposed to be my assignment," Hetty whispered as she picked up the yarn ball and started winding it vigorously. "I should be the one who's dead."

Mimi stared at her friends without seeing them. "Maybe your information is wrong, Kees."

Kees shook his head grimly. "My source saw it happen. Maria was raped and shot by an Orpo officer—Gerald Hess."

Mimi froze while she considered this new information. Her anxious eyes settled on the bed where Maria had slept when she wasn't with Kees.

"It's my fault," said Hetty absently. "I was supposed to teach her how to protect herself."

She began to weep, quietly at first, but soon she lost control completely; her body convulsed with heaving sobs.

"No, it was my job to take care of her," said Kees, biting his lip. "I loved her so much."

Suddenly Mimi stood up. "Do the Germans know that she lived here? Should we leave Leiden and shut down?"

"No one would blame you if you quit," said Kees in a raspy voice.

"That might be best," murmured Mimi.

"I've seen people hang their heads like you are, Mimi," said Kees evenly. "Boxers do it when they are ready to give up."

"I do feel like giving up." Tears flowed down both of her cheeks.

"I know," said Kees with quiet determination. "But when I felt that way as a boxer, I always got up and took another swing. Sometimes I won, sometimes not. But the other guy had to knock me senseless if he wanted to win the fight."

Hetty stared at Kees, thinking about his words. Then she stood up and threw a book across the room.

"You can be sure that I'm *not quitting*. It's not our fault," she shouted. "That bastard Hess did it. And Hitler. Not us."

"Maybe we should discuss this later," Mimi whispered anxiously. "I don't want to end up like Maria."

"You two lay low until we find out whether the Germans have linked you to her." Kees's voice wobbled, his confidence of a moment ago evaporating. "Watch the street. If the Germans come, leave by the back stairway."

"What are you planning?" asked Mimi, her voice trembling.

Kees put his hand on the doorknob. "For the last couple of weeks, I've had someone watching a tavern where a lot of the Germans go."

"I know the place," said Hetty. "What about it?"

Kees put on his coat. "I'm told that Hess is there every night—always the last one to leave the bar."

"I remember him," said Hetty coldly. "He's the one who likes to whip people."

"Don't go to the tavern." Mimi crossed the room and blocked the door. "He's not worth the risk."

"I'm not stupid enough to try to kill him. He'll be heavily guarded," said Kees as he gently moved Mimi away from the door. "I just want to see what the bastard looks like."

"I hope he doesn't do something stupid," said Mimi when the door closed behind him. She brought whiskey and two glasses from the kitchen. "He'll try to kill Hess if he gets the chance."

"Why the hell do you care what happens to Hess?" said Hetty incredulously. "I'm more worried that the bastard will get away with what he did to Maria."

"We can't risk provoking the Gestapo." Mimi set the whiskey bottle on the table and handed Hetty a glass as she started to pour their drinks. "They'll swarm Leiden and catch us if we kill a German officer."

"Stop worrying about what the Germans will do to us, Mimi." Hetty downed her whiskey in one gulp and poured another. "For us, there are no more rules—not when the Nazis rape and murder our women."

"Aren't you scared that they will do the same thing to us?" Mimi's thin voice reminded Hetty of a mouse scurrying for cover. "Just thinking about it petrifies me."

"Then stop thinking about it," Hetty shouted, shoving her chair violently against the wall. "If they try to rape me, they'll have to fuck my corpse."

In the middle of a city block, between a darkened dress store and a butcher shop, cheery light poured through the thickly beveled glass windows of a tavern. The door opened, and with it that same honey-colored light poured briefly into the street as the last few drunken revelers stumbled into the chilly night.

Across the street, folded into an alcove between two buildings, Kees waited and watched. It was too dangerous to attack Hess tonight, he knew. German security would be out in force following the murder of a resistance courier. But Kees wanted to know when Hess might be vulnerable, and for that he needed to be able to recognize the killer. Now hidden, Kees could not take his eyes off the tavern. If his intelligence was correct, Hess should be in the pub, lingering over his drinks.

Suddenly there were voices. Kees shrank into the shadows. Two Orpo policemen on night duty walked down the sidewalk speaking rapidly to each other. Kees held his breath, but unnecessarily: without even glancing in his direction, the police crossed the street to the pub; there was the same flash of ironic light as they went inside. The door closed behind them with a *thunk*.

Looking in both directions, Kees crossed the street stealthily and peered through the thick, blurry glass. The two policemen stood on either side of an officer seated at the bar. It had to be Hess. The officer drunkenly waved the men away and slid his shot glass nearer to the bartender, indicating another pour. When the police headed toward the door, Kees scurried back to his hiding place.

The two Orpo policemen were patrolling the street when Hess emerged. They returned to him, speaking in German.

Expecting to abandon his watch the moment they were gone, Kees froze when Hess waved away the Orpo police. Both policemen saluted, turned, and walked briskly down the street and out of sight, leaving Hess standing alone in front of the tavern.

Kees's hand gripped the hilt of his dagger. He thought about the promise he'd made to Mimi, but he hadn't anticipated that Hess would be so completely alone. *He must not have told anyone about Maria*, Kees reasoned. *Security is light because they have no idea that he needs it.*

Hess stumbled on his first step into the street.

"Let me give you a hand, my friend," said Kees in Dutch, reaching out to steady the German officer.

Hess did a double take at the Dutchman before his face broadened into a hazy grin. "Most of you Dutch don't have a good word to say for us," Hess slurred, speaking in heavily accented Dutch. Up close, Kees could tell that Hess was drunker than he first appeared.

"Happy to help." Kees steadied the tottering Hess. "Which way is home for you?"

Hess pointed, and the two men walked slowly down the street, Kees guiding the officer by the elbow.

"Where are you from, Lieutenant?" asked Kees casually.

"Munich." Hess continued to slur. "My mother still lives there."

"I lost my mother a few years ago," said Kees with a sad expression. "Do you have brothers or sisters to take care of her?"

"She only has me," said Hess shaking his head. "My father was killed during the Great War."

Kees watched the sidewalk ahead with a sober expression. Could he be feeling sympathy for this monster? "I think I've seen you at the checkpoints," said Kees, hoping to learn something useful about German security. "It must be dangerous work."

"Not dangerous at all," Hess bragged. "Nothing ever happens." Then Hess winked at Kees. "But it does have its benefits."

"Benefits?"

Hess chuckled. "Women. You can take any that you want. I had a young one today, in fact."

Without thinking, Kees hit Hess in the face with his fist. The startled officer recovered quickly, and with surprising strength, shoved Kees to the ground. When Hess reached for his pistol, Kees realized he was about to die.

Suddenly someone darted up from behind and hit Hess on the head with a big rock. He collapsed in a heap, dropping his pistol on the sidewalk.

"Hetty! What are you doing here?" said Kees, scrambling to his feet.

Recovering faster than Kees had expected, Hess struggled to his knees and clutched his weapon. Before he could point it at Kees, Hetty leaped onto the Orpo policeman's back and yanked his head by the hair, exposing the delicate skin of his throat. Out of her pocket she produced a knife—Gerhardt's killing knife—its razor-sharp blade flashing across the German's throat.

"This is for Maria," Hetty hissed through clenched teeth.

The Orpo Lieutenant gasped, his blood pumping out and spurting onto Kees's face and clothes, Hetty's face and arms, and flowing down the German's chest onto the sidewalk. He collapsed forward, face first. His eyes were vacant by the time Hetty stabbed him three more times in the back, grunting with each thrust.

After catching her breath, Hetty extended her finger to remove the friendship ring that Maria had given her. She stared at it for a moment, then kissed the ring and shoved it in Hess's mouth.

The sound of the door to her flat being unlocked startled Mimi awake. Rubbing her eyes, she opened it and stepped back, her mouth agape. "Oh my. What happened to you, Kees?"

Then she saw Hetty standing behind him, covered in blood head to toe. "Where did you go?" the astonished Mimi asked, glancing toward Hetty's empty bed as she closed the door behind her friends. "I didn't hear you leave."

"Turn around, Kees," Hetty ordered to give her privacy while she removed her blood-stained clothes before throwing them in the waste basket. "We need to sink our clothes in the river," said Hetty as she entered the bathroom. "Get out of that bloody outfit while I have a shower."

Kees did as he was told while Mimi faced the wall. "Do you have something to drink?" he asked, with a hint of desperation in his voice as he wrapped a towel around his waist.

"We have some whiskey," said Mimi, who went to the kitchen and returned with the half-empty bottle that she and Hetty had shared earlier. "Is that Hess's blood?"

Hetty returned in her bathrobe, using a towel to dry her hair.

Kees sat down heavily in the only chair, staring blankly at the whiskey bottle. "What have we done?" He ran a hand through his hair. "We just killed a German officer in cold blood. There will be reprisals."

"We need to run!" Mimi said urgently.

Hetty turned calmly toward Kees. "You'd better take a shower."

He stood up with a dazed expression as Hetty handed him a fresh towel from a shelf in the bathroom. "Wash your hair; it's caked with blood."

Then she went to the closet and gathered a pair of pants and a work shirt. "Try these on. Karl left them here before the war."

Kees sat down on Maria's bed. "I need a minute." He put Maria's pillow against his face and inhaled. "I can smell her, like she's still here."

"You promised not to kill him," said Mimi, huddled on her bed.

"I wasn't going to," said Kees, lighting a cigarette. "Then Hess said something terrible about Maria, and I lost my head. Still, if Hetty hadn't saved me, I'd be dead right now."

"What were you thinking, Hetty?" said Mimi. "You shouldn't have left without telling me."

"Would you have let me go?" asked Hetty.

"Thanks to you, the Gestapo will be crawling around Leiden like ants looking for us," said Mimi, her voice agitated.

"He needed killing," Hetty said sharply, plucking the cigarette from Kees's mouth. She took a deep drag and coughed.

"You're wrong. We would all be safer if you two had left Hess alone," said Mimi, pacing the floor. "And what about the night Gerhardt killed Brecht? You didn't say he needed killing."

"I was wrong about Brecht but not about Hess," said Hetty, smoking the cigarette in rapid puffs. "We need to stay focused on what's important. I should not have asked Maria to take my place on yesterday's assignment just because I wanted to be with Pier. She died while I was having a meaningless fuck. We have to stop that sort of nonsense. Our war against the Nazis has to come first from now on, always."

Corporal Schultz stood at attention in front of Major Jacek's desk, his SS uniform less than a perfect fit for his large girth.

"Tell me about Lieutenant Gerald Hess," Jacek scowled.

"He was murdered last night—"

"I know he was murdered, you idiot." Jacek slammed his hand on his desk. "Tell me who killed him."

Corporal Schultz scowled at the nasty rebuke, but he'd collected himself by the time Jacek glanced up at him. "We don't know yet, sir. Our investigation just started."

"I must report this to Berlin tomorrow." Jacek lit a cigarette, inhaling deeply. "They will be furious that one of our officers was murdered in the street." He flicked the ash from his cigarette in Schultz's direction. "When I make my report, shall I also tell them my incompetent assistant has no fucking idea who killed him?"

Schultz stared straight ahead while he composed himself. "No, sir." Using his kerchief, Schultz wiped the ash off of Jacek's desk into his hand and put it in the wastebasket. "We think it was the resistance."

"Now you're trying to cover your ineptitude by making things up," Jacek frowned. "There's no resistance in Leiden."

"Do you remember Peter Brecht, sir?" asked Schultz.

"Wasn't he the informant who went missing?" Jacek scratched his earlobe absentmindedly. "He's another of your unsolved cases, isn't he?"

"We never found Brecht's body, sir," Schultz acknowledged as he fished in the pocket where he kept his cigarettes. He grunted when he found the package empty. "But he failed to show up for his appointment with you the same night we found a lot of blood on the street just a block from here."

"That doesn't prove it was Brecht," said Jacek, exasperation on his face.

Schultz reached into his shirt pocket and produced a lighter. "We also found this."

Jacek snatched the lighter out of Schultz's extended hand, noticing the SS symbol embossed on both sides.

"I gave this to him," Jacek recalled. "Remember? But even if Brecht was killed that night, there's no evidence that it was done by your phantom resistance."

"We suspect that the people who killed Brecht also killed Hess." Schultz inhaled deeply on his cigarette. "It's the same M.O. Both were alone on the street after curfew when they died. And both left a lot of blood on the street."

Jacek narrowed his eyes and leaned forward. "What tells you it was the resistance?"

"Hess killed a girl just before he died." Schultz paused to let that sink in. "His corporal told us that the girl was in the resistance."

"And you think it was a revenge killing?" Jacek leaned on his desk, staring coldly at Schultz.

"That's how we see it right now. Yes, sir." Schultz nodded.

"Why wasn't I told that this resistance creature had been apprehended?" Jacek stubbed out his cigarette in an ashtray. "I would have had her interrogated."

"None of us knew, sir." Schultz cleared his throat. "Hess concealed it. We think he didn't want anyone to know he had raped her."

"Has the girl been identified?"

"Unfortunately, no, sir." Schultz finished his cigarette and stubbed it out in Jacek's ashtray. "Hess had his men burn her body and her ID."

"What have we done about Hess's men?"

"They're on a train to the eastern front, sir."

Jacek nodded his approval. "And reprisals?"

"Our men are rounding up city leaders," said Schultz with a nod.

"Good," said Jacek. "At least I can tell Berlin we have taken action—and that we have a lead."

"There's one more thing, sir." Schultz placed a tiny ring made of yarn on Jacek's desk. "We found this in Hess's mouth."

"This is an act of sentiment." Jacek put the trinket in the palm of his hand and examined it. "It must have been a woman, Schultz. That's where you should start. Look for a woman who works for the resistance—in Leiden."

In the early light of dawn, the gallows appeared as a looming shadow in the Leiden town square. Five nooses in all. Putting on her scarf against the cool morning breeze, Hetty spotted Mimi a block away but did not acknowledge her. They had agreed to come separately.

"Damned resistance," said a man standing next to her. "They're going to get all of us killed." Hetty turned the other way, but the man persisted. "Do you know anyone in the resistance?"

"Never met one," Hetty shrugged. "Maybe there isn't a resistance in Leiden."

"Then why are they going to hang hostages?"

"Hush," said Hetty. "Here they come."

The bespeckled Mr. Aalders was the first to enter the square. The father of one of her classmates, Lennard Aalders had been acquainted with Hetty since she was a young girl. When he saw the gallows, Aalders dropped to his knees; his body convulsed, unable to move. Two Orpo police lifted him by the armpits and dragged him up the scaffold. Hetty did not know the four men who followed single file behind Aalders, but she was impressed that they kept their composure as they lined up next to the nooses that had been prepared for them.

An SS officer held up his hands for quiet. "I am Major Jacek," he said curtly. "An Orpo officer—Lieutenant Gerald Hess—was murdered in cold blood on the streets of this city. Someone here knows who killed him."

The crowd murmured but went silent when Jacek pointed toward the men standing at the gallows.

"Give me the murderer, and these men will return to their homes and families unharmed."

Hetty glanced quickly toward Mimi, whose stoic expression did not change.

"You have five minutes," said Jacek, raising his voice.

Everyone in the crowd started talking at once. A young woman ran toward the gallows. "No," she screamed. "Not my Ethan." The Orpo police restrained her.

"Let her through," said Jacek. The sobbing woman was allowed to climb the steps of the gallows to embrace one of the condemned men. "Everyone must see the price being paid for this town's silence," said Jacek. "Give up the killer, and this young couple can leave together."

Jacek surveyed the crowd, then glanced at his watch. "Time's up." The woman uttered a guttural scream as the police led her away. Taking his time, a single policeman placed a noose around each man's neck, careful to cinch the knot tightly. "One last chance. Tell me who killed Lieutenant Hess!" Confused sounds spread through the crowd, but no one identified the killer.

Jacek gave a slight nod. Suddenly five trap doors opened, and five lives were ended.

Hetty and Mimi were both in tears when they returned to their flat. "We did that," said Mimi, unable to control her grief. "I don't mind risking my life for the resistance, but I never meant to harm others. What if one of those men had been your brother?"

"The Nazis killed those men, not us," said Hetty, struggling to regain her composure. "I'm just glad it's over."

"It's not over." Mimi shook her head. "The Gestapo has barely started its search for us."

CHAPTER 14

WHEN HETTY ARRIVED AT HER family home in The Hague, the usually quiet residential neighborhood buzzed with activity. She had known most of her neighbors since childhood, and she had never seen them so frightened as they rushed to move their possessions into the street. The neighbors paused to watch a convoy of military vehicles roar past them, wondering where they would live when the Germans demolished their homes.

Surrounded by old maple trees, the Renaissance-style home where Hetty grew up rose like an elegant fortress, fending off imagined enemies with its beauty. The steep roof featured dormer windows with white shutters, and the brick front looked as if it had been built by highly skilled stone masons in medieval times.

In the kitchen, Hetty put ersatz coffee on the table with two cups while Jan produced some biscuits he'd found in the cupboard.

Jan sipped his coffee, lost in thought. "Do you think Mimi might come from Leiden to help us move?"

Hetty flashed an affectionate grin at her brother. "You'll never let go of your schoolboy crush, Jantje."

"Give me some credit," said Jan, buttering his muffin and taking a bite. "I know that Mimi will always treat me like a little brother. I just enjoy having her around."

Hetty knew he was lying. Jan had secretly loved Mimi since he was fourteen and hoped that he would one day win her heart. No one was aware of this except Hetty, who knew all of her brother's secrets.

"I'd like to see Mimi too," said Hetty wistfully. "But she's in France."

Jan looked at her quizzically.

"You're not supposed to know," Hetty continued, "but she's escorting Allied pilots to the Pyrenees so they can get back to England. It's good that she's not in Leiden."

"Good?" Jan spilled his coffee. "Aren't you worried for her?" He stood up to get a towel.

"Not as worried as I would be if we were still there," said Hetty, using her napkin as a dam to prevent the spilled coffee from pouring onto the floor. "Leiden is thick with Gestapo. They're trying to find the person who killed an Orpo officer."

"Do you know who did it?" Jan stopped wiping the table and stared at his sister. Then a light went on in his eyes. "It was you, wasn't it?"

Hetty said nothing as she refilled Jan's empty cup.

They sipped their coffee in silence, contemplating the significance of what Hetty had just revealed.

"So the German order arrived yesterday?" asked Hetty, changing the subject. "How can we possibly move everything out in five days? And where would we put it?"

"You haven't heard?" Jan asked as he used a knife to slice another muffin. "Our whole family is moving to Oma Betje's house. It's big enough for most of the antiques and artwork, and the rest will go to storage."

While Hetty made more coffee, her thoughts drifted to the huge wisteria vine that Karl had climbed the night they made love in her bedroom. "After we leave, I suppose they'll destroy everything," she reflected.

Jan nodded. "The Nazis are razing the whole neighborhood for gun emplacements."

"They're stealing our memories," said Hetty bitterly. "Just like they stole Karl and Maria from me."

Willem paced around his study. "I can't believe the Germans denied my request for a moving van."

The sounds made by their neighbors scurrying to save their belongings entered through the open window.

"Only collaborators get them, Papa." Hetty was seated in the brown leather guest chair, trying not to get caught up in her father's agitation. "They're in short supply, because the German order covers so many homes."

The bookshelves in Willem's study were dark and foreboding, reflecting the mood of its principal occupant. Located near the center of the large home, only one small window connected Willem with the outside world. Most of the light was provided by two small lamps, which cast shadows across the cloistered workspace.

Willem sat down in the large leather chair behind his desk, eyeing the boxes of books on the floor that had already been packed. Then he stared wearily at the books still on the shelves. "I thought I had done enough to warrant a moving van," he said sullenly.

The telephone rang, and Willem answered it.

"Hello, Reiner," he said as he held his hand up in a gesture that said this would be a short call with his civil service friend. "No. I can't reveal the confidences of my clients." He listened for a moment, then responded before slamming the phone back in its cradle, "Tell the Germans I will send them the files when they get me a moving van!"

"What was that about?" asked Hetty.

"The Germans suspect that one of the companies I represent is disguising Jewish ownership."

Hetty was incredulous. "And you're going to give up their confidential files for a *moving van?*"

"The Germans will find nothing in those files," her father said calmly. "I don't have any Jewish clients."

Suddenly the throaty sound of a large vehicle entered the study. Hetty went to the tiny window to see what was going on.

"That son of a bitch!"

"What's wrong?" asked Willem.

"A moving van just pulled up across the street."

"That's incredible," said Willem, bringing his fist down on the table. "Why can't I get one?"

"That's not the point," said Hetty, resuming her seat. "Our neighbor must be a collaborator, or he wouldn't be able to get a moving van."

"There's a war on," said Willem. "We all do what we have to."

"Don't you understand why it's wrong to collaborate?"

"Calm down," said Willem, making a quieting gesture with his hand. "I'm not collaborating. I'm just helping my friend Reiner."

"Helping the Germans in exchange for a moving van is collaboration," said Hetty, punching the air with her index finger. "Besides, Reiner is a collaborator too. He helps the Germans run the government in return for favors."

"Reiner has a job to do," said Willem. "You have no idea how much pressure the Germans put on him as head of the tax bureau."

"How can you make excuses for him? The Nazis are about to demolish our home." Hetty wiped angry tears from her eyes with a quick swipe of her hand. "You should resist them, not kiss up to them."

"There are a lot more people like me in Holland than there are resist-ers," said Willem, his cheeks turning bright red. "Your little group is so small and ineffectual that you couldn't even prevent the Nazis from closing your university."

"At least we fight them." Hetty glared back at her father.

Willem leaned forward in his chair, his nostrils flaring, but then sat back and took several breaths. "Do it my way, Hetty," he said more qui-etly. "Keep your head down and wait this out. It's the safest way to deal with an unpleasant situation."

"Tell that to the Jews," said Hetty tersely. "How unpleasant do you think it is for them?"

"No one can do anything about the Jews." Willem lit a cigarette and was surprised when Hetty reached for the package to take one.

"Maybe this once," she said in her quiet voice. Hetty did not know why she was reluctant to tell her father she'd taken up smoking. Perhaps it was residual deference from a time when she cared what he thought about her.

Willem studied his daughter skeptically before lighting a cigarette for her. "We need to concentrate on protecting ourselves," he said.

"You're wrong." Hetty inhaled her cigarette as she stood to leave. "We have a duty to fight evil, not collaborate with it."

"It won't end well for you—not if you keep working for the ineffec-tual resistance." Her father cleared his throat, then added, "And you have put your brother in danger too."

Hetty stopped in her tracks. "What's Jantje got to do with this?"

"He's been trying to join the resistance," said Willem. "Following your footsteps, I suppose."

Looking like a fighter who had just taken a sharp right to the jaw, Hetty sat down slowly in her chair. "I thought someone would tell me if he did that."

"It appears that the right hand of your ragtag group doesn't know what the left hand is doing," said Willem. "Talk to your brother before he makes a terrible mistake."

The phone rang again.

"Hello, Reiner," said Willem. "You got a van for me!? That's great news. Send it over, and I'll have my assistant bring the file you asked about."

"Papa's not going to talk me out of it," said Jan, his jaw set as they sat side by side on the floor of the loft they had always used as their private sanctuary.

"Umm, actually, he sent me to talk you out of it." Hetty took her brother's hand. "How did you contact the resistance without me knowing about it, Jantje?"

"The people you work for are focused on helping people in hiding. I avoided them because you made it clear you didn't want me to join."

"Then who does Papa think you've been talking to?" asked Hetty.

"The people who kill Germans. You don't know them."

Hetty's eyes narrowed. "I've heard of patriots who engage in combat, but I never met one. The resistance should be better organized—work together against the Germans."

"Obviously," said Jan. "But I want to know why you've become Papa's messenger. It's such a betrayal."

Since childhood, Jan had always wanted to be just like Hetty. She mastered three languages, so he did too. She was kind to people who were different, so he was too. And this morning she had admitted, in so many words, that the Gestapo was chasing her for killing a German officer. Jan wanted to become part of the resistance too, and like his sister, he was stubborn enough to get what he wanted.

"You know I would never betray you." Hetty touched her brother's face. "You betrayed yourself. If Papa knows what you are doing, then the Germans know it too."

Hetty inspected the tiny loft until she found what she was looking for. "Remember the day we carved our names in the floor?" She placed her hand lovingly on the inscription. "'Friends Forever' we said." Hetty brushed her hand through her thick curly hair. "You're my brother, Jantje, but you're also my best friend. I can't imagine how I would live without you. Plus, it wouldn't be fair to Mama and Papa to lose both of us."

Jan's eyes flitted around the loft. "I'll miss this place when the Germans demolish it." He picked up three crayons tucked away in the corner and handed them to his sister. "Will you keep these as a memory of our secret meetings here?"

She studied the crayons in the open palm of her hand and held back tears. "We're not children anymore, Jantje. This isn't a game. If you join the resistance and get caught, the Germans will kill you."

"You keep reminding me of that," said Jan. "But as long as the Nazis occupy our country, I can't sit home and do nothing." Resolute, he stood up and walked out before Hetty could say another word.

CHAPTER 15

"Just tell me what the prisoner said, Corporal." SS Major Jacek glared impatiently at his assistant. "Save me the details about how you broke him."

Corporal Schultz stood at attention in Jacek's office at SS headquarters in Leiden. "The prisoner's name is Pier Arden, sir. He was caught organizing Dutch worker strikes. The details are in that report."

Jacek thumbed through the multipage document, stopping at the third page. "So—the prisoner identified the other ringleaders of the Hengelo and Limburg strikes. That's excellent intelligence."

"Gestapo in those jurisdictions is already rounding them up, sir." Schultz brushed a piece of lint from Jacek's shoulder with his fingertips. "He also named two leaders from the Philips factory shut down at Eindhoven. I will notify SS in Eindhoven as soon as we are finished here."

"Good work, Corporal." Jacek produced an opened package of cigarettes from his pocket and offered one to Schultz. "What is the prisoner's status?"

"Awaiting your orders, sir."

Jacek smiled mirthlessly. "You know my answer. German soldiers died at Limburg."

"I'll take care of it, sir."

"Did the prisoner say anything about the resistance in our jurisdiction?" asked Jacek.

Schultz flipped through his notes and landed on a page with the intel Jacek requested. "He identified one Leiden operative, sir. The prisoner had a liaison with a university student here. He was very reluctant to give her up, but no one can hold out against our methods."

"Her name?"

"All we have is 'Hetty,'" said Schultz, still standing at attention. "No last name."

Jacek raised his eyebrows. "How thorough was the interrogation?"

"He was well beyond his pain threshold when he cracked, sir. He would have given up his own mother if she had anything to do with the resistance."

"Does she?" Jacek managed a slight smile.

"His mother died before the war." Schultz frowned. "But he has two aunts in The Hague, both involved. Their names are Rini and Thyrza Arden, his father's sisters. Gestapo has already staked out their house."

"Interrogate them now." Jacek's face grew more sullen. "This girl, Hetty, must be linked to the murder of that officer. What was his name—Hess? There can't be many women in the Leiden resistance."

"The prisoner knew nothing about the murder," said Schultz, shifting his weight uncomfortably. "Do you really think a girl could kill a trained Orpo officer?"

"She either slit Hess's throat or knows who did. Find the fucking girl!" Jacek slammed his hand on the desk, causing a box of paperclips to fly off.

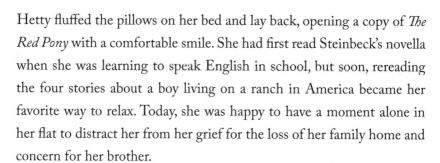

Hetty fluffed the pillows on her bed and lay back, opening a copy of *The Red Pony* with a comfortable smile. She had first read Steinbeck's novella when she was learning to speak English in school, but soon, rereading the four stories about a boy living on a ranch in America became her favorite way to relax. Today, she was happy to have a moment alone in her flat to distract her from her grief for the loss of her family home and concern for her brother.

She was interrupted by a pounding on her door. "Hetty," Kees yelled. "Let me in."

Laying her book on the nightstand, Hetty opened the door a crack. "What's wrong?" she asked anxiously as she opened the door wider to let him in.

Kees pushed past her. "You and Mimi need to get out of town right now!" He glanced around the room. "Where is she?"

"She's away on an assignment."

"Good. Then we only need to worry about you for now."

"Worry about what?"

"The Gestapo captured Pier."

Hetty was silent while she processed the news. "When?"

"They shot him this morning."

"Bastards!" Hetty sat down on her bed, too stunned to cry. "Even though we're not together, I always cared for him."

"C'mon. Get dressed. I'll help you pack." Kees grabbed a suitcase from the closet. "We have to assume he told them about you."

Hetty's eyes widened, realizing the danger. "Where am I supposed to go?" She slipped into the closet to put on her clothes. "Maybe Mimi and I took too big a chance returning to this flat after I killed Hess. The Gestapo could show up here any minute."

"Did Pier know about Hess?"

Hetty shook her head. "We haven't spoken since we broke up the day before Maria was killed." She picked up a blouse, then threw it on the floor. "Kees, they know who I am! Anywhere I go, they'll find me."

"No, they won't—not if we hurry." Kees brought clothes from her closet. "I'm organizing a safe house for you and Mimi, but it will take some time. Is there someplace you can stay in the meantime?"

"I can't fit all my clothes into one small suitcase," said Hetty, tossing a dress on the floor. "What should I pack?"

"You have to concentrate if you want to live," said Kees, holding her by both shoulders. "Let's start with finding you a place to sleep tonight."

"I s-suppose I could stay with my parents," she stammered. "But won't the Gestapo know where they live?" Hetty's body was shaking.

"Pier didn't know your last name, right?"

Hetty nodded.

"They'll probably figure it out eventually, but not for a while," said Kees, tossing some shoes into the suitcase. "Come on. We need to get out of here."

Hetty stopped cold with a frightened expression. "Has anyone told Pier's aunts? Rini and Thyrza are in terrible danger."

"Nothing can be done for them. You need to save yourself." Kees studied his courier, knowing her headstrong nature. "Don't go to their house, Hetty. The Gestapo has it under surveillance."

"But those poor women are all alone," said Hetty, worry lines deepening on her forehead. "They need someone to watch after them."

Kees grabbed Hetty by the chin, forcing her to look at him. "I just gave you a direct order. Don't be stupid about this, or we're all dead. *Do you understand?*"

Hetty nodded but refused to say another word. Her jaw clenched, she tossed the suitcase onto the floor. Then she found a backpack and filled it with the few items that fit.

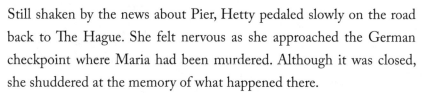

Still shaken by the news about Pier, Hetty pedaled slowly on the road back to The Hague. She felt nervous as she approached the German checkpoint where Maria had been murdered. Although it was closed, she shuddered at the memory of what happened there.

When she entered the city, she followed a circuitous path until she entered the neighborhood where her parents lived at Oma Betje's house. A man stood on the street corner. She inhaled deeply and held it. Was he watching her? When he disappeared into a drug store, Hetty exhaled. Thinking about Kees's order, she started to turn down the street where her parents lived.

Then she made a sharp left turn toward Pier's house. *To hell with Kees*, she thought. *He's never even met Rini and Thyrza.* Her heart was pounding, but she needed to find out whether it was possible to warn Pier's aunts. She told herself she would turn around if there was any sign of Gestapo.

"Papers please." The unexpected gruff voice hit her like a hammer. How could she have missed two Gestapo agents standing in front of Pier's house? Not far away, behind a tree, she glimpsed a third man, but he ducked into the shadows.

One of the Gestapo agents flung down his cigarette and moved toward Hetty. She swerved to avoid his grasp, then sped up. "Hey! Stop!" the man shouted, reaching for his pistol. The other man grabbed Hetty's shoulder and tried to bring her down, making his partner hold his fire. Then the Gestapo agent tripped over himself, leaving his partner with a clear shot at Hetty, who ducked just before two bullets zipped over her head.

She pedaled as fast as she could. *Kees was right*, she thought—and *he'll be furious*. Hetty considered keeping her visit to Pier's house a secret, but she knew she had to tell him so he could plan around the damage she'd just done. She kept pedaling hard until the agents were out of sight. Then she slowed a little, riding evasively through the neighborhood until she arrived at her grandmother's house.

"Kees!" Hetty slowed to a stop in front of him, panting for breath. "I almost did something really stupid." She shook her head, trying to collect her thoughts. "No. I *did* do something stupid."

"I *told* you to stay away from Pier's house," Kees exploded.

"H-how did you know?" Hetty stammered, still disoriented from her narrow escape.

"I was standing behind a tree when those two goons almost caught you." Kees paced up and down the sidewalk, waving his arms.

"That was you?"

"What the *hell* were you thinking?" Kees shouted. "You could have been killed."

"I *was* almost killed." Hetty flung her bicycle to the pavement, tears of fury in her eyes. "Can't you just leave me alone?"

"Stop it," Kees ordered. He slapped her across the cheek, not hard since he knew what a real slap by a trained boxer might do to her, but enough to make a point. "You aren't the only one at risk here."

Hetty felt remorse. "Of course you're worried that the Gestapo might come after you too," said Hetty, her shoulders slumping. "How could I be so stupid?"

"Did you ever tell Pier about me?"

"Of course not," said Hetty.

"Then I'm not in more danger than usual," Kees reflected.

"But if they catch me, they'll make me tell them about you," said Hetty, her eyes growing wide at the implications.

"Not just me." Kees nodded. "You'd be forced to tell them about Mimi, Aldon, Yacov, Rachel, and everyone else you've met in the resistance. That's why you risk more than your own life when you act recklessly."

"Of course, you're right," said Hetty, staring at the pavement. "You must hate me for being so reckless."

"I can't hate you for following your instincts," said Kees, wrapping his arms around her. "You're a lioness who looks after the other members of your pride." He paused for a moment. "It's what made you save my life when Hess had the drop on me."

Hetty touched his cheek with her fingertips, grateful for his kind words. "What I did tonight was reckless, and I'm sorry. But never slap me again. I will not tolerate it."

"Fair enough." He shrugged and handed her a cigarette, striking a match to light it for her.

"I can't sleep here." Hetty glanced toward her grandmother's house. "The Gestapo will search this neighborhood."

"You need to leave," said Kees decisively. "You can never return to Leiden now that they know your name."

"Mimi wanted me to go to France with her," said Hetty. "She has an assignment there. I told her it was a crazy idea."

"Do it," said Kees, picking up her bicycle from the curb. "You'll be safer in France than here."

CHAPTER 16

"Only half a day's ride before we get to Paris," said Mimi as she and Hetty navigated their bicycles down a narrow road through a French forest.

"I hope your cousin lets us stay with him," said Hetty, her blouse soaked with sweat from the sweltering day. "We haven't had a bath since we left Holland."

"Francois will never turn *me* away," Mimi laughed. "I'm his favorite. He lives in a castle, Plaisance, a few miles north of Paris. I practically grew up there."

A glint of light in the forest caught Hetty's eye. She raised her hand, and Mimi immediately pulled her bike off the road with Hetty right behind her.

"What was that?" whispered Hetty as she and Mimi hid in the underbrush. Then she saw it again, recognizing the reflection of filtered sunlight off a belt buckle, but the source had moved.

"There," whispered Mimi. "I count five people in the forest—and they're armed. Do you think the Germans are looking for us?"

Hetty thought about the danger they had already overcome on their long bicycle journey. They surely would have been caught at a checkpoint when they crossed into Belgium were it not for two Dutch children who showed them how to crawl through the brambles at an unwatched place on the border.

When she got a closer look at the five people walking stealthily through the forest, Hetty relaxed. "They're not Gestapo," whispered Hetty. "They're partisans. Their weapons aren't military issue."

Mimi started to stand up, but Hetty pulled her down behind the bushes. When the small column of French resisters had passed out of sight, Hetty and Mimi mounted their bicycles to continue their journey.

"Why didn't you let me speak to them?" said Mimi as she pedaled down the narrow forest road. "They might have been able to tell us about German checkpoints."

"I told you before that I don't trust the partisans," answered Hetty, mounting her bicycle. "Come on. We need to reach your cousin's house by nightfall."

For the rest of their journey, the friends encountered neither Germans nor partisans.

Suddenly it appeared, Château de Plaisance, like an elegant toy castle in the distance. "It's magnificent," said Hetty, shielding the sun from her eyes. Both women dismounted and gazed at the fourteenth-century castle, poised on the verdant hillside.

"We have three days until my partisan contact will take me to my pilots," said Mimi, gazing at the valley below. "That's plenty of time for a holiday at Plaisance."

"We both need a vacation," said Hetty, wiping her neck with a kerchief. "But you shouldn't risk your neck with those unreliable partisans again."

"This is the third time I've taken pilots to the Pyrenees," Mimi replied, irritation in her voice. "My partisan contacts haven't let me down yet." Riding on in silence, Mimi expertly guided her bicycle on the winding descent to Plaisance. "Out here, it seems impossible that we lived in Leiden only two weeks ago."

"Do you think we'll ever be able to go back?" asked Hetty, following closely behind her friend.

"Only after the goddamn Nazis leave," Mimi replied.

"I miss the days when all of us planned our futures at the university," said Hetty. "I thought I would marry Karl, have kids, and enter the law like my father."

"You know who I miss from those days? Arie and Mieke." Mimi chuckled at the memory of their delightful friends as they emerged from the forest into a landscape of rolling hills covered with green grass.

"Have you ever met two people more perfect for each other?" Hetty asked. "Funniest couple I know."

Mimi smiled. "Remember when Arie declared schnapps the greatest drink in the world?"

"'It's cheap and it has alcohol,'" Hetty said, laughing as she mimicked him. "He was joking as usual. One time, Mieke and I helped him finish a whole bottle of whiskey, and he never said a word about schnapps."

"Let's make some time to see them when we get back," said Mimi, turning down a long, narrow driveway that led to the gate. "I heard they moved to The Hague."

Hetty was taken by the magnificence of Château de Plaisance up close. "If the Gestapo catches us, at least we'll die in a beautiful place."

"Relax." Mimi dismounted her bicycle and walked it toward the open gate. "Nothing bad can happen to us at Plaisance. It's magical."

As they walked through the gate, a mature woman in a dark green peasant dress swept into their path. She was tall, with gray streaks in her dark hair, and had a powerful physique.

"Madeline, oh my dear Madeline." Mimi embraced the older woman, speaking excitedly in French. "How have you been? Keeping everyone safe I hope."

Mimi turned to Hetty, continuing to speak in French. "This is my Madeline." Mimi bubbled with enthusiasm. "She's tended the gate since I was a little girl."

"Welcome." Madeline's smiling eyes glowed. "We weren't expecting you, Mimi. This is a delightful surprise."

"We had no safe way to let Francois know we were coming," Mimi explained, still beaming. Then she turned to Hetty. "Whenever I was being poorly treated by the adults in my family, I came to Madeline for comfort. We cuddled in the gatehouse while she told me stories about medieval times. She never let me down." Mimi hugged Madeline again and kissed her cheek.

Madeline grabbed the girls' backpacks. "Monsieur Francois is in Paris on business. We expect him back this afternoon." She smiled warmly at Mimi and performed a girlish hop before moving briskly up the path.

"I hope we won't be a burden," said Hetty, hesitating at the gate. "I'm sure he has his own problems with the Germans without taking on two women wanted by the Gestapo."

"I told you to stop worrying. Francois can take care of himself. Now, let me show you around." Mimi led Hetty by the hand toward the spacious gardens that surrounded the imposing castle. "Afterward, you can have your bath."

Hetty tilted her head back to view one of the monumental spires as they walked next to the house. "When was the castle built? I've never seen such beautiful architecture."

Mimi enjoyed the chance to show off Plaisance to her friend. "Oh, this is just a farmhouse in a French meadow. The oldest parts were built in the fourteenth century, but the main house was constructed in the sixteen hundreds."

"Some farmhouse," Hetty chortled.

Oh, the joy of being clean again! Soaking in a good, hot bath was one of Hetty's favorite pastimes. Like everything else at Plaisance, the bath was luxurious, and the temperature of the water was perfect, with French fragrances on the shelf that Hetty had not experienced before.

Hetty had nearly fallen asleep, so peaceful was this corner of Plaisance castle, when Mimi burst through the door. "Germans are at the front door."

"What? Do they know we're here?" Hetty stood up in the bathtub, naked and dripping wet, her heart racing.

"Not yet," said Mimi, reaching into a cupboard for a robe. "Follow me. No time to lose."

Mimi pulled the plug to drain the bath before leading her friend to a secret opening in a closet. From there they crawled on their bellies through a narrow pathway inside the walls of the castle until they reached a small room. "Where are we?" whispered Hetty.

"Above the living room," whispered Mimi. "This was my favorite hiding place when I was a little girl. Look." She put one eye against a slight crack in the wall, then moved aside for Hetty.

Hetty held her breath. A German general in full uniform stood inside the entryway. "It's about time," said the German. "I've been waiting for thirty minutes."

"My apologies," said a young man who had just entered the living room. "I've just returned from Paris and had to freshen up."

"That's Francois," whispered Mimi.

"To what do I owe the honor of your visit, General?" asked Francois.

Furnished in a baroque style, the floor of the massive living room featured a mosaic of inlayed hardwood. Delightful antiquities seemed to be everywhere. An oil painting nearly covered one wall. Was it an original portrait of Louis XIV, Hetty wondered?

"We have reports that a partisan by the name of Cedric has been seen in these parts," said the general.

"I haven't seen any partisans—and no one by that name," said Francois. "I know everyone who lives nearby, and I would have been told if there was a stranger lurking about. You are welcome to search my house, of course."

The general motioned to two soldiers waiting outside, and they bounded up the stairs. The sound of doors being opened and slammed shut upstairs jolted the living room. There was a crash, which made Hetty wonder what household heirloom they had broken.

She glanced at Mimi with a worried expression.

Suddenly one of the soldiers appeared at the top of the stairs. "Someone took a bath, but I can't tell how recently she was here," he reported. "There were perfume scents." The general raised an eyebrow toward Francois.

"I, uh, occasionally entertain female guests," said Francois with a wink. "A single man alone needs distractions. She was here last night and apparently lingered to take a bath. But she was gone by the time I returned from Paris."

A knowing smile spread across the general's face before he glanced at the soldier. "Did you find anyone up there?"

The soldier shook his head.

From her vantage point, Hetty was bewildered that the general did not ask more questions. The reason became clear when he clasped Francois's hand to say farewell. "I hope you don't mind that we have taken a suckling pig from your stable for a banquet we are having tomorrow night. Fresh meat is hard to come by, even for the Reich."

So the general had no real interest in searching Francois's house, thought Hetty. It was the pig he was after. Lucky break.

"Consider it a gift," said Francois, closing the door behind the general and his men. Holding his nose while he made his way across the living room, he waved his hand to refresh the air. Then he poured whiskey and sat down in his favorite chair with a thud.

"He's the pig," he muttered, before taking a large gulp of whiskey.

Mimi burst into the living room and embraced her cousin. "I'm surprised they didn't find our backpacks."

"They weren't really looking for partisans—though a lot of them live around here," said Francois *sotto voce*. "The Nazis came here to steal one of my pigs. It's a little arrangement I've made with them. I don't complain when they steal food from my farm, and they mostly leave me alone."

"This is my friend, Hetty," said Mimi. "She was in the bathtub when the Germans arrived."

"That is a tragedy, for which I apologize," said Francois, shaking her hand with a welcoming smile. "A good bath should never be interrupted."

Francois carried himself the way one would expect of a direct descendant of Guillaume de Plaisance, who built the castle in 1304. In truth, Francois was not related to the famous aristocrat; his family had acquired the castle in the 1700s. But they had adapted well to patrician ways. Even though Francois had just traveled from Paris on a hot afternoon, the clean-shaven French nobleman dressed impeccably, wearing a dapper ensemble that featured a waist coat and ascot. He had a slightly awkward manner, but Hetty decided it was just a charming ruse that enabled him to maintain civility while still getting what he wanted—as he had done with the thieving Germans.

"In Paris, everyone is talking about the Allied invasion of Italy," said Francois. "It happened a week ago, but I don't have to tell you that news travels slowly in an occupied country. With rescue on the way, nothing would make me happier than to have the two of you stay with me until the war ends."

"That's a tempting invitation," said Hetty, admiring the portrait of Louis XIV, which she knew now was an original. "But too many people depend on us. So Mimi and I are committed to the resistance until the last German leaves Holland."

Mimi moved around the living room, fondly touching priceless antiques. "I promised Hetty a vacation at Plaisance," said Mimi, admiring a vase. "So far, it's hardly been that."

"Let me show you around," said Francois, taking Hetty by the elbow. "When the Germans aren't intruding, this place can be a haven from the war." He led the way to a courtyard outside a reinforced wall. "This was the entrance to the original fort—before the castle was built."

Hetty pointed to a twenty-foot-high stone tower. "What's that beautiful structure?"

"We call this the pigeon tower because it was built to attract nesting pigeons. During times of siege, pigeon eggs—and sometimes the pigeons themselves—became the food of last resort. Fortunately, no one eats them today," Francois laughed.

A roar of vehicles interrupted them. All eyes went to the road, where five heavy trucks drove past, each loaded with Nazi soldiers. Hetty and Mimi exchanged worried glances. "They're not after us," said Francois in an amused voice. "They already have my pig."

Mimi swung her backpack onto her shoulders. "I have to leave," she said.

"And end all of this?" With a relaxed smile, Hetty removed her sunglasses and propped herself up on the lounge chair where she'd been sunbathing every afternoon for the past three days. "It seems like we just got here."

"We've had three glorious days—free of Germans," said Mimi, raising her eyes to the fresco in the ceiling. "But this is the day I meet my pilots."

"I know, but I don't want it to be over." Yawning, Hetty stretched her arms above her head.

Francois arrived with toast and jam on a plate as Hetty was standing up. "Leaving so soon, cousin?"

Mimi nodded. "Duty calls." She bit into her toast. "I'll miss your good food while I'm traipsing through the woods with my pilots."

"I wish we had woods in Holland," said Hetty.

Mimi rolled her eyes. "You always say that."

"It's true," said Hetty defensively. "When we saw those partisans in the forest, I envied how easily they concealed themselves. There's nowhere like that forest to hide in Holland."

"All the more reason for you to be especially careful when you get back," said Mimi. "I'm counting on you to find us a safe place to live."

"Kees is already working on it," said Hetty.

"I wish you wouldn't go," said Francois, hugging his cousin. "Maybe the war will be over soon."

"When the war ends, Hetty and I will come back to Plaisance for a long vacation." Mimi kissed Francois on the cheek.

"You will both be welcome." Francois hugged her again, smiling bravely when they separated before disappearing into the house.

Hetty followed Mimi to the front gate, where she put her backpack on the ground. "Francois will let you stay here as long as you like."

"I can stay for a few more days," said Hetty. "But Kees has work for me back in The Hague."

"Stay alert when you get there." Mimi hugged Hetty at the entry gate and then embraced Madeline, who seemed determined not to cry, before walking briskly down the path toward the road. Mimi waved as she called out over her shoulder, "*Au revoir.* Schnapps with Arie and Mieke when I get back."

The Paris café was empty, except for one guest seated at a table and one waiter.

"Cedric, so good to see you again," said Mimi, giving him a hug when he entered the café.

The waiter brought two cups of ersatz coffee then retreated to the kitchen. The other customer finished his coffee and left.

"The Germans were asking about you at Plaisance," said Mimi with a frown. "Is our operation safe?"

"You know I'm dependable," said Cedric. "Nothing will go wrong."

He held out a red scarf. "Wear this." He tied it around her neck with a neat bow. "This will allow Gloria to recognize you. She'll approach you when she sees your scarf." Cedric led Mimi into the street. "When she calls you by name, you must respond with hers. Don't hesitate. We are using names instead of passwords."

Mimi knew Paris well from the days before the war, but she didn't recognize any of the streets where Cedric took her. Suddenly he guided her into the alcove of a bookshop, where they pretended to admire the books displayed in the window. A squad of German soldiers marched past them in goose step. The moment the soldiers had passed, Cedric guided Mimi onto a side street, then through an alley into a labyrinth of Parisian walkways and alleys. They came upon a busy plaza ringed by shops and restaurants. Mimi admired the birds splashing in the center of the fountain.

"This is where I leave you." Cedric pointed to a bench near the fountain while he scanned the plaza. "Remember, your names are the passwords. If she doesn't call you Mimi, run. Got it?"

"Got it." Mimi lit a cigarette as she watched Cedric disappear into a side street.

Cedric had been gone five minutes when Mimi heard a silky voice behind her. "Hello, I'm Gloria." A slender woman with dark hair and brown eyes sat next to Mimi holding a purse. "I noticed your red scarf." Gloria adjusted her beret, which she wore at a fetching angle. "What's your name?"

Kees had trained her to follow password protocol strictly. *She didn't say my name,* Mimi thought, glancing left and right for an escape route as she dropped her cigarette on the pavement. *She doesn't know the password!* Fixing her eyes on the smoldering cigarette, Mimi tried to appear casual while she stubbed it out slowly with the sole of her shoe.

Gloria quietly moved her purse from her lap to the bench beside her. Noticing the likely signal, Mimi stood abruptly and turned to flee. A man's powerful hand grabbed her hard by the right arm. She jerked free long enough to clutch her dagger. But another man clenched her wrist with a vise-like grip, making her drop the knife. The two men snatched the petite Mimi like a rag doll and handcuffed her.

"Wait," said Mimi, flashing her best smile at the French policeman who held her. "There's been a mistake. I'm just waiting for a friend."

Most men would have melted at Mimi's smile, but the policeman only tightened his grip. Mimi screamed in French to the people on the crowded sidewalk, "Please help me. I am being arrested for no reason!"

No one met her gaze. A group of people exited a nearby café in response to the commotion, but they walked away quickly when they saw the police. In handcuffs, Mimi continued to cry out for help, but no one paid attention.

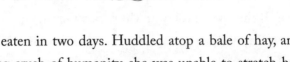

Mimi hadn't eaten in two days. Huddled atop a bale of hay, an island in the stinking crush of humanity, she was unable to stretch her arms because every inch of space was occupied. *Thank God they didn't interrogate me*, she thought. Because her French was flawless, she'd been able to convince the French police that she was only the girlfriend of a partisan who had gotten in over her head. This saved her from a painful interrogation, but they still put her on this train. Mostly, her fellow passengers stared at the floor, but when she caught the eye of one of them, she saw only despair.

A blinding flash of sunlight entered when the door of the railcar slid open. Mimi gulped the fresh air, which tasted sweet after three days jammed into the rolling box filled with the stench of human waste and fear.

A sharp pain stabbed her left ankle when she landed on the ground amid the cascade of bodies that tumbled from the railcar. German soldiers barked orders while her fellow passengers called out for loved ones.

"Good morning," said the German officer ironically with the condescending air of a man who knew he held absolute power over his prisoners. Mimi shuddered at his commanding voice. "I am Major Schmidt, commandant of Saarbrucken Camp."

CHAPTER 17

THE SOUND OF GREASE SIZZLING in a skillet greeted Kees when he entered his unassuming flat in a working-class neighborhood of The Hague. "I've found a better place for you to live," he said to Hetty.

"About time," she replied from the kitchen. "I've lived here too long, especially since you and Aldon are such slobs," she teased.

Kees followed his nose to the kitchen. "Where did you find those eggs?"

"Do you want some?" Hetty flipped the eggs onto two plates and put them on the table. "Kidding aside, thank you. I don't know how I could have survived without you this past year."

"You were in pretty bad shape when you came home from France," Kees agreed, as he hungrily shoveled a bite into his mouth. "Besides, you needed a safe place to hide."

"At first, I was certain that Mimi would turn me in," said Hetty, staring at her eggs without touching them. "She's my best friend, but everyone cracks under torture. She knows I killed Hess."

"They must not have tortured her," said Kees. "Mimi is a clever girl."

"She's probably dead by now," said Hetty morosely.

"She's not dead," said Kees, taking a sip of coffee. "She's at Saarbrucken Camp."

Hetty had been wary over the past year and didn't want to get her hopes up, only to be let down again. She had learned her lesson after Karl went missing. "She was arrested nearly a year ago. How do we even know your news is current? And it's not only Mimi," she continued, staring at her hands. "I miss Karl so much I can barely get out of bed some mornings."

Kees gave her a knowing look. "I feel the same way about Maria. I never understood what she saw in me, but I was so obsessed with her that sometimes my whole body aches."

"She was an amazing friend," Hetty agreed.

"The list is growing too long," said Kees with a forlorn expression.

To distract herself from her grief, Hetty decided she should go back to work. "Karl would have told me to get going. We have a war to fight." Hetty took a small bite of her eggs, reflecting on what she had just said. "It's been killing me to be idle for so long."

"I've given you some courier runs."

"Those are boring, Kees—short, infrequent, and extremely safe." Hetty sipped her coffee. "It's time for me to take on meaningful assignments again."

"I'll decide when it's safe for you to fight again," said Kees, wiping egg yolk from his mouth.

"So, where is the new safe house?"

"I hope you like to do farm work."

"It's a farm?"

"Kees nodded. The owner, Katrien, is loyal to the resistance and will take good care of you."

Aldon burst through the front door out of breath. "I have news. The

Allies are in France!" He took off his hat and flung it across the room. "They invaded at Normandy on Tuesday. Caught the Nazis flat-footed."

"Yahoo!" Kees stood up and improvised a lively dance, which made Hetty and Aldon laugh.

"Do you think we'll be rescued by the Allies next week?" Aldon asked.

"I doubt it will be that soon," said Kees, joining hands with Aldon and Hetty as they danced in a circle. "But Normandy is only three hundred miles from here! So anything's possible. And if they come soon enough, maybe you won't have to resume dangerous assignments at all, Hetty."

"The Allies invaded Italy nearly a year ago, and they're still bogged down." Hetty had stopped dancing, and her smile disappeared. "I hope they move more quickly this time, but we can't be sure they will. As long as the Germans are in Holland, no one is safe."

"Katia, this is Hetty," said Kees to the girl who greeted them at the gate of a neatly arranged farm. A skinny girl for whom puberty had arrived late, Katia's coveralls hung loosely on her lanky body, and her long red hair framed a freckled face with blue eyes and a reserved smile.

Katia nodded at Hetty shyly.

"Have you heard that the Allies invaded France?" said Kees enthusiastically. "We just found out today."

"No. We're the last to hear any news out here," Katia lamented. "Where did they land?"

"Welcome, Kees," said Katia's mother, Katrien, bustling toward them from the back door of the house. "We haven't seen you in a long time." Heavier than her daughter, Katrien had red hair and blue eyes like Katia, but she wore her hair in a short, practical bob.

"This is Hetty," said Kees. The two women shook hands. "We just learned that the Allies are at Normandy. Can Hetty stay here until they come to Holland?"

"Amazing news," said Katrien ecstatically, grabbing her daughter and twirling her. "And we're glad to have Hetty," said Katrien with a smile.

"When do you think the Allies will get here?" asked Katia. The unvarnished elation in the teenager's voice made all of them laugh with joy.

"Maybe we should take things slowly until we know more about the Allies' plans," said Kees, recalling Hetty's caution on this subject. "They might decide to liberate Paris before they come to the Netherlands."

"Don't be a killjoy," said Katrien, squeezing his hand. "We know Hetty has to stay here until the Nazis actually leave, but it doesn't hurt to dream. This is the first good news we've had in a long time."

"Let's be clear," said Hetty, raising her voice. "Unless the war ends next week, I plan to return to the front lines of the resistance—no matter what Kees says."

Ignoring the obvious disagreement between Kees and Hetty, Katia took Hetty's hands in hers. "But I hope you don't leave too soon. I've always wanted a sister."

A border collie barked, tugging at the end of a long chain fastened to the house. To the dog's delight, Hetty scratched his belly. "I love dogs," she said, sliding both hands up to scratch behind its ears. "My father never let us have one. He did give me a rabbit named Sherlock, which is almost as good."

"This is Jasper," said Katrien, giving him a pat on the head. "We have a strict rule that he stays on the chain unless he's in the house. He gets after our neighbors' chickens."

"Then Jasper and I will become friends while he's on the chain," said Hetty, continuing to pet the dog while she glanced up at Katrien. "I hope I won't be too much trouble."

"We can use an extra pair of hands." Behind her smile at the news of the Allied invasion, Katrien's face wore the haggard look of someone who worked too hard and worried too much. "My husband was killed by the Gestapo a year ago. It's not easy managing the farm without him." Katrien put an arm around Katia, who leaned her head against her mother's shoulder.

Swish! Swish! Swish! Hetty's strong hands coaxed the cow's milk into the bucket between her knees. She was pleased with the competence she had acquired during her weeks working on Katrien's farm.

"Tell me a story about the resistance," said Katia, never tiring of her favorite subject. "My mother won't let me join." She used a pitchfork to pile hay into the horses' stalls.

"You should listen to your mother," said Hetty, continuing her milking. "Besides, most of the time, the resistance is pretty boring."

"I don't believe you," said Katia, who brought her pitchfork with her to stand next to Hetty. "You must have done something exciting to get the Gestapo on your trail."

"You sound like my little brother," Hetty chuckled. "He wants to join the resistance too—sees it as a great adventure, but it's far from that."

"You have a brother?" asked Katia excitedly.

Hetty nodded. "Jan."

"How old is he?" asked Katia. "Maybe we can join the resistance together. Can I meet him?"

"He's twenty, the same age I was when the war started," said Hetty, smiling at Katia's eagerness for companionship. The farm was certainly isolated.

"Twenty seems old enough to be in the resistance," said Katia with a toss of her red hair. "Is he handsome?"

"Are you looking for a boyfriend?" Hetty laughed. "Or a comrade in arms?"

"Why not both?" said Katia, leaning on the handle of the pitchfork.

"My brother tried to join the resistance last year—in combat, where there are the most casualties," said Hetty lifting a full bucket of milk. "When I got wind of it, Kees helped me stop him. I didn't want to be a nag, so we compromised, and I let him join as long as he stays away from combat." She carried the milk toward the main house. "So he's helping a forgery expert create false documents for people in hiding."

A murder of crows settled into a fruitless mulberry tree in front of the house, driving away the songbirds and making a huge racket. *Caw! Caw!* A chill went down Hetty's back as she stopped to watch them.

Katia waited for the noise to die down. "Please take me with you to The Hague, Hetty. Maybe I can meet your brother."

Hetty shook her head as she hefted the milk bucket onto the porch. "There won't be time. I'll only be there for one day to visit my mother." A clap of thunder made the crows fly away. Hetty turned her eyes toward the stormy sky and grabbed her bicycle.

"Looks like rain."

Bored with his job making false papers, Jan had broken his word to Hetty and now he lay in a foxhole on his first mission for the combat resistance. The rain had slowed to a drizzle, but it left the ground around him soggy. The glow of a full moon peeked through the parting clouds, penetrating the dark, overcast sky.

The nearby road that ran alongside the canal was empty. Windmills and farmhouses formed shadows in the moonlight. Jan reached under his coat and felt for the sten submachine gun he'd put there to protect it from the rain. Light automatic weapons known as sten guns had become the preferred firearm of the resistance ever since the British began smuggling them into the Netherlands.

Niels startled Jan when he suddenly appeared next to his foxhole. "Are you ready, New Guy?"

Jan's resistance leader, the thirty-year-old Niels was surprisingly agile considering his sedentary prewar occupation as a doorman at a large office building in Rotterdam. His dour countenance suggested a hard life, but there was a steely determination in his eyes.

"I'm as ready as anyone can be with only one day of training," said Jan, wiping the rainwater from his face with the back of his hand.

"I wish we could have given you more practice with that weapon," Niels said, tucking his own sten gun under his coat. "But we only learned yesterday that the collaborator would be on this road tonight."

The wind picked up, and Jan wrapped his scarf around his neck.

"Nice scarf," said Niels.

"It's too green for me," said Jan. "But my sister knitted it for me, so I wear it."

"Sister?" Niels became serious. "What's her name?"

"Hetty. Why?"

"I know a guy named Kees who knows her." Niels used a small telescope to survey the road and the positions of his men. "She won't be happy when she finds out you signed up for combat. She thinks you're making false papers."

"That's Hetty all right." Jan managed a slight smile. "Please don't tell her."

"Stay alive today, my young friend." Niels checked the road again with his scope. "Maybe the Allies will get here before we have to worry about telling your sister anything." Niels silently waited for his target to arrive. "Pretty soon, you'll see a car on this road." Niels glanced at

Jan reassuringly as he pointed. "A collaborator, Joseph Sloan, will be in that car. He's a petty little prick who gave up a hundred Dutch Jews to the Nazis."

"I hate him already," said Jan.

"Good, because we're going to shoot him."

Jan swallowed hard, his hand trembling slightly while he checked his weapon. "I've never killed anyone."

It stopped raining, but the ground remained soggy.

"Quiet!" a team member called in a loud whisper from a nearby foxhole. Muted headlights appeared on the winding canal road as moonlight provided a clear view of the advancing vehicle.

"I count four occupants." Niels's calm voice was reassuring to Jan.

Jan tried to chamber a round in his submachine gun, but it jammed.

"Let me have that." Niels reached for the weapon. In one motion, he cleared the round that was stuck and chambered another. Returning the weapon to Jan, he peered through his telescope at the oncoming car. "I make out Sloan as one of the passengers, but who are the other three?"

Jan squinted, waiting for the car to come closer. "One of them is a woman."

"Do you think that bastard brought his wife?" Niels whispered. "That means there are only two soldiers in the car. Good."

Niels removed his cap and waved it across his body. For a silent instant, Jan wondered what the signal meant. Suddenly there was a flash of light when an explosion ripped through the quiet, lacerating the front end of Sloan's car before it swerved off the road and slammed into a tree. The woman screamed, and the driver's head ricocheted off the steering wheel. An armed guard in the right rear seat lunged from the car without his helmet, screaming as he lumbered toward a large bush, where he directed a fusillade of lead.

"*Arrgh*." Aaron, one of the resistance fighters, cried out from behind the bush. Erik, another fighter, stood up from his hiding place, perfectly located behind the German. But his sten gun jammed.

"Fuck!" Erik dove headfirst into the dirt as the German whirled the muzzle of his gun around to erase him from the battlefield. But before he could fire, the soldier's forehead burst open, spraying blood. With a stunned expression, Jan held his sten gun pointed toward the German, a waft of smoke emerging from the barrel.

Quickly, Jan swung the muzzle of his weapon back toward the collaborator's car. "Stop! Please! Don't shoot!" The woman inside screamed, waving both arms in surrender.

Niels pointed his gun at a balding fat man in the passenger seat. "Get out, Sloan."

The driver was slumped over the steering wheel. Another team member, Raf, flung the car door open, placing his hand on the dead driver's neck before turning off the ignition. "Got him," said Raf staring across the vehicle at Niels. Raf pulled the driver's corpse from the car and collected the man's weapons.

"Don't shoot." Sloan held his hands up as he scrambled from the car.

Raf bent down behind the bush where his colleague had screamed. "Aaron's dead," Raf reported.

Niels nodded toward Raf. "You and Erik. Make a sling to carry Aaron's body out of here."

"What about them?" Erik gestured toward the bodies of the German soldiers.

Niels glanced at the corpses. "Leave them."

He turned back to the woman standing next to Sloan. With a stylish hat cocked at a jaunty angle and a red evening dress with a pearl necklace, she was dressed like someone who hoped to make a grand entrance somewhere. "Got yourself a mistress, have you, Joseph?" said Niels derisively.

Sloan said nothing. Niels hit him in the face hard with his gloved fist. "I asked you a question, Sloan. I know this woman isn't your wife. Who is she?"

"I have never seen her before," said Sloan.

"Good. Then you won't need this." Niels fired his weapon into the ground, barely missing Sloan's crotch. Joseph screamed, grabbing his manhood protectively.

"I won't miss next time," Niels said coldly.

Niels turned to the woman. "Who are you?"

Her eyes were frozen on the pistol in Niels's hand. Niels cocked his gun and put it in her face. "Are you his mistress?"

"Yes." She nodded her head, glancing nervously at Niels's weapon. "We haven't known each other very long."

"See. That wasn't so difficult." Niels returned his attention to Sloan, who had a humiliating wet stain spreading in his pants.

"Sloan, you fat bastard, you have betrayed your country," Niels snarled, putting his face close to the collaborator's. "Hell, you've betrayed the whole human race." Niels stepped away, glancing at Jan. "New Guy, shoot him."

"No. Please," Sloan begged, his face contorted with fear.

Jan stared at Sloan, and then hesitated. "Maybe you should do it, Niels." Jan's voice quivered as he lowered his sten gun.

Raf called out from where he was making a sling for Aaron's body. "You just killed this other German bastard, kid. Do it."

"That was different," Jan whispered.

Sloan's gaze shifted anxiously from Jan to Raf and back again.

Niels held his pistol out to Jan. "What will it be, kid? Do I have to put this Jew-killing bastard out of his misery?"

"No. I'll do it." Jan reluctantly took Niels's pistol.

"Go ahead," Raf sneered. "Finish him."

Jan used two hands to steady the weapon, its muzzle inches from Sloan's head. Then he pulled the trigger. Sloan's body slumped immediately. Jan began to tremble, the pistol dangling from his finger.

"I'm glad that was hard for you, kid," said Niels, clapping Jan on the shoulder as he retrieved his pistol. "It should never be easy to kill a man."

"Won't there be reprisals?" Jan asked quietly. "Someone will surely die for this."

"Probably, but we can't fight the Germans if we worry about that."

Jan nodded toward Sloan's mistress and whispered. "What should we do with her?"

"That's enough killing for today," said Niels, gesturing to Raf to tie the woman up. Then he glanced down at Sloan. "We've sent our message."

"Don't leave me alone out here," the woman begged. "I'll die of thirst."

"Would you rather end up like him?" Niels pointed toward Sloan's corpse. "Someone will come along and find you." He handed her his canteen.

After the resistance fighters had carried their dead comrade away and buried him, Niels held up his hand. "Before you boys leave, I have a request from leadership. They want volunteers. A dangerous mission they tell me." His eyes locked on each man in turn. None of them moved.

"They've asked for men without families," Niels added. "So I won't be leading this one."

Jan started to raise his hand, but Erik, the man he had just saved, pulled his arm down. "No," whispered Erik. "This sounds like a suicide mission."

"None of you has to do it," Niels emphasized.

Jan took a deep breath. Then he raised his hand again. "I'll go."

CHAPTER 18

JAN FOUND IT TEDIOUS WAITING for orders on his new assignment. Increasingly he spent his afternoons at a bookstore about a mile from where he lived with his parents at Oma Betje's house.

"Do you like American authors?" The soft female voice came from behind Jan, who had been thumbing through *The Grapes of Wrath.*

"My, uh, sister recommended this," said Jan awkwardly. "I suppose I'll give it a try."

"An educated man. I like that." The woman held out her hand. "I'm Marleen."

"I'm Jan," he said, already smitten by the auburn-haired beauty with the alluring voice.

Marleen spoke with the confidence of one who is accustomed to being heard. "Shall we have some coffee?"

"Right now?" said Jan, surprised by her boldness.

Marleen smiled. "Why not?"

They exited the bookstore, enjoying the July sunshine. Jan headed toward a café across the street.

"They only have ersatz coffee there." Marleen winked at him with a conspiratorial smile, placing a hand gently on his arm. "Guess what? I have *real* coffee at home."

"And sugar?" said Jan enthusiastically.

"Mm-hmm." Marleen nodded.

Jan's eyes shone with excitement. "Where did you get it?"

"You don't want to know." Marleen laughed. "Do you want some or not?"

"Don't make me beg," said Jan with a big smile.

"This is me." Marleen gestured toward a residential building as they turned the corner. "This flat belonged to my parents." When they walked inside, Jan thought of his parents for a moment and wondered what it must be like to speak of them in the past tense. He hoped it would be a long time before he had that experience. After opening the door, Marleen put her key away as she ushered Jan inside. "They were arrested a few weeks after the invasion."

Marleen extended her arm toward the living area as she walked into the kitchen to get the coffee started.

"That must have been hard for you." Jan sat down on the sofa. "Why were they arrested?"

Marleen watched the coffee percolate on the stove. "They were outspoken opponents of the Dutch Nazi Party. The Germans shot both of them last year."

Jan lowered his eyes toward the floor. "The Germans demolished our family home for gun emplacements," said Jan, walking over to the kitchen and putting his hand on Marleen's. "But that doesn't compare to what happened to you."

"Sometimes I get angry," Marleen said as she poured the steaming coffee into two cups. "Mostly, I try to concentrate on the small things that make me happy; this coffee for instance."

Jan leaned toward the cup and sniffed the aroma with his eyes closed.

"That's a good philosophy," he said with a smile, anticipating the rare treat.

Marleen nodded as she produced a sugar bowl and held it open.

"I can't believe you have sugar." Jan put the precious grains of sweetness into his coffee and took a sip. "Mmm. It's been so long since I've had real coffee—with sugar no less."

"I'm happy you're enjoying it." Marleen smiled coquettishly as she led Jan to a velvet sofa in the living area. She sat down, her leg casually touching his as she tried her first sip. "Mmm," she said. "I only have a little of this, but I like sharing it with you." She turned her full attention to Jan with a slight flicker of her pretty eyes. "Tell me about your sister. You seem proud of her."

"How do you know I have a sister?" asked Jan, an eyebrow raised.

"Your sister recommended the book you were reading in the bookstore. Remember, the Steinbeck novel?"

"Um, right," said Jan, recalling nothing about their conversation except the way Marleen made him feel. "Her name's Hetty." Jan smiled at the thought of her. "She's four years older than me and still tries to tell me what to do."

"About what?"

Jan paused, thinking about the fights he'd had with Hetty about joining the resistance. "Nothing important," he said casually. "Why are you so interested?"

Marleen put her hand on his inner thigh, and he jumped. "No reason," she chuckled. "I'm more interested in you." She kissed him on the mouth, flicking her tongue against his.

The airfield was tiny, just a short runway and a dilapidated shack sur-rounded by farmland. Jan held his sten gun out of the mud as he watched the shack from an irrigation ditch, lying against the berm next to Jip, the mission leader. The front of their clothing was soaked by the wet ground.

Five years older than Jan, the diminutive Jip had an involuntary tick that made it appear as though he were winking when he talked. When Jan agreed to the assignment, Niels told him to ignore the tick; Jip was one of the bravest men he knew.

The weather had cooled, and Jan extracted his green scarf from his backpack. Jip glanced at him before resuming his surveillance of the airfield.

Tygo, another resistance fighter whom Jan had just met, was in a prone position to Jan's right. "*Achoo!*" Tygo sneezed, lifting his hand, too late, to muffle the sound. Already showing a bald spot on the crown of his head, Tygo appeared older than his twenty-one years.

"*Shhh.*" Jip lifted a finger to his lips, his tick making him wink.

"Is it just the three of us?" whispered Jan.

Jip shook his head. "More are coming." He gazed at Jan, who fidgeted nervously. "Don't worry. If the others don't show up, we'll abort the mission."

"What exactly is the mission?" asked Jan.

"A high-ranking German officer, probably a general, will land at this airfield," Jip whispered. "As you can see, the runway is only suitable for small planes, which means he won't have room to bring an armed escort. If all goes well, we're going to kill him and then run like hell to my car, which is parked in those trees."

Jan could barely make out a glint from the trees where Jip had ges-tured—probably the sun's reflection off the car's chrome bumper, he guessed. "Those trees are at least three hundred yards away," said Jan, worry lines forming on his forehead.

Just then another man arrived, flopping down on the far side of Tygo. The youngest of the group, Mick had fuzz on his face instead of whiskers.

Almost immediately, Siem, another fighter, slid in silently next to Mick, a scowl on his face. "No one's ever seen Siem in a good mood," Mick smirked.

"Good," Jip whispered to Jan. "We have enough fighters. Now we just need our target."

Suddenly, out of the corner of his eye, Jan saw a familiar flash of auburn hair. Before he knew it, Marleen was lying on the far side of Siem, holding her own submachine gun and ready for action.

"What the hell are you doing here?" Jan whispered. "Why didn't you tell me?"

Marleen held a hand to her ear and shook her head, indicating she could not hear him.

Jan turned to Jip on his immediate left. "We need to abort the mission," he whispered.

"Too late," Jip shook his head. "Why?"

"I don't trust that girl," said Jan urgently. "We slept together last week, but she never said she was in the resistance. It can't be a coincidence that she's here."

"I imagine you didn't tell her that you were in the resistance either. So why would she bring it up?" Jip gazed at Marleen. "I can't blame you though; she's tempting."

"I'm serious, Jip," Jan pressed. "Something's wrong." He looked back at the young woman, who smiled at him and winked.

"*Shhh!*" Jip's eyes were focused straight ahead.

A German soldier with a rifle slung over his shoulder emerged from the shack about a hundred feet away, wearing a helmet and green battle fatigues. Using his hand to block the sun, the soldier stared toward the berm where the resistance fighters were hiding. Marleen momentarily forgotten, Jan touched the trigger of his sten gun, ready to fight if the soldier found them. The German lit a cigarette and turned away, walking slowly in a loop around the dirt runway. When his journey brought him to the irrigation ditch, everyone held their breath. Only five feet away from them, the sentry inspected the runway. Jan's heart raced as the sentry stepped toward them. Then the German threw his cigarette butt on the ground and walked away.

As the soldier approached the guard shack, a German Shepard emerged and ran toward him. The dog's ears went up as it faced the irrigation ditch, its tail flicking slightly. The sentry produced a small piece of cheese for the dog as he scratched its ears. They returned to the guard shack. Jan wondered why the soldier hadn't picked up the dog's signal. Was he setting a trap? Jan glanced at Marleen. She was aiming her gun at the guard shack, seemingly concentrating on her target.

"Good. Our intelligence was accurate." Jip stared at the airport building. "No extra guards have been assigned on the ground."

Jan gestured at the road, which disappeared beyond a sharp turn a hundred feet past the airport building. "Could there be guards hiding around that turn?"

"Not likely." Jip's tick made him wink, and he scratched his head. "They would have to know we were coming to go to that trouble."

"What if they know?" Jan whispered urgently as he stared down the line at Marleen, who was inspecting the clip in her weapon.

"Marleen only volunteered for this mission yesterday. Even then, we didn't tell her the details," said Jip before turning toward Jan suspiciously. "Did you tell her something?"

"I don't know what I said for sure," said Jan nervously. "I wasn't paying much attention to the conversation."

His voice was drowned out by the buzz of a small airplane, which swooped in close for a landing. "No time to worry about her now," said Jip. "There's our target. Get ready."

Tygo put a cigarette in his mouth with no intention of lighting it, a slight tremor in his lower lip. Siem whispered a short prayer, made the sign of the cross, and checked the mechanism on his sten gun.

The plane landed, coming to a stop near the shack at the far edge of the runway. A man stepped out of the plane in full uniform. Three rows of medals with brightly colored ribbons glinted in the sunlight.

"That's him." Jip focused his small telescope. "He's a general all right." Jip didn't hesitate. He pumped his fist and shouted. "*Go, go, go!*"

Guns ready, the fighters jumped out of the irrigation ditch and ran toward the building. Suddenly the roar of truck engines filled the air. A column of armored personnel carriers stormed the runway from around the bend in the road and slammed on their brakes, launching forty screaming soldiers at the resistance fighters.

One of the vehicles was armed with a machine gun, which fired a burst at the commandos. Mick went down first with a bullet to the head. Struck by two rounds in his left arm from the machine gun, Tygo fell where he stood. Still breathing but whimpering softly, Tygo's right hand covered the bullet wounds, where blood seeped through his fingers.

Jan dove for the ground, his face spattered with Tygo's blood. He managed to fire a burst, but his sten gun collapsed when a single bullet fired at him by the Germans destroyed it. Jan frantically searched his own body for wounds—but there were none.

"Hands in the air!" A German officer barked his orders.

Jip raised his hands slowly, glancing around for an escape route. Lying prone on the ground, Jan raised one hand in the air while he propped himself up with the other. "Face down on the ground." The officer pressed the muzzle of his submachine gun against his head.

A German soldier walked briskly to the place where Tygo lay bleeding and fired one round into his head. He stopped whimpering.

Gun still in hand, Marleen walked straight toward the officer in charge. "What's she doing?" Jip whispered to Siem. "She'll get herself killed."

"I told you she's bad news," whispered Jan.

The officer's face wore a skeptical expression as Marleen approached. Then he hugged Marleen and kissed her cheek. "Good job, Diede."

Lying with his face in the dirt, Jan sucked in his breath and exhaled quietly. *I'm such a fool*, he thought.

After they were handcuffed, the remaining members of the resistance team were marched to a waiting truck. To their left, Marleen chatted with the German officer. "Time to pay what you owe me," she said with a flirty smile. Brimming with confidence, she held her hand out.

"I always pay what I owe," said the officer with a twisted smile. He drew his pistol and fired two shots into Marleen's head.

CHAPTER 19

HETTY CARRIED EGGS FROM KATRIEN'S henhouse in a clay bowl. Enjoying the warm day, Jasper rolled lazily in the dirt, unaffected by the chain that tethered him to the barnyard. "Kees is here to see you," said Katia, out of breath as she ran toward Hetty.

Hetty glanced past Katia with a smile. "Kees! I've missed—" Her smile disappeared when she saw what was in his hands: a light-green scarf with blood on it. She staggered backward, remembering what she had said to Jan about the day Kees had brought her Karl's sweater. "What are you doing with Jantje's scarf?"

Kees turned toward Katia. "Is there a place where we can talk inside?"

"Tell me now!" Hetty insisted, her voice rising. "What's happened to my brother!?"

Using the toe of his shoe, Kees pushed straw around on the ground. "He was captured in a commando raid."

The clay bowl slipped from Hetty's hands as she fought to save it.

Most of the eggs broke in the dirt before she gave up and let everything fall, breaking the bowl.

"The Gestapo has him." Kees hung his head. "I'm so sorry."

"Oh, Hetty." Katia grabbed her tightly.

In a daze, Hetty knelt down and pushed the broken pieces of clay around aimlessly in the filthy egg yolk. "Can we get him out?"

Kees shook his head grimly. "We don't have the resources. Your father paid a bribe to get information about Jan." Kees's voice was almost a whisper. "But no amount of money will persuade the Germans to let him go. He tried to kill a German general."

Hetty fought back tears. "When Jantje told me his work was limited to false papers, you promised to keep an eye on him. What was he doing on a commando raid?"

Kees averted his eyes.

"You knew!" Hetty shrieked. "You bastard!" Hetty hit Kees in the chest with her fists. "How could you keep something that important from me?"

"Jan was needed," said Kees in a quiet voice. "All of us are needed—sometimes for the most dangerous jobs. Your brother understood that." He tried to hug her, but she pushed him away.

Hetty brushed away a tear with the back of her hand then leveled a cold stare at Kees. "Go away! Leave me alone!" Hetty's voice was terse and threatening.

It pained Kees that he could not comfort Hetty, but he realized he was not welcome. "All right," said Kees in a gentle voice as he turned to retrieve his bicycle. "Stay put until you hear from me."

Jan stared down at the bodies of Jip and Siem, still warm in the trench below. He forced himself to stand up straight, which required effort by a man who had endured three days of torture since his capture on a lonely airfield.

He closed his eyes and remembered the day he discovered the loft at their family home when he was seven years old. There he found an oil painting of a nude woman that their mother thought she'd locked away from the prying eyes of children. "Hetty, come quickly," he'd shouted that day with breathless enthusiasm. "I've found a naked lady."

Jan smiled at the memory of that day—his eleven-year-old sister's admiration, the total love in her eyes. Then a bullet passed through his brain, ending his life twenty years after it had begun.

"It's the waiting that's killing me." Hetty stared into the fireplace, where Katia had made a roaring fire against the evening chill. "It's been three days since the Gestapo arrested Jantje. I know he's being tortured. Every day he stays alive is another day of agony for him—and for me. It needs to end."

"Do you think Kees could be mistaken?" asked Katia, leaning her head on her friend's shoulder. "Maybe Jan wasn't captured."

Hetty shook her head sadly. "Kees showed me the scarf I knitted for Jantje. It had blood all over it."

"But where did he get that scarf?" Katia wondered. "Maybe another resistance member picked it up and Jan is in hiding somewhere."

"You're a sweet girl." Hetty stroked Katia's red hair. "But there's no mistake. My father paid a bribe to learn what happened to my brother. His contact will send a note when he's gone."

Katrien squeezed her hand. "I am sure Jan's suffering will be over soon."

"I'm so glad you don't lie to me, Katrien—not like Kees."

"Don't blame him." Katrien placed her hand on Hetty's shoulder. "Someone had to give you the news."

But Hetty was inconsolable. "He knew my brother had volunteered for combat and never told me."

"I don't think he lied to you, Hetty. He just honored your brother's wish. I'm sure they didn't want to worry you."

Still in her coveralls from a hard day's work, Katia went to the kitchen and returned with tea on a tray. "I never got to meet Jan, but I know I would have liked him."

"He would have liked you for sure." Hetty clutched the young woman close to her.

Outside, the front gate creaked open. Katrien exchanged a worried glance with Hetty before approaching the front door. She had a mumbled conversation with someone and returned holding a note.

Katrien started to speak, but words failed her. She handed the note to Hetty, her face contorted in pain.

"Oh no." Hetty convulsed in tears as she dropped the message on the floor.

The three women hugged and cried together. Then Hetty stared, dry eyed, at the front door.

"What are you planning to do?" asked Katia warily.

Without a word, Hetty went to her room and returned, holding her coat and hat.

"You can't go outside," said Katrien, placing her hand on Hetty's shoulder. "It's after curfew."

Hetty donned her coat. "I have to be with my family." Hetty opened the front door, then turned around. "Don't worry. I'll stay in the shadows."

It was late morning when Hetty crept through the neighbor's backyard and climbed the fence so that she could enter Oma Betje's house from the back. She approached the kitchen door, which opened to a side yard that was screened from the street by a high fence. She had taken this route dozens of times as a child playing at the homes of her grandmother's neighbors, but those were just games of hide and seek, never real people with guns trying to hunt her down.

In the kitchen, Hetty found Oma Betje, who greeted her with an embrace that Hetty was in no hurry to end. The familiar scent of her grandmother's talcum powder comforted her.

Oma Betje was a short, heavyset woman with rosy cheeks and glasses. Too often lately she stared at people with vacant eyes, but today her dementia did not protect her from the awful truth. "Come, Hetty. Everyone's in the living room."

Inside, the doors and windows were shut tightly, leaving nowhere for stale breath and cigarette smoke to escape. The drawn drapes yielded a semidarkness that reflected the mood. Embers of a fire smoldered in the fireplace untended.

Henriette sat in a big stuffed chair in one corner of the room, weeping. Oma Corry held her daughter's hand, sitting in a straight-backed wooden chair. Two friends of the family were huddled in whispered conversation. Everyone else stared ahead quietly, lost in their own thoughts.

Willem's foghorn voice shattered the silence. "How dare you come here, Hetty. My boy is dead because of *you*."

Hetty took a moment before replying quietly, "I loved him too, you know." She searched her father's face for a sign that they might find a common bond in shared grief, but she saw only hatred and hostility.

"Get the hell out!" Willem shouted.

"I couldn't stop him, Papa," Hetty cried out in frustration. "He was a twenty-year-old *man*—not a *boy*." Angry tears filled her eyes. "Real men—the brave ones like Jantje—can't be stopped when they decide to die for their country. You will never understand what that's like."

"How dare you insult me on this of all days," said Willem, choking back tears of fury. "I will never forgive you."

Hetty turned her back on Willem and stepped toward her mother, who seemed to have aged considerably from the last time she saw her.

"Don't listen to your father." Sussje, Hetty's and Jan's nanny, chimed in from her rocker. Hetty bent down to embrace Sussje, who gave her a big hug in return. "People die in wars," Sussje continued, rocking Hetty gently in tiny, nearly imperceptible circles. "I lost a brother who fought against the colonialists in Indonesia. I was loyal to your Dutch family because you and Jan were my first priority, but I still grieve for him. What happened to your brother is no one's fault, sweetheart."

As she held Hetty, Sussje hummed a song under her breath. The tune was achingly familiar.

"I remember that tune as if it came from a previous life," said Hetty as she clung to her.

Sussje smiled through her tears. "That was our sweet boy's song, a lullaby I made up one night to quiet him when he wouldn't sleep, and it always seemed to make him feel better. Remember?"

"Yes, I remember now." Hetty's throat tightened at the memory. "Jantje hummed it for me the day I learned that Karl was dead."

"You always came when your brother cried," Sussje continued with a comforting smile. "You laid at my feet until you knew he was all right."

Hetty held the nanny's face in her hands. "Thank you—" She started to say more but could not.

Sussje gave her a loving smile. "Go see your mother."

Hetty crossed the room to embrace her mother, who was weeping quietly in a corner. "I'm here, Mama."

"Our boy is gone." Henriette slurred her words through her tears as she reached out a limp hand toward Hetty. Her eyes were dreamy and unfocused.

Hetty frowned at her grandmother. "What the hell is my mother taking?"

"I asked the doctor to give her something to help her sleep." Oma Corry was the best-dressed person in the room, wearing a high-collared dress with tiny jewels stitched around the edges.

Hetty stroked her mother's cheek. "She shouldn't be sedated so heavily."

"She needs her pills to dull the pain, dear." Oma Corry put her hand on Hetty's arm. "She's not strong like you and me."

"What makes you think—?" Hetty's voice, raspy from crying, broke in mid-sentence. "I am barely holding myself together."

"You came here, despite personal risk." Oma Corry kissed her granddaughter's forehead. "You are stronger than you will admit."

"What do you know about my personal risk?" Hetty glanced toward her mother, who had fallen asleep.

"Isn't it obvious?" Oma Corry gently placed a small pillow behind Henriette's head. "You and Jan told each other everything. Now the Germans know it too."

"Jantje would never give me up." Doubt flickered across Hetty's face as soon as the words left her mouth.

"The Nazis make everyone talk, Hetty." Oma Corry's voice was soothing, despite her grim message. "I wish you could have remained naïve about these things forever."

"I'm not naïve," said Hetty. "One of my lovers gave me up under torture."

"Now they know your full name and where your parents live." Her grandmother sighed. "It's time for you to run, Hetty. Go through the back; they're waiting for you out front."

Hetty opened a tiny crack in the curtains and inhaled sharply. Two Gestapo agents sat in a car across the street. She closed the curtains quickly and struggled to catch her breath.

Sussje was the first to speak after the tense moment. "Are those men outside searching for you?"

"How do you know about those men?" Hetty stared into Sussje's inscrutable eyes. "I just saw them myself."

Sussje's reassuring smile calmed her. "Oma Corry is right. You should leave before they know you're here."

"I need to say goodbye to Mama first." Hetty turned toward her mother.

"Not so fast, young lady." Willem's voice was loud enough for all to hear. "We haven't finished our conversation."

"I don't have time for this, Papa," said Hetty urgently. "The Gestapo is outside."

"*What?*" Willem glanced toward the front door. "You've put our whole family in jeopardy." His eyes moved to Sussje, who beckoned Hetty to the stairs. "Leave this house! At once!"

After Hetty had hugged her mother, she started to leave through the kitchen door—the same way she'd come in.

"Wait. I have a safer way," said Sussje as she guided Hetty up the stairs to her parents' bedroom. "No one can see this window from the street." Through the open window, Hetty climbed onto a thick branch of a maple tree. She glanced around quickly to be sure she could not be seen by the men out front. Then she clutched another branch of the tree and dangled from it briefly before dropping into the flower bed below. She stood next to a seldom-used gate in the far back corner of the yard and waved to Sussje, who smiled back from the upstairs window.

Once she slipped out the back, Hetty zigzagged through the same streets she had shown to Maria so long ago. She glanced over her shoulder repeatedly but saw no Gestapo. At first she ran, but she quickly realized the Orpo police would view this as suspicious if they saw her.

Then she froze. Somehow she had found her way to Pier's home. For a moment, she was overcome with emotion while she imagined the terrible things the Gestapo must have done to Pier and his aunts—the same things they surely did to her beloved brother. Unsure where to go next, Hetty began walking aimlessly through the residential streets of The Hague, her brain in a fog from grief for her brother. She walked for two more hours before she arrived at Kees's front door.

"You're shivering." Kees placed a blanket around Hetty's shoulders and held her close. He went into the kitchen and prepared a bowl of chicken broth for her.

"I've been walking around The Hague for hours." Hetty said as she sipped the broth. "I went to my parents' house," she confessed sheepishly. "The Nazis were there, but I gave them the slip."

"That was reckless." Kees gently guided her to the sofa.

"Are you going to slap me again?"

Kees gave her a quick glance to see if she was kidding, then shook his head. "You've been through enough. Besides, I'm the one who deserves to be slapped for not telling you Jan had joined our combat forces. Maybe you would have talked him out of it."

"It wouldn't have done any good." Hetty shook her head with a forlorn expression. "I tried over and over. I really tried. I'm convinced he'd already made up his mind the first time we talked about it."

Kees reached under his mattress for a pistol.

"I stole that pistol from a German," said Aldon proudly as he emerged from the bathroom. Then he paused and faced Hetty. "Sorry about your brother, Hetty."

Hetty nodded solemnly and reached out as Aldon gave her a big, comforting hug.

"You are so mature," said Hetty, hugging him back. "Sometimes I forget that you're a child."

Hetty knew that Aldon didn't like being called a child; he was, after all, ten years old with much experience dodging the Germans. But this time he did not protest, offering only a sad smile and glistening eyes.

"The pistol is just a precaution," said Kees, putting bullets into the cylinder. "Did Jan know where you were staying?"

Hetty shook her head. "The last time I saw him was before I moved in with Katrien. So he knew nothing about the farm." Hetty finished the broth and turned her eyes toward Kees. "He knew nothing about you either, Kees. I was careful about that."

"Then this flat should be safe for you tonight," said Kees. "Tomorrow, I'll take you back to the farm."

Hetty nodded, barely able to keep her eyes open.

CHAPTER 20

HETTY RODE HER BICYCLE ALONG the canal road toward The Hague to visit her mother. It was the first time since she escaped the Gestapo at Jan's wake that she felt brave enough to leave Katrien's farm. Suddenly her bicycle struck a pothole. She was flying headfirst toward the canal when *whap!*—her face encountered a dead tree stump. A bottle of milk Katrien had given her shattered on impact.

Stunned by the blow to her face, Hetty rolled over to take stock of her injuries. The front wheel of her bicycle had come off, and the handlebars were twisted. A fish that she had brought from the farm stared up at her from the road.

Hetty sat on the tree stump and ran her hands over her arms and legs gingerly, finding abrasions but no broken bones. Shards of thick glass from the milk bottle glittered on the dirt road. "What next?" she shouted at the sky. "Haven't I been through enough?"

"It can't be that bad," said a familiar voice. "At least you're not in the Orange Hotel."

A smile spread across Hetty's face. "Kees! What are you doing here?" She flung her arms around him. "It's been weeks since I've seen you."

"I was riding along this canal road," said Kees with good humor, "and I thought 'why is this beautiful damsel so sad?'" He wet his kerchief in the canal and cleaned the dirt and pebbles from Hetty's face.

She winced when he touched a cut on her forehead with a kerchief. "Is it bad?"

"Just superficial wounds."

Kees plucked a shard of glass from her forehead and handed it to her while he staunched the blood with his kerchief. "Here—a souvenir from that milk bottle. You'll be right as rain when we get you cleaned up."

He picked up the fish and dipped it in the canal to clean off the dirt. "Come home with me tonight, and we'll make a fine dinner from this fish."

"You and Aldon get half," she clarified. "The rest is for my mother."

"Do you think it's a good idea to see your mother?" asked Kees. "The Gestapo might have her under surveillance."

"I know they're watching her house, but I'm not going there," said Hetty almost nonchalantly. "I've arranged to meet her at an ice cream shop where we used to go when I was a little girl. She'll make sure no one follows her. How is Aldon?"

"Don't ask," said Kees pressing the palm of his hand against his chest. "The boy will give me a heart attack with his reckless stunts."

"Like what?"

"Three days ago, he decided to steal a bayonet from a Nazi soldier who was indulging himself in a liaison with a woman in some bushes," said Kees, picking up Hetty's bicycle to examine it.

"I can fix my own bicycle, Kees."

"Let me do this for you," he beseeched her gently. "I'm still trying to make amends for not telling you that Jan joined the commandos."

"Go ahead," said Hetty, gesturing toward the bicycle with her hand as she sat back down on the stump. "I told you I understood. Now, please finish your story about Aldon."

Kees nodded, satisfied that Hetty was no longer upset with him, and then continued. "The soldier burst out of the bushes and grabbed Aldon by the shirt."

"That's terrible," said Hetty, forgetting about her own injuries. "How did he get away?"

"His shirt ripped," said Kees, simulating ripping with his hands. "The soldier couldn't give chase because his trousers were around his knees."

Hetty laughed. "Poor Aldon got an education that day, didn't he?"

"Nothing he didn't already know," said Kees, examining the bike. "A child grows up fast in a war."

"Still, it's a funny story." Hetty was still laughing. "It feels good to laugh. Thank you."

"That's what friends are for," said Kees, examining the broken bicycle.

Hetty watched Kees work on her bicycle. "Is it a lost cause?"

With a grunt, Kees twisted the handlebars so that they were almost straight. "I think I can fix it enough to get you to The Hague." Reaching in his pocket, he produced a pocketknife and went to work.

After a few minutes he said, "I need to tell you something." He stopped working and turned toward Hetty. "I came to ask you to do a job."

"So you just pretended to run into me by accident?" said Hetty with a smile that said she hadn't been fooled. "More lies?" she teased. But her face said she was pleased that he had an assignment for her. She yearned to get back to work.

"*Shhh*," Kees whispered. "This job is sensitive. We have to be careful."

Hetty's eyebrows went up. "Isn't the war almost over? It's been nearly four months since Normandy."

Kees shook his head grimly as he reattached the wheel of Hetty's bicycle. "There was a huge battle at Arnhem last week—Operation Market Garden. The Germans won and sent the Allies packing."

"Oh no. I hadn't heard." Hetty threw pieces of the broken milk bottle into the canal. "Not much news comes to Katrien's farm."

"Market Garden was our best chance for early rescue, and it failed. So Holland will be occupied longer than we hoped," said Kees, concentrating on the bicycle. "Now we're short of seasoned couriers." He used a rock to tap the wooden wheels into place. "During Market Garden, thousands from the resistance were exposed when they helped the Allies, and they've gone into hiding. That's more mouths to feed and fewer of us to feed them."

"I can help," said Hetty. "I'm itching to do something productive. Any news about Mimi?"

"She's been transferred to Buchenwald—her third camp."

"I can't believe she's still alive," said Hetty. "You were right. Mimi's a fighter. God knows what hell she's gone through."

"I'm afraid we have bad news for her when she returns." Kees tilted the bicycle onto its wheels and pushed it in a circle while he examined its mechanisms.

"Did something happen to her mother?"

"Gerhardt is dead," said Kees somberly. "He recruited a courier in Maastricht who turned out to be a collaborator. When the Gestapo came for him, he crunched a cyanide pill. They said it ended quickly."

"At least they couldn't torture him," Hetty mused. "But you're right. Mimi will be devastated. She really loved him."

"We don't know what Mimi will be like when she comes home," said Kees, staring vacantly across the canal toward the horizon. "We might never know the horror she has endured in those camps." Kees shook his head to bring himself back to the moment. "Here." He pushed the bike toward Hetty. "Good as new."

They rode side by side toward The Hague on the canal road, wheat fields on their left and cornfields on their right. "What's the job you want me to do?" Hetty asked, watching a feral cat chase a mouse across the road in front of them. "You didn't come all the way out here only to ask me to deliver ration cards."

"It will be dangerous," said Kees. "You've earned the right to say no."

"I'll do it," said Hetty insistently.

"You don't even know what it is yet."

"I know what they did to Jantje," said Hetty grimly. "Give me the damn assignment."

CHAPTER 21

HETTY STARED AT THE HAND grenades tucked tightly into the suitcase she had opened on the floor of Kees's living room. "I wonder what would happen if one of these little guys went off right now?" She felt the weight of one of them in her hand.

"It would obliterate every living thing in this room." Kees stared at the tiny bomb. "But they're safe as long as you don't pull the pin."

"I've been daydreaming about what our boys will do to the Germans with these." She carefully replaced the hand grenade and closed the suitcase. "I just need to get them to Delft, right?"

Kees nodded. "Meet your contact behind the warehouse across the street from the tram station," he said, taking a bite of toast. "The Germans haven't been searching the passenger luggage at Delft station recently. So this should be relatively easy."

"An easy trip sounds good," said Hetty as she practiced carrying the suitcase around Kees's living room.

"In case it isn't easy—" Kees held a small white capsule with his fingers. "Hide this."

Hetty glanced skeptically at Kees.

"Cyanide," he whispered, dropping it into her hand.

"Oh," said Hetty, examining the capsule between her fingers. "You don't think this will be easy at all, do you?"

Hetty stood still on the platform, waiting for Tram No. 1 to arrive. Before the war, she had come many times to Den Haag Hollands Spoor, the largest rail terminal in The Hague, but this was her first visit to the huge building since the war began. She felt puny standing inside the immense neo-renaissance structure with its high ceilings and ornate sculpture.

Then she saw it, Tram No. 1, a streetcar version of a railcar, pulling into the station before stopping in front of her. She waited for two armed soldiers to pass her before she lifted her suitcase with confidence and offered her ticket to the conductor.

"Where are you heading, Miss?" The conductor reached for Hetty's suitcase.

Despite being nervous, Hetty responded with a polite smile, "End of the line." Hetty glanced across the tracks toward another platform, where passengers were boarding another tram.

On her own platform, the two German soldiers who had just walked past her confronted a young man, who fumbled in his pockets to produce identification. Using his rifle, one of the soldiers shoved the young man against a wall while his colleague examined the papers.

"Delft is our last stop." The conductor smiled congenially, studiously ignoring the unpleasantness on the platform.

Hetty smiled in response before turning to find a seat.

The conductor lifted Hetty's suitcase onto the luggage rack. "*Oof.*
Your bag is heavier than it appears."

"You know how ladies are," Hetty chuckled. "We never travel light."

Hetty found a seat next to a window, where she continued to watch
the soldiers outside. They had freed the young man, who was leaving the
station in a hurry, but now the soldiers had stopped a young woman. One
soldier held the terrified woman by the arm, while the other rummaged
through her purse. Hetty shuddered at the thought that it could have
been her who the soldiers chose to search.

Hetty stole a glance at the other passengers when the tram rolled
out of the station. All averted their eyes the moment Hetty's gaze fell
on them. The conductor walked down the aisle. "Ten minutes to the
next stop."

Hetty leaned her head back and closed her eyes, prepared to doze off.
"Good morning." Her eyes popped open. A German officer loomed over
her. "I'm Major Ackerman," he said in a friendly tone, offering his hand.
"May I?" He gestured at the empty seat next to her.

Hetty wiped her sweaty palm on her skirt before she shook his
hand, nodding her assent as the officer sat down next to her. An armed
enlisted man stood at the rear of the car, watching the passengers. *Must
be Ackerman's bodyguard*, she thought. She glanced outside. The tram had
already arrived at the next stop. After the new passengers had boarded,
the enlisted soldier took a seat.

"I'm Alida," said Hetty, borrowing the name of a high school class-
mate. She desperately tried to keep her voice steady.

"Where are you going, Alida?" Ackerman asked.

A passenger shot her a scolding glance, then quickly returned to a
book she was reading. It was frowned upon for Dutch girls to make
casual conversation with German soldiers. Hetty cleared her throat and
managed to string together a complete sentence. "My grandmother

is sick in Delft." She spoke in German. "I try to visit her at least once a week."

"You speak German very well." Ackerman removed his hat and put it on a hook above them. "Where did you learn?"

"Mostly in school." Hetty glanced nervously at her suitcase on the rack at the front of the car. "I spent a summer in Zurich to get the accent right."

"*Ugh*," Ackerman said good-naturedly. "The Swiss don't know how to speak German. You should visit Berlin someday."

"Maybe I will," said Hetty, wondering how long she could keep up the charade before Ackerman caught on. Or had he figured it out already? "After all, we're all part of the Reich now," she said in her most agreeable voice.

Ackerman smiled approvingly at this response. "I'm surprised I haven't seen you on this tram before. I ride it to work nearly every day."

"I sometimes get a ride from my cousin." *Another lie!* thought Hetty. *I've got to stop answering questions.* "Why do you ride the tram, Major? Most officers I've seen have their own cars."

"It feels normal to me," said Ackerman. "Back home, I took the tram to work every day before the war."

"Are you stationed in Delft?" Hetty resolved to keep asking questions as she eyed the bodyguard nervously.

Ackerman followed her gaze. "Don't worry about him. He's a hazard of the job." For Ackerman, men carrying guns was the norm, Hetty knew. As they pulled into the next stop, Ackerman pointed out the window toward a military installation. "I work over there."

At first, Hetty was relieved; *is it possible that this Nazi will leave the tram without suspecting?* Then her heart sank. The military installation where Ackerman worked was located where her old neighborhood had been. She'd grown up here and didn't recognize it now. Gone were the beautiful Renaissance homes and towering maple trees, replaced by huge cannons that were plainly visible from the tram's window. She had not returned here since the Germans seized her family's home.

"It would be nice to see you on this tram again, Alida," said Ackerman, shaking Hetty's hand as he stood to leave. "I hope your grandmother recovers soon." Hetty managed a slight smile but did not trust herself to say anything.

Hetty took quick, choppy breaths as she watched Ackerman and his bodyguard leave the tram, barely aware that other passengers were boarding. Her mind was swirling. She turned toward the window and watched Major Ackerman disappear into the crowd.

"I was about to give up looking for you." The familiar voice startled her. Hetty stared at her new seatmate. "Aren't you going to say something?" Karl said while she stared in disbelief. Slowly, tentatively, she touched his hand as if to be sure that she was not dreaming. He smiled his quiet smile.

Suddenly a dam burst within Hetty. She threw her arms around Karl's neck. "Is it really you?" Her voice quivered. "They told me you were dead."

"Not dead," said Karl, who had shaved his beard but otherwise, looked the same, "but nearly so. I've been living in Friesland with Uncle Jef. I came here to find you when he died in a truck accident."

"Oh no," said Hetty. "How did that happen? And how did you avoid getting caught by the Germans? They found your body by the side of the road."

Karl glanced over his shoulder at the other passengers. "Let's get off at the next stop. Then I'll tell you everything."

Hetty shook her head. "I can't get off the tram, Karl." Her voice quivered as she glanced toward her suitcase filled with explosives. "I need to go to Delft."

A quizzical expression crossed Karl's face. "You're not married, are you?"

Hetty laughed, shaking her head with glistening eyes. "No, not married."

"That was my biggest fear," said Karl exhaling in relief. "Why don't I just ride along with you to Delft? After you do your business there, we can talk."

"You must get off at the next stop, Karl." Hetty nervously surveyed the car, but no one seemed to be listening. "I'll find you tomorrow back in The Hague. I promise."

The screeching of the tram's brakes penetrated the air as passengers came and left at the next stop. A mother shushed her crying baby as she searched for an empty seat.

"Obviously, something is up," Karl whispered, glancing at the other passengers, who seemed to ignore them. "No matter what it is, I won't leave you—not ever again."

Hetty touched his cheek with the back of her hand, then sighed and turned toward the window.

"I went to Leiden but found no trace of you," Karl continued, taking her hand.

"I didn't want to be found," she said brusquely.

"That seems pretty clear," said Karl, regarding her curiously. "I got on this tram after looking for you in your old neighborhood. What the hell happened to your house?"

"They destroyed it for gun emplacements," she said quietly, studying her hand in his. "It's a sad story, but too long to tell it now."

They said nothing while the tram made another stop. Karl gently rubbed his thumb across the back of Hetty's hand. She had forgotten how big his hands were. "OK. If I let you come to Delft with me, you must promise to pretend that you don't know me."

The tram pulled into the Delft station.

"Delft. End of the line," called the conductor, as he moved suitcases from the rack to the floor of the tram.

"Please stay quiet," Hetty hissed.

Karl nodded his assent with a worried look.

Then she glanced out the window and her heart sank. Two German soldiers, armed with submachine guns, smoked cigarettes while they prepared a passenger checkpoint. *Kees was wrong about the checkpoint*, she thought before turning to Karl. "I need to do this *alone*."

Sensing the emotional distance that Hetty had suddenly placed between them, Karl touched her face. "Please let me help," he whispered. "I know you're in trouble."

"Leave me alone, or we'll *both* be killed," she whispered urgently.

People began to get up and gather their things. Hetty stood and walked slowly toward the exit of the tram, standing behind the other passengers who lined up to retrieve their bags. Karl followed stubbornly behind.

"Karl," Hetty hissed, "I can't do my job if you don't—"

"Miss?" The conductor was staring at Hetty. Her heart dropped to her toes. "Don't forget your suitcase." He glanced at the bag, which he had placed on the floor with a grunt.

Hetty eyed the activity on the platform beyond the tram door. Two lines for luggage inspection were forming in front of the Nazi soldiers, who politely insisted that each bag be opened.

Karl suddenly snatched her suitcase off the floor before she could stop him.

"No. Please, don't do that," Hetty said too loudly. The conductor and other passengers turned to see what the commotion was about.

"Is everything OK?" asked the conductor.

Hetty smiled at the conductor while she touched Karl's face affectionately. "No problem. Just a disagreement with my boyfriend."

"If I am still your boyfriend," whispered Karl, his hand gripping the suitcase handle firmly, "then let me carry your bag for you. Whatever danger you're in, I want to share it."

Hetty relaxed and gave Karl her prettiest smile. Waiting another moment for the other passengers to go about their business, Hetty put her arms around Karl's neck and held him tight, using the momentum created by her movement to leverage Karl to take a step or two away from the other passengers. When Karl felt her body press against him, he closed his eyes to enjoy the familiar embrace. Hetty placed her mouth next to his ear and whispered, "*The suitcase is full of hand grenades.*"

Karl gave her a startled glance and then went slack as though he'd been shot at close range. He released his grip on the suitcase with a muddled stare out the door, where the Nazis were checking luggage. Hetty wasted no time snatching it up in a single, confident motion. Then she exited down the stairs of the tram. As Hetty approached the checkpoint, she caught her breath.

"You're next, Fraulein." The corporal glanced up at Hetty as he closed the luggage of the passenger in front of her.

Hetty glanced to her left, where Karl was making his way to the checkpoint set aside for passengers without luggage. Karl looked away from Hetty until he had been waved ahead. Then he glanced at her over his shoulder and walked across the street.

Hetty walked toward the German soldiers with a sway to her hips and her pretty smile. She swung her suitcase easily by her side as though it were filled with linen underwear.

"Herr Corporal." Hetty's voice lilted in German as she glanced furtively at his submachine gun, wondering if she would feel anything when he shot her. "This day is too beautiful for anyone to have to work." She sat her luggage down lightly on the ground next to her feet as she sidled up to the soldier. Inhaling the scent of her perfume, the corporal stared at Hetty with desire in his eyes. A chain-link fence had been erected behind the sentries, and beyond the gate was a wide road with an old warehouse on the opposite side. Most of the passengers had already left the platform when Hetty approached.

"Yes, it is a lovely day, Fraulein." The corporal gave her a big smile. "But my work is so much nicer when I have a beautiful girl to talk to."

"You must not see many girls out here if you call me beautiful," Hetty laughed. "Besides, you probably have a pretty wife at home who won't like you flirting with a Dutch girl."

"I'm not flirting, only being honest." The soldier glanced at her suitcase before refocusing on her dancing hazel eyes. "No one we see here is as pretty as you."

"Honest with me and every girl you meet is my guess." Hetty giggled and rolled her eyes. "But I don't mind. You're a lot more fun than the boys around here." She began rocking shyly. "I have an appointment with my grandmother and her doctor on the other side of the village in ten minutes. But if you help me get there on time, I won't have anything to do until the afternoon tram. When do you get off work?"

Hetty hadn't touched or even acknowledged the suitcase since putting it down by her side, allowing the bag to prove its own innocence. "So what's in the suitcase?" the soldier asked in a friendly voice.

Hetty didn't hesitate. "It's full of hand grenades. What else?" She let out a perfect, delighted laugh at her hilarious joke, while inside, her stomach churned.

"*Ha. Ha.*" The corporal laughed from deep in his belly. "Don't blow anything up." He waved her through the checkpoint. "I get off in an hour. Don't forget."

"See you then." Hetty waved jauntily as she carried her suitcase toward the gate.

Hetty sauntered through the exit, careful not to seem in a hurry. She stopped to glance back over her shoulder. The soldier who had let her pass was lighting a cigarette, chatting with his colleague. Suddenly both of them turned toward her.

She took slow, deep breaths as she continued toward the warehouse, where she stopped to trace the outline of a picture a child had drawn on the wall. She risked another glance. The sentry who had let her pass was walking toward her. Hetty went back to the child's drawing, not wishing to seem in a hurry even though every synapse in her brain yelled *run*! Then his colleague said something that made the man return to his post.

Hetty held her breath until she turned the corner of the warehouse. Karl! His hair and shirt soaked with sweat, he leaned against the warehouse as though he had been built there by a carpenter to hold the building up. Hetty peeked around the corner toward the guards, but she saw no one. The tram had left the station for its return to The Hague. She hugged Karl tightly, sobbing as she pulled him closer.

"Thank God you came back to me," Hetty whispered.

"I thought those soldiers were going to kill you," said Karl, kissing her deeply. Then he froze.

"Hey, you two, break it up," said a bald man in a cocked hat, who stood behind Hetty. He was short and in need of a shave, a change of clothes, and a bath. "I'm the cobbler. Did you order a pair of shoes?"

Hetty recognized the man. He had opened the door for her long ago when she met Yacov's parents. Karl looked back and forth between the two, curious.

"No, but I have some shoes in this bag that need attention." Hetty pushed the suitcase forward with her right foot. The man lifted the suitcase and walked away without another word or sign of recognition.

"So is that guy your contact?" Karl asked curiously.

"Yes, but we need to go. That soldier will be looking for me soon."

Hetty produced a bicycle from behind some bushes.

"Where did that come from?" Karl inspected the wooden wheels.

"A fellow named Kees left it here for me." Hetty fastened her hand-bag to the bicycle.

"The resistance thinks of everything." Karl scratched his face where his beard used to be. "Can't wait to hear about it."

Hetty jotted an address on a slip of paper and handed it to Karl as she pedaled away. "See you tomorrow at noon."

CHAPTER 22

SITTING ALONE IN HER SECOND-FLOOR flat, Hetty chewed her fingernails until there was nothing left. Karl was late. That morning, she'd watched the Gestapo going door to door in residential buildings down the street. *What if they've arrested Karl? Does he even have papers? He's too new at this*, she fretted.

Hetty paced back and forth. She couldn't bear the wait. She was about to risk another peek outside her window when she heard a soft knock at the door.

Tap, tap.

Hetty's heart pounded in her chest. She leaned her back gently against the door, wondering who it was. The Gestapo? Or was it Karl? She held the doorknob for a moment, then closed her eyes and bravely opened it.

The moment Karl walked in, Hetty flung herself into his arms and kissed him, opening her mouth to drink in all of him. He returned her kisses, four years of pent-up desire finding a home in her passionate embrace.

Then he nudged her backward. "Hetty, this will have to wait," he said urgently. "German soldiers are searching the buildings on this street. They'll probably come here next."

"I know. But this might be our only chance," she said, unbuttoning her blouse. She looked out the window and saw soldiers enter a building down the block. "We still have a little time before they come."

"That's cutting it too close," said Karl, hugging her tightly but resisting the urge to do as she wanted. "After we get out of here, we can make love whenever we want to."

"I wish we could be sure of that," said Hetty, reflecting on the people she had lost.

"Is there a way out of here?"

Disappointed, Hetty buttoned her blouse and refocused on the urgency of the situation. Gestapo agents made a racket as they entered her building from the street below. "They're here. We'll go out the back way."

Hetty opened the window that faced the back alley and dropped one end of a long rope over the edge. The other end was tied to the steam radiator, which was bolted to the floor.

"Follow me," Hetty said as she climbed down the rope.

Outside the city, Hetty and Karl rode their bicycles on the canal road toward Katrien's farm, wheat fields on their right and cornfields on their left.

"I liked that flat," said Hetty wistfully. "Now I can never go back there."

"Can we live at your parents' house?"

Hetty shook her head. "It's under surveillance. Our best hope is Katrien's farm, where I've been safe before."

They pedaled along in silence before Karl spoke.

"What was going on back at your flat? It would have been insane to make love when the Germans were so close."

"I suppose it was reckless."

"Then how do you explain—?"

"Back in Delft, I was sure I was going to die. And then I didn't."

Karl nodded knowingly.

"Maybe I've had so many close calls that I'm becoming inured to the danger. I might even like it," Hetty reflected in a voice so distant that she might have been talking to herself. "All I know is that just for a moment back in my flat, I needed you so much that I was willing to risk every-thing. It was like a premonition that we might not have another chance."

Karl tried to reassure her. "We have a lifetime to be together now."

"I hope so. I still can't believe you're alive," said Hetty more enthusi-astically. "Why didn't I hear from you before now?"

Karl furrowed his brow. "How could I have been so stupid?"

"What do you mean?"

"I left a note with Brecht. He was supposed to give it to you if I went missing. Do you think that idiot let it fall into the wrong hands?"

Hetty frowned. "Brecht's dead. He was a spy."

Karl fell silent while he processed the news. "Guess that explains why we were ambushed," he said at last, pedaling past a cornfield on their left.

"Ambushed?" Hetty turned her head toward Karl.

"Yes, Uncle Jef was shot when a squad of Germans attacked us from out of nowhere," Karl explained.

"I was told that your bodies were found by the roadside," said Hetty. "They said police investigators saw your IDs."

"I'm sure they found bodies next to Uncle Jef's truck, but we left our IDs on dead Germans before we escaped." Karl veered his bike around a pothole.

"Uncle Jef swerved off the road when he was shot. I was knocked silly for a moment but managed to jump from the truck before it crashed in the ravine. I hid behind some rocks. The Germans who came after us thought he was dead—so did I—but he was just pretending. When he killed the ones closest to him, I shot at the others from behind. We put our clothes and IDs on two of them."

"That explains the bloody sweater," Hetty's eyes opened wide at the revelation. "But what about your ID photos?"

"We had six German bodies to choose from and managed to match two of them up. We must have been lucky because they never searched for us."

Suddenly a border collie came out of the cornfield and barked at them. Karl dismounted and scratched the black and white dog behind the ears. "Look, we've found a new friend."

"Something's wrong," said Hetty with a frown. "That's Jasper, Katrien's dog. He's not supposed to be out. We walk from here."

From behind the bushes growing near Katrien's front gate, Hetty saw a German military jeep parked beside the house. "They must be looking for me," said Hetty, grabbing Karl's hand. "Let's hide in the barn." Jasper followed them in.

Hetty and Karl hid their bicycles under a pile of hay. Then they ducked into a stall where she usually milked the cow, leaving the gate of the cow's stall open. The cow mooed at their presence.

"Hush." Hetty patted the cow on its side. Then she lay down on the floor, clutching the border collie close. Barely breathing, Karl slid in behind her, spoon style, and wrapped his arms around her.

"What do you think the Germans want?" Karl whispered.

"They're probably searching all the farms in this area." Hetty whispered into his ear. "If they knew I used to live at this farm, they would have burned the place down by now."

Outside they could hear someone meandering around the barnyard and tapping a foot against the baseboards of the house.

Hetty glanced back at Karl. She knew the Germans were just outside the barn.

The border collie suddenly rushed from Hetty's grasp into the court-yard, barking at the intruder.

"Who's in there?" the man shouted in German. "Come out immediately!"

Through the open barn door, Hetty could make out an SS officer pointing his pistol toward the inside of the barn. She could see Jasper maneuver to cut off the officer's path. Snarling, the dog bit the man's ankle.

"Ouch! Fucking dog."

Hetty heard Katrien come out onto the front porch. "Jasper, I've been looking everywhere for you." Her familiar voice went on. "This is my dog," she explained. "We try to keep him chained so that he doesn't bother the neighbor's chickens—or bite visitors."

Hetty saw an enlisted man appear at the barn door next to the officer, who had turned toward Katrien.

"That dog attacked me, Schultz." The officer's eyes darted around the barnyard, distracted from his search for intruders by his anger toward the dog. "He bit my ankle. Look. He tore my trousers."

"He did not." Hetty recognized Katia's voice. "Jasper never bites anyone."

The officer aimed his pistol in the direction of Katia. "No," she shouted. *Pop! Pop!* The officer fired his pistol.

Inside the barn, a cry of horror rose in Hetty's throat, but Karl put his hand over her mouth, holding her close. Had the Nazi just shot her friends?

Then she heard Katia crying. "No! Why did you shoot my dog?"

"It's time for you to go, Major Jacek," said Katrien. "This has been a wild goose chase from the start, and now look what you've done."

"This is a lesson." The officer holstered his weapon. Then Hetty heard the doors close on their jeep. Before he turned on the ignition, he added.

"If I find out you've been hiding traitors, you and your daughter will end up like that dog."

Coughing from the exhaust of the Germans' jeep, Hetty emerged cautiously from the barn with Karl.

"Are you two OK?" she asked, her eyes darting from Katrien to her daughter.

"Hetty!" Katia squealed as she ran across the barnyard. "I didn't know you were hiding in there." She flung herself into Hetty's arms.

"I saw the cow's stall wasn't how I left it," said Katrien with a knowing nod.

Still clinging to Katia, Hetty reached out to take Katrien's hand. "I'm lucky to be alive," said Katrien. "That officer would have shot me if the corporal hadn't pulled me away from the dog."

Hetty hugged the two women for a long time before untangling herself. Then her eyes moved toward Jasper, whose body lay in a pool of blood. She knelt on the ground next to the border collie, running her fingers through his blood-soaked fur. "My old friend Jasper," she whispered, hugging the dog. "Gone so soon. Why is it that everyone I love keeps dying?"

Katia stood silently for a moment with her hand on Hetty's shoulder. Then she turned toward Karl who quickly remembered he was a stranger.

"I'm Karl," he said, extending his hand.

"Karl?" Katia studied him with surprise. "Aren't you supposed to be dead?"

CHAPTER 23

HER TEETH CHATTERING, HETTY STOOD still as a stork, watching for signs of Gestapo surveillance. "The last time I was in this backyard," she whispered, "I was at Jantje's wake five months ago. I sneaked in over the fence the way we just did."

"I'll bet it wasn't this cold," said Karl, flapping his arms despite his heavy winter coat.

"No. Jan died in the summer, so it was hot. This is the coldest winter ever. Look at the windows," she said, pointing with a hand trembling from the cold. "My parents have boarded them up." She pulled her hat down further over her ears and wrapped her scarf high to cover her face. "We've had plenty of cold winters before this, but they've never put boards on the windows."

Karl's breath produced a thick fog the moment it came from his mouth. "Can't we go inside where it's warm?"

"I think it's safe now," said Hetty, nodding her head. "We've been watching the street for half an hour, and I didn't see any signs of Gestapo surveillance. Did you?"

"I doubt the Gestapo wants to be out here any more than we do," said Karl, putting his gloved hands over his ears to prevent frostbite as he guided her toward the house.

They entered through the kitchen door, the same place Hetty had been welcomed by Oma Betje when she came to Jan's wake. Instantly they felt the comfort of the warm house.

"Did you watch for surveillance?" asked Henriette, welcoming her daughter in the kitchen with a hug.

"Everything's clear," said Hetty, removing her heavy coat.

"That's a relief. After your brother died, the Germans watched the house day and night from across the street."

"Where's Oma Betje?" asked Hetty, glancing toward the stairs. "I haven't seen her since the wake."

"She's upstairs sleeping, dear," Henriette replied with a hint of sadness. "But she's not well—doesn't recognize anyone these days, not even your father."

"Then I'll peek in on her when she wakes up," said Hetty hugging her mother. "I wish I'd said goodbye when she still remembered me. I'll miss her so much."

"Come into the living room and get warm. Your father installed a pot-bellied stove in there since you were here last. We only have firewood to heat the house these days."

Hetty took her mother's arm while they both turned toward the living room, but Karl delayed their progress by placing his hands gently on Hetty's shoulders. "I'd like to say hello to Willem. I haven't seen him since I had dinner with your family before the war. Is he around?"

"Yes, he's in his study," said Henriette, pointing toward the hallway. "It's at the end of the hall."

In the living room, Hetty and her mother warmed their hands near the pot-bellied stove, which stood like an armored sentry in the middle of the tastefully appointed room. "I don't think we could survive this godawful winter without this big, wonderful stove. It heats the whole house."

"This is the coldest I remember," Hetty agreed. "No wonder they're calling it the Hunger Winter. People are starving all over the city." Hetty lifted the lid to the huge pot sitting atop the stove to have a peek inside. "Ugh." Hetty held her nose while she replaced the lid on the boiling caldron. "That syrupy sweet smell is everywhere. Is it really necessary to have those beets stewing all day long?"

"Sometimes I think a steady diet of stewed beets is worse than starving," said Henriette with a laugh, holding her hands out toward the stove. "Then I think about all of the people who are starving in this city, and I thank God every day that your father secured a basement full of beets."

"Still, the smell is horrible," said Hetty. "At least you have meat roasting tonight."

"It's our first meat in three weeks," said Henriette, taking a seat on the sofa. "But please remember to thank your father for the beets, Hetty. He's a prideful man."

"Has he stopped blaming me for Jantje's death?" asked Hetty sharply.

Henriette stared at her daughter, shaking her head slowly. "I'm afraid that will take more time."

"Then why should I be nice to him?" Folding her arms, Hetty paced in a circle. "He hates me, Mama. That won't change."

"He's grieving in his own way," said Henriette. "But Willem has promised to be civilized tonight. You should too."

Henriette sat down next to Hetty on the sofa. "It's been so long since we heard from you," she said, stroking her daughter's hair. "I wish I knew where you and Karl are living."

"We're safe, Mama; that's all I can say." Hetty wanted to tell her mother that for the past two months, she and Karl had been living in a safe house in the small village of Voorschoten just outside Leiden. Besides them, only Kees knew the location. "I can't tell you where we live. One slip-up, and the Germans will catch me."

"But I'm your mother."

"If I tell you where we live, what will you tell the Germans when they ask?" said Hetty, putting her hand gently on her mother's shoulder.

"I see your point," said Henriette reluctantly. "Still, I worry—"

"That's why Karl and I came tonight; we don't want you to worry," said Hetty. "We wouldn't have taken the chance just for the meat." Hetty kissed her mother on the cheek. "How are you coping?"

"The same as you, I guess. I miss your brother so much." Henriette glanced at her daughter with a haggard look, her hands trembling slightly.

"I miss him too," said Hetty sadly, stoking the fire inside the pot-bellied stove with a metal poker.

"I had one good dream where Jan appeared to tell me he was OK," said Henriette, clutching her daughter's hand. "Mostly, I have nightmares about what will happen to you."

"I don't sleep well either," said Hetty, placing her arm around Henriette's shoulders. "But the war might end soon, and we'll all be safe. The Allies liberated Paris in August. That was four months ago. Holland could be next."

Henriette led Hetty into the dining room, where they were first to take a seat.

Hetty's eyes tracked Willem and Karl, who engaged in congenial conversation as they made their way to the dinner table. Anika, the cook, served beet stew to everyone.

"Thank you for stocking up on beets, Papa," said Hetty. "Good foresight."

Henriette smiled and squeezed her daughter's hand.

"Mm-hmm," Willem grunted, slurping beets with his spoon. "They're all we could get when the famine came," he said tersely. Even making small talk, he could not conceal his hostility toward his daughter.

"Hetty and I saw two frozen bodies beside the train tracks when we rode here today," said Karl, glancing at Hetty for affirmation. "The Nazis have done a decent job of cleaning up the dead, but sometimes, there are just too many of them."

"It was gruesome," Hetty added. "The corpses looked like they were huddled around a campfire, but the fire ring was covered in ice. So were the dead—a man and a woman, who died holding hands."

"The famine is getting worse, no doubt," said Karl, lifting a spoonful of stew to his mouth. "We're grateful to share your food, Willem."

"Look," Henriette said cheerfully as Anika entered with a big platter. "Here's the meat."

They patiently waited until Anika had served all of them before taking first bites.

"Yum," said Hetty, savoring the skin and fat in her mouth. "It's been weeks since I've eaten meat. What is this?"

Henriette exchanged glances with her husband. "I told you this was a bad idea, Willem." Then she turned toward Hetty. "Don't you recognize the flavor of roast rabbit, dear?"

"You know I don't eat ra—" Hetty abruptly put down her knife and fork and stopped chewing. "Where did you find this one?" she asked tentatively, dreading the answer.

"We didn't exactly find it." Willem hesitated. "More like it was already here."

Hetty spat the meat onto her plate. "Are we eating Sherlock? How dare you, Papa!" Her eyes shot daggers at her mother for her complicity.

"Everyone in The Hague is eating their pets," said Willem defensively. "It's my job to put meat on the table."

"Sherlock was *my* rabbit—a gift from you, Papa," Hetty shouted. "Do you hate me that much?"

Willem put a forkful of roast rabbit in his mouth, glanced toward his daughter, and shrugged.

Karl continued to clean his plate, licking his fingers as he stripped the last vestiges of meat off of a tiny leg bone. Hetty stared at him as though he were a stranger. "Am I alone in this? Why aren't you defending me?"

Karl put the bone on his plate with a confused look. "Aren't you over-reacting? We are in a war after all—and living through a famine created by the Nazis."

"You just don't get it!" She grabbed Karl severely by the arm. "Come on. We're leaving."

Karl had barely unlocked the front door of their Voorschoten cottage when Hetty shoved past him, flinging her coat on the floor. "You'd better figure out where you're sleeping tonight," said Hetty, slamming the front door behind them. "Because it's not with me."

The rickety dwelling shook when Hetty slammed the door. Built over fifty years ago in a humble neighborhood where every home looked alike, the gray cottage had seen better days. But the bickering couple knew they would have frozen to death weeks ago were it not for the protection of its dilapidated roof and flimsy walls.

"C'mon," Karl protested. "You're being unreasonable."

"How could you keep eating after you knew it was my pet?" Hetty spat the words as she grabbed a blanket and pillow from their bedroom and threw them onto the sofa. "Couldn't you have been a man and stood up to my father?"

"Wait, Hetty. Can't we talk about this?" Karl touched her arm. "I know

I should have said something to your father, but we were only starting to know each other. Sooner or later, he and I will have to get along."

Hetty sat down heavily on the sofa with folded arms. Then she reached for Karl's hand. "This damn Hunger Winter has everyone acting crazy."

"Blame the Germans, not me," said Karl, using both hands to hold hers. "They're the ones who shut off the supply chain from farm country."

"Only evil maniacs would cause a man-made famine," said Hetty, putting her hand on Karl's cheek, rubbing the stubble where he was trying to grow back his beard.

He leaned into her touch, and Hetty's stern expression softened. "Do you admit you were a complete barbarian?"

"I do, and I'm sorry," said Karl, sliding closer.

Hetty brushed her lips across his mouth as she unfastened his belt and reached inside. "This doesn't mean I forgive you," she said as she kissed him again, pulling him toward the bedroom.

Karl gently unbuttoned Hetty's blouse. They were so eager to make peace they fell over before getting into bed. Laughing, he helped her up and lay her gently on the bed. Hetty smiled and pulled him close and kissed him passionately. He reciprocated and then pulled the blanket over them to keep warm.

It was easy for them to be together. The time apart and false news of Karl's death had made their daily lovemaking that much more passionate since they arrived at the Voorschoten cottage. This had been their first quarrel, and neither of them liked it. Afterward they lay peacefully under the covers of their bed, cuddling and enjoying the warmth their conjoined bodies made.

"This is *much* better than sleeping on the couch," Karl chuckled, squeezing Hetty toward him.

"Mm-hmm," she cooed while she played with his hair. "I hate when we fight."

"Me, too. How about we do something better?"

Hetty looked at Karl with questioning eyes.

A big smile spread across Karl's face. "Marry me."

"What?" Hetty propped herself up on her elbow and stared at Karl. "That's crazy. The Gestapo might catch me tomorrow. Where's the future in that?"

"That's why we should get married now," said Karl, hugging her tightly. "Before the future catches up to us."

"I'll happily marry you when the war's over," said Hetty with a loving smile as she gently kissed his cheek.

"Why wait?" said Karl, returning her kiss. "I love you. Why not next week—or even tomorrow?"

"I still have my work for the resistance," Hetty replied, reaching for her robe. "Tomorrow, I have to deliver fifty ration cards."

"Don't do it," Karl insisted. "Ask Kees to find someone else."

"Besides me, there's no one but children left," said Hetty, sitting up on the bed. "Do you know how many couriers have died or gone into hiding since we began four years ago?"

"That's my point," said Karl, tugging her gently to lie down next to him again. "Every time you go on a mission, I worry you won't come back."

"Do you remember what we fought about just before the invasion— the night you climbed the wisteria vine to come into my bedroom?" asked Hetty, putting her head back on his shoulder.

Karl nodded. "You begged me not to go to Rotterdam."

"Now I understand why you had to go," she said, pressing her cheek against his. "It was your duty. I have a duty too."

"Haven't you done enough?" He pleaded stubbornly. "The war is almost over. Why take more risks?"

"People in hiding need to eat."

"And I need you to live," Karl begged.

"Too many people I loved have died." Hetty stood up and walked toward the kitchen. Then she paused and looked back over her shoulder with a resolve that made Karl proud. "I *won't* let them down."

Hetty glanced into her purse, making sure the fifty ration cards, bound together with a string, were easily available as she strolled down the sidewalk in the crowded central shopping district of The Hague. It was still bitterly cold, but when the sun came out, a large crowd of people ventured to the shopping district hoping to find food for sale. The faces of the people around her were hollow as Hetty wondered who among them might be her contact.

Suddenly an Orpo policeman stood in front of a checkpoint ahead. She turned left into the crowd, away from the checkpoint. Then she tied a blue scarf over her head so that her contact could identify her. Hetty reached into her handbag but froze when a strong hand grabbed her gruffly by the elbow. "Stop, Fraulein!" The Orpo policeman smelled of garlic. "I saw you turn off the main street. Were you trying to evade the checkpoint?"

Hetty's mouth felt like cotton inside, but she mustered her prettiest smile. "What checkpoint?" Hetty fluttered her eyelashes. "I always cooperate with the police." While the policeman was fixated on her hazel eyes, Hetty reached carefully into her purse—slowly, slowly—until she found the ration cards.

"Come with me," said the policeman.

Hetty tried to control her breathing as she closed her grip on the ration cards and slowly, slowly moved them from her purse to her side. "Of course, Herr Corporal. I have nothing to hide." Holding the cards next to her hip, Hetty was wondering what she would do next when they were suddenly snatched away by someone in the crowd. Hetty inhaled sharply just as another Orpo policeman arrived. Together, they took Hetty to a quiet alley, where they searched her thoroughly.

Hetty's heart was still pounding while they rummaged through her purse.

"You can go," the policeman said at last. He was already scanning the crowd for new suspects. "Next time, heed the checkpoint."

"Why did you take such a risk?" Karl could not restrain his anxiety when she returned to the cottage. "You could have been killed."

The inside temperature was still recovering from the brief moment the front door had been opened for Hetty to let herself in, allowing sub-zero winds to penetrate the warm living room. She kneeled next to the fireplace to warm her hands.

"I need comfort right now, Karl—not criticism." Agitated after describing her close encounter with the Orpo police, Hetty removed her hat and scarf. "I was almost caught today. If my contact had been a split second later—"

"You have a right to be scared." Karl enveloped Hetty in his arms and rocked her until she calmed down. "So do I," he whispered.

Karl found a bottle of whiskey in the kitchen and brought it into the living room with some glasses. He poured the whiskey and handed a glass to Hetty, who gulped hers quickly and poured another before setting the bottle on the table.

"I remember when you didn't drink whiskey," said Karl, kissing her forehead.

Hetty frowned. "You were gone a long time." She drank another glass and filled it again. "A lot has changed." She put her arms around him and pressed her face into his neck.

"You're the bravest person I know," said Karl, kissing her forehead. She turned her face toward him, and he kissed her on the mouth. His hand cupped her breast reflexively even though he'd not intended to be romantic.

Suddenly Hetty was aroused, kissing him passionately and unbuttoning his shirt. "Maybe you were right."

"About what?"

"After what happened today, I don't want to wait for the war to end before we get married." She kissed him again, her body melting into his.

Karl and Hetty shook the snow off of their coats on the porch as Arie and Mieke opened the door to welcome them to their home in The Hague in the Bezuidenhout neighborhood near the woods of Haagse Bos Park. "Lucky I ran into you in the park," said Mieke, kissing Hetty on the cheek. "It's been so long since we've seen each other."

"It feels like yesterday to me," said Arie, hugging his guests with a friendly smile. "That's how it is with good friends."

"Actually, I'm keeping a promise to Mimi," said Hetty, producing a bottle of schnapps from her handbag. "The last thing she said to me the day they caught her was 'schnapps with Arie and Mieke.' So, let's drink some."

Arie poured the schnapps and held up his glass. "To Mimi. May she return to us safely."

"Maybe Mimi will be freed soon," said Karl, sipping his schnapps. "The Allies have the Reich on the run after their victory in the Ardennes. But it's sad that so many Allied soldiers had to die during the Christmas holiday."

"The end of the war might not be as close as you imagine," said Arie, pouring more schnapps for everyone. "The Germans have deployed V-2 rockets in Haagse Bos Park—just down the street from here. Sometimes we see them flash across the sky on their way to England. They say those rockets will change the war in their favor. Even if that's mostly propaganda, their new weapon could prolong the war."

"I hope you're wrong," said Mieke. "This war can't end soon enough for me."

"Won't the Allies try to destroy them while the rockets are sitting in the park?" asked Hetty, glancing out the window. "Are we safe here?"

"We are more than a mile away from the park," said Arie with confidence. "The Allies would never bomb a Dutch residential neighborhood. So we're safe."

"Well," said Mieke dismissively. "There has been no bombing yet. And I hope it never starts."

"I hope it does—and soon," said Hetty, staring coldly at her friend. "The Allies must destroy those rockets on the ground."

"They're too close for my comfort even if Arie thinks we'd be safe," said Mieke.

"I always try to stay safe," said Hetty. "Still, if that's how I die, so be it."

Silence filled the room until Karl changed the subject.

"We brought bacon and potatoes," said Karl, taking the food to the kitchen. "I can cook them now, if you like."

Mieke and Arie nodded, eager to feast on the meal their friends had brought—and, for Mieke, put the fear of bombing raids out of her mind. Good food was still hard to find and was mostly procured by people willing to travel to farm country, as Karl had done to obtain the bacon.

"Where are you living these days, Hetty?" asked Mieke, watching Karl as he retreated to the kitchen.

Hetty was saddened that she couldn't disclose her location, but it was for everyone's safety. She patted her friend on the shoulder and said, "Sorry, but I can't tell you where we live. Keeping that secret helps me stay one step ahead of the Gestapo."

"That sounds serious." Mieke brought her hand to her mouth. "We knew you were in the resistance, but you never talked about it."

Soon the sizzle of bacon and potatoes wafted in from the kitchen, taking their minds off of unpleasant things for a moment as they took in the aroma of the hearty meal Karl was preparing.

Hetty sipped her schnapps. Eager to change the subject, she asked, "What have you two been doing since we last saw you?"

"Arie works nonstop on his family business," said Mieke. "I've tried to keep up on my studies since they closed the university."

"I'm sure the university will reopen when the Allies get here," said Hetty, shivering at the icy wind penetrating the cracks in the flimsy cottage.

"Will you return to your law studies when it reopens?" asked Mieke, pulling a shawl around her shoulders.

Hetty shook her head. "Karl and I plan to reopen his family's bicycle factory in Rotterdam."

"Are you getting married?" Mieke squealed as she leaped up to hug her friend.

Karl stepped out of the kitchen. "We're going to tie the knot as soon as the canals thaw and restore the supply chain from the farms. Then we will have food for our guests."

"Let us plan it for you," said Arie enthusiastically.

"We won't take no for an answer," Mieke added. "As soon as the supply routes reopen in the spring, come back here so we can plan and celebrate."

CHAPTER 24

WILLEM RUSHED THROUGH THE DOOR of Reiner's office without knocking. "Your note said it was urgent—" He froze. An SS officer sat serenely in the chair Willem usually occupied.

Pretending not to notice Willem's anxiety at encountering him—but with a subtle glance that revealed he was secretly pleased by it—the officer smiled congenially.

"Major Jacek," said Reiner, the veins on his neck standing out. "Please meet Willem Steenhuis."

"Please sit, Mr. Steenhuis," said Jacek, gesturing to one of the big leather chairs. He poured whiskey into a glass and handed it to Willem. "I told Reiner about the rumors I've been hearing, and he suggested that I discuss them with you in person."

Willem swallowed hard as he sat down and crossed his legs, his heel bouncing nervously in the air. "Rumors?"

"Some of my friends in the Gestapo think you're an enemy of the Reich," said Jacek in the same tone that most people use to talk about the weather. "Your friend Reiner assures me that you are a loyal servant. Which is it?"

"Loyal servant, for sure," Willem blurted as he loosened his tie. "I've never done anything to deserve such an accusation."

"What about your daughter?" Jacek asked nonchalantly. "We know she is active in the resistance."

"That has nothing to do with me." Willem's face flushed. "Besides, the war is almost over. Why question me about her now?"

"I disagree with you about the progress of the war, Mr. Steenhuis," said Jacek confidently.

"I meant no offense—" Willem began.

"The Allies are feckless," Jacek interrupted sharply. "The Fuhrer bent them to his will at Munich in 1938, and he will do the same when an armistice is signed."

"I haven't heard about any talks," Willem replied, fidgeting with his cuff link, shocked that anyone would think the Nazis could still win the war.

"You are determined to upset me," said Jacek, the veneer of his non-chalance disappearing with each word. "No matter. I will be surprised if the armistice doesn't give Germany control over all Aryan territories. That includes the Netherlands."

Willem knew the war was not going well for the Germans but did his best to conceal his skepticism. "What does this have to do with my daughter?"

"Have you heard of Hannie Schaft?" asked Jacek as he lit a cigarette.

"Everyone has heard of the red-haired girl from Haarlem," said Willem, the dryness in his throat making it difficult to pronounce her name.

"Fraulein Schaft is an assassin who has murdered many soldiers of the Reich," said Jacek, anger rising in his voice. "Do you imagine the Reich will ever give up before that whore is dead?"

"My daughter never did anything like that."

"You're wrong. She killed an Orpo officer in Leiden," said Jacek, showing Willem a photo of Hess's body lying on the sidewalk in a pool of blood.

"That can't be right," said Willem. "Hetty is not a murderer."

"We think she is." Jacek was careful to conceal that Hetty's brother was his source. Under torture, he revealed the conversation he'd had with his sister shortly after she killed Hess. "But even if your daughter didn't wield the knife, she knows who did," said Jacek, tucking the photo back in his file.

"I don't know anything about it," said Willem, beginning to wonder whether he had missed a murderous side of his daughter.

"But you know where she is, right?"

"Actually I don't," said Willem, relieved at his own ignorance. "She doesn't live with us."

"Certainly there must be family gatherings that you both attend?" suggested Jacek in an oily voice.

"Nothing like that is planned."

"Make plans," said Jacek with a casual smile but a voice that sent dread through Willem's heart. "Otherwise, my friends at the Gestapo might believe that you really are an enemy of the Reich." The smile disappeared from Jacek's face. "You can imagine the consequences."

Willem watched as Jacek left the room, slowly and deliberately.

"What the *hell* am I supposed to do, Reiner?" Willem exploded the instant the SS officer had left. "I can't give up Hetty to the Gestapo. She told her mother she's planning to get married. When they set the date, does Jacek expect me to give him that information?"

"I've known Major Jacek for a long time," said Reiner, shaking his head slowly. "For him, violence is just a tool to get what he wants. And he obviously wants Hetty."

"Don't tell me I have to choose between giving up my daughter or whatever that maniac will do to me," said Willem, gripping the lapels of his friend's jacket.

"It might not come to that," said Reiner in a measured tone. "You don't have to do anything until you know where Hetty is. Maybe the war will end before then."

"Sorry we had to make this a morning meal," said Hetty, hugging Mieke as she crossed the threshold into their cottage. "I have some business to attend to this afternoon, and it's time to plan our wedding. Farm food has been flowing into the city for a week now that the spring thaw has opened the canals."

"Where's Karl?" asked Arie, enveloping his friend in a warm embrace.

"He'll be a little late," said Hetty, removing her coat and sniffing the air at the fragrance of sizzling eggs. "He found a source for fresh tomatoes and is waiting at the dock for them to arrive. But he said we should start without him."

"It's been so long since we've had fresh tomatoes," said Arie as he took a seat next to Mieke on the sofa. "Worth waiting for."

"Will you get married at your family's church?" asked Mieke.

"The pastor said we can have the ceremony on March 17." Hetty nodded. "Saturday is a good day for a wedding. You're the first people I've told."

"That's only two weeks away," said Mieke.

"Mm-hmm. Can we have the reception here?"

"Why not have it at your parents' house?" Mieke suggested. "It's much bigger than our tiny cottage."

"There will only be a few people," Hetty explained, scanning the small living room to imagine where guests might sit. "Besides, my father still holds me responsible for my brother's death, and I don't want him to make a scene."

"Sometimes I think we'll never be able to put the war behind us," said Mieke. "The other day we lost one of Arie's cousins, who worked for the resistance."

Hetty sat up. "What happened?"

"Nick, my mother's second cousin, was a member of the Haarlem Resistance Group," said Arie, leaning back in his chair.

"I've heard of the Haarlem resistance," Hetty said, taking a seat on the sofa. "They blew up the railway between Ijmuiden and Haarlem."

"Right." Arie nodded. "Nick was captured about a month ago. The bastards tortured him for three days before they shot him."

A sudden sadness at the memory of her brother's ordeal swept through Hetty. "Can I have some schnapps, Arie?"

"Isn't it a little early?" said Arie, rising to his feet as he reached for the bottle.

Suddenly, the wailing of air raid sirens interrupted the conversation.

"So it begins," said Arie.

"Is there a shelter?" asked Hetty calmly.

"We won't need one," said Arie with confidence. "This is the third Allied attack this week, and the bombs never come close to us."

Kaboom!

The sudden explosion split their eardrums and sucked the oxygen from the room.

Hetty threw herself on the floor face first.

Kaboom!

Every window in the cottage shattered from the next explosion.

"Follow me," Arie shouted over the din as he scurried on his belly across the floor, blood running from several cuts in his face. Mieke was right behind him. One after another, the bombs dropped, seemingly right on top of them.

A jabbing pain ran from Hetty's knee up through her tailbone. There was no time to check for injuries.

Kaboom!

Hetty coughed from inhaling the dust and smoke. Arie grabbed Hetty by the wrist, and she low-crawled into the kitchen, wincing each time her skinned knees touched the floor.

Arie opened a small door, then rolled over sideways into a musty, shallow basement. Hetty and Mieke were close behind. Once inside, Mieke lit a candle. They found themselves in a vegetable closet filled with sugar beets.

"We're not out of danger," said Arie, his voice quivering.

"I'm not going anywhere." Hetty grabbed Arie's wrist while the bombs kept exploding. "Those bombs must be coming from the Allies."

"How could they be so far off target? The German rockets are that way," said Arie, pointing in the direction of Haagse Bos Park.

Mieke, meantime, lay face down on the sugar beets and crossed her arms over her head. "Are we going to die, Arie?"

"Nah," said Arie. "But if we do, I love you."

"I love you too," Mieke whimpered.

Shards of wood rained down like shrapnel with each impact, one just missing Hetty's eye and leaving a deep scratch on her cheek. Hetty squeezed harder on Arie's wrist with each explosion.

They huddled quietly among the sugar beets, their bodies quaking long after the bombing had stopped. When Hetty finally let go of Arie's wrist, it was covered in bruises showing the unmistakable imprint of Hetty's fingers.

Hetty had no idea how long they waited in that vegetable cellar after the bombing stopped. Finally, she ventured outside, searching for

Karl. She was shocked by the devastation. Whole buildings had been destroyed, and fires still burned fiercely only a few blocks away. She winced when her skin fought the scabs forming on her knees, limping across the street where the bomb crew stood around a body. Hetty's heart went into her mouth. Both arms of the corpse had been blown off. But the long hair was blond. Still numb from the shock of the bombing raid, Hetty vacillated between relief that the body was not Karl's and horror at what the bombs had done to a woman her age.

Dust hung in the air where a building had stood only the night before. Twisted steel bars stuck out of collapsed brick walls, like stubble on the chin of an old man who forgot to shave. Two men in coveralls, wearing kerchiefs over their faces, carried a body on a stretcher covered with a tarp. Approaching them slowly, Hetty lifted the tarp. She emitted a quiet sigh of relief. It wasn't Karl.

Hetty walked three blocks before she saw him, curled fetus-like against a bush, with no obvious cuts or bruises on his body, giving the appearance that he was sleeping peacefully. Lumpy red liquid had spread from beneath nearby rubble. Hetty pushed some bricks aside. Squashed tomatoes.

Hetty fell to her knees, unable to move as she stared at him. Then the tears came, slowly at first and then in heaving sobs. "Oh, Karl, my love." She stroked his cheek, taking in the familiar texture of his beard. "It should have been me."

Willem paced on the sidewalk in front of the civil service building, rehearsing in his mind what he would say to Reiner. He had tried to avoid knowing where Hetty was, but there was no escaping the terrible news about Karl—and that the wedding planned at the Presbyterian

Church this Saturday would now be a funeral. He needed to talk to Reiner about what to do with that information.

Willem smelled smoke the instant he entered the building. Following his nose, he bounded up the stairs to Reiner's office. Smoke trickled from beneath the door. Willem rushed in, ready for action, only to find his friend sitting calmly at his desk with suffocatingly thick smoke around him, tossing papers into a small fire in his trash can. Willem rushed to the open window and put his head outside to breathe some fresh air.

"Hello, Willem," said Reiner calmly, continuing to feed the contents of his desk drawers into the simmering blaze. A flame erupted angrily, consumed itself quickly, and sent a plume of dull grey smoke toward the open window.

"What the hell are you doing?" Willem stood in front of his friend's desk, coughing and waving ineffectually at the smoky air. "How can you be so calm at a time like this?"

"The Americans crossed the Rhine today, and the German army just surrendered in Italy. It's the beginning of the end for our German friends," said Reiner as he continued to feed the flames. "Some people want to punish me for collaboration when the war is over. I won't let my private records hang me."

"Have you forgotten that I have an impossible decision to make?" Willem closed the door and locked it before going to the open window again. "Stop trying to burn the building down and listen to me."

He tried to pour some whiskey, but his hands were too shaky and he spilled it. Reiner came to his rescue and filled their glasses.

Reiner plopped down in one of the red leather chairs, coughing to clear the smoke from his lungs. "Now, what's this about your big decision?"

"Hetty's boyfriend, Karl, died last week," said Willem as soon as he had settled. "Killed by a stray bomb in an Allied raid."

"I heard the bombs falling," said Reiner, taking a big gulp of whiskey. "The Allies sure made a mess of it. Over five hundred civilians killed, they say. Too bad about the boyfriend. Tell Hetty I'm sorry for her loss."

"Now I know where Hetty will be on Saturday," said Willem without enthusiasm. "If I give you that information, can you guarantee that the Germans won't bother my wife and me?"

Putting his whiskey down, Reiner stared at Willem. "You know what they'll do to her, right?" The small fire crackled indiscernibly. "She's your daughter, for Christ's sake."

"I'm trying to save my family, Reiner—what's left of it," said Willem with knitted eyebrows. "You heard Jacek threaten me. He's given me no choice."

"You have a choice—run and hide," said Reiner. "It wouldn't be for long. The war is almost over."

"With what money?" said Willem, breathing hard. "Jacek closed my bank accounts."

"You're worried about money?" Reiner raised both eyebrows incredulously as he offered Willem all the cash in his wallet. "Take this and run. Surely Hetty can help you find a hiding place."

"Stop lecturing and answer my question," said Willem, waving his hand at the money being offered. "Will Jacek leave us alone or not?"

"Jacek is a man of his word—within limits," said Reiner with resignation in his voice. "If you are certain you want to give him Hetty—and I advise you to think about it before you make a rash decision—I am sure you and Henriette won't have to worry about the Nazis."

"What about my bank accounts?"

"Do they matter more than Hetty's life?" said Reiner sharply, shaking his head in exasperation. "Please think about what you're doing."

"I *have* thought about it," said Willem. "Tell Major Jacek that Hetty will attend Karl's funeral at our church on Saturday morning."

CHAPTER 25

A GERMAN SOLDIER PUSHED A cart overflowing with documents toward the smoldering oil cans in the courtyard of SS headquarters. Major Jacek put his hand on the man's arm. "Work faster. Berlin wants everything destroyed immediately."

"How long will Berlin even be there, sir?" Corporal Schultz stood next to his superior with a glum expression. "The Russians are advancing on Berlin from the east, and the Americans are getting closer from the west."

"I'm sure the Fuhrer is negotiating a favorable armistice as we speak, Corporal."

Schultz had seen this side of his boss before. When the Allies invaded at Normandy, Jacek insisted that the Reich would push them back into the sea. He had disregarded the facts on the ground to match his unquestioning belief in the Fuhrer's leadership. It took Schultz two months to steer Jacek back to reality on that occasion, but he was not so sure this time.

"What do you have for me?" Jacek asked as if this were business as usual.

"We have some intelligence from the man you met with last week at the civil service building, sir," said Schultz, shouting to be heard above the hubbub.

"Willem Steenhuis?"

"Yeah." Schultz nodded.

"I knew that man was weak," said Jacek with a satisfied smile. "Let's go to my office where we can hear ourselves talk."

In the relative quiet of Jacek's office, the SS Major lit a cigarette and offered one to Schultz. "What did Steenhuis say?"

"The woman we have been looking for in Hess's murder, Hetty Steenhuis, will be at her fiancé's funeral Saturday morning at the family's church," said Schultz, looking at his notes. "He was killed in that Allied raid. I have the address here."

"Good," said Jacek, his expression brightening. "Tell Gestapo in The Hague to post surveillance at the church and apprehend her when she shows."

Schultz inhaled deeply on his cigarette. "All SS personnel have been reassigned. Many are helping the Reich Commissariat to relocate; others are helping with document destruction and other priorities, sir."

"What the hell is that supposed to mean, you idiot?" Jacek slapped Schultz across the face.

Schultz took a deep breath before responding. "It means we can't order surveillance, sir. No one is available, here or in The Hague."

Jacek paused, considering his options. "Then you and I will perform the surveillance ourselves," he said as he went to the window and stared at the street. "The murder of one of our officers in cold blood is the biggest blot on my record in Leiden. I aim to solve it even if others have cut and run."

"Are you suggesting that you and I arrest her alone?" said Schultz, his voice bordering on insubordination.

"A child could finish the job," said Jacek with a disparaging glance at Schultz. "I already did the hard part when I persuaded her own father to give her up."

"Which one is Hetty?" Jacek peeked out the window of an office building across the street from the Presbyterian church. The sky was overcast and gloomy.

"We don't know what she looks like, sir," said Schultz, repeating what he'd told Jacek three times already.

"Let's get closer." Jacek produced a small telescope from his pocket and surveyed the grounds around the church. "Someone will do something to give her away."

"Why not just barge in, pistols drawn?"

"Her family will clam up," said Jacek, staring at the growing group of mourners. "Then you'll have to shoot some of them to make the others talk. That will be messy."

Standing behind his boss, Schultz raised his eyes to the ceiling. "Great plan, sir," he said with an ironic smirk that Jacek couldn't see.

"Psst! Hetty," someone whispered as she walked toward the church.

Unsure whether she had heard anything, Hetty glanced left and right but saw no one.

"Over here," the voice whispered urgently.

Curious, Hetty walked down the sidewalk, a tall building on her left. When she came to the end of the block, she peeked around the corner. "Kees. What are you doing here?"

Grasping Hetty's forearm, he pulled her toward him. "Don't go into the church," he whispered. He suddenly stepped back, shocked by Hetty's appearance; her usually pale face had been reduced by grief to translucent paper, and the skin under her chin sagged as if she had aged thirty years in the past few days.

"It's Karl's funeral," said Hetty, pulling her arm away. "This is my atonement for not protecting him."

"It's not your fault," said Kees, wrapping his arms around his courier. "Even a lioness can't protect everyone. It was just bad luck."

Hetty leaned into his shoulder for a long moment, then stepped back. "Why are you slinking around in front of a place of worship?"

"We're getting reports from all over the country that the Gestapo is hunting down our resistance friends," whispered Kees insistently. "You need to stay out of sight."

"Does the Gestapo know I'll be here today?"

"Not that I know of," said Kees, shaking his head. "But why take the risk with the war nearly over? Come and stay with Aldon and me."

"I appreciate how you try to look after me," said Hetty, taking his hand. "But I am going to say goodbye to Karl today no matter the risk. If you want to know the truth, with Karl gone, I don't really care what the Germans do."

"You're the most stubborn woman I know, Hetty." Kees looked down at his feet in exasperation, then put his hand gently on her cheek. "Come back to this spot as soon as the service is over. I'll be here to take you home."

The minister used his hand to shade the sun from his face as he joined the mourners emerging from the church. "Please know that Karl is in heaven, Hetty. And you will see him again," he said, hugging her a long time.

"That's *her*!" Jacek whispered excitedly. They hid behind bushes located across the street from the church. He handed his telescope to Schultz. "Watch. She's the one getting all the attention."

"Shall we arrest her?" Schultz peeked around a tree.

"Let's wait until she's alone."

"Papa's not here." Hetty cast a bitter glance toward her mother as they stood outside the church. "Why am I not surprised?"

"He wanted to come, but something came up at the office," said Henriette, hugging her daughter tightly. "Your father liked Karl."

"Let's not pretend." Hetty stepped back from her mother's embrace. "Papa will never stop hating me, no matter what he thinks of Karl."

"Maybe he'll learn to forgive when the war is over," said Henriette in a soothing voice.

"I'm not sure I will." Hetty stared down the sidewalk to the corner of the building where Kees promised to wait for her. Then she hugged her mother briefly and walked away briskly in the opposite direction, where she had parked her bicycle.

Moments later, Hetty made a left turn and pedaled down an empty side street. The cool air felt good on her face.

Suddenly her handlebars were jerked from her grasp and two strong hands seized her around the waist.

"Help!" Hetty screamed, looking around wildly for assistance. A face appeared briefly in a window across the street; then it disappeared behind the curtains.

Jacek put his hand over her mouth. "Now we'll get some answers about Lieutenant Hess."

Hetty's bicycle clattered to the sidewalk as the two SS soldiers dragged her toward their sedan. Desperate, Hetty bit Jacek's hand as hard as she could, sinking her teeth into his flesh. She was rewarded with a slap that rattled her teeth. Her lip began to bleed.

"Help! Help me!" Hetty dug her heels into the pavement, using all her strength to resist getting into the car, but her captors pushed her, inch by inch, toward their objective. A woman stepped out of a nearby building, but she scurried back inside at the sight of SS uniforms.

Jacek opened the back door of the sedan with one hand, clutching Hetty tightly with the other. "Shut up, stupid girl," Jacek snarled.

Breathing hard, Hetty gripped the handle of the door, her last anchor, but Schultz pried her hand loose. Jacek slammed the door, leaving her alone in the back seat. Panting, disheveled, and in shock, Hetty put trembling fingers to her bleeding lip.

Carefully, she chanced a look out the car window. Jacek stood only inches away, his eyes focused on something behind the car. Hetty took a deep breath and with trembling hands found the cyanide capsule in her pocket. Outside, Jacek and Schultz seemed to be arguing. Hetty stared at the pill, then popped it into her mouth. The words Kees said when he gave her the suicide tablet echoed in Hetty's mind: *Just bite down, and the war will be over quickly for you.*

Blam!

A gunshot startled Hetty. She spat the pill into her hand, satisfied that she had not crushed the ampoule to release the poison, and looked out the car window. Jacek was on the pavement, blood spurting from his head. Ears ringing from the gun blast, Hetty used the car door to push Jacek's body aside, making an opening large enough for her to squeeze through. She stumbled to her knees and threw the cyanide pill into the gutter.

"Fraulein!" She looked up. Schultz stood three feet away with a smoking pistol in his hand. Slowly, Hetty put her hands in the air, wishing she still had the cyanide.

"There will be tribunals after the war," said Schultz, holstering his pistol. "Maybe you will tell them I saved your life." He walked briskly down the sidewalk and disappeared down an alley. Hetty stared after him in shock, still trembling next to Jacek's body.

CHAPTER 26

"IF YOU FALL DOWN, THEY will shoot you," whispered an emaciated woman, who limped alongside Mimi as they joined the column of twenty-eight thousand prisoners leaving Buchenwald camp near Weimar. Mimi did not respond, preferring to save her energy for the march, which had no known end. They trudged eastward—*toward Czechoslovakia?* she wondered. The date was April 6, 1945, but Mimi had lost track of the calendar long ago.

The next day, Mimi's companion collapsed from exhaustion and was shot where she fell.

Life in Buchenwald and the other camps had been hard. Death was routine, and Mimi could not remember a day when she wasn't hungry. Nevertheless, always, each day was invested in living until the next. So she kept walking, step after weary step, for a few more days, when a woman ahead of her faltered. Mimi moved to the opposite side of the column and watched. There was no moon, so the woman appeared only as a shadow when she collapsed. When the guard turned his back to dispose of the person he viewed only as a whimpering heap, Mimi made a slight right turn into the woods. Two other prisoners followed her. The guard did not notice; he chambered a round in his rifle and shot the woman who had fallen.

By the time the guard realized that three of his prisoners were gone, Mimi and her companions were deep inside the dark forest of beech-wood trees. Too tired to sound the alarm, the guard trudged forward with the prisoners who remained in the column.

Once inside the woods, Mimi and the others headed west. None of them spoke. Unable to see in the darkness, the group of escapees stumbled with their arms outstretched for three hours before they stopped to rest.

At first, the voices they heard were too far off to distinguish. Were they Germans giving chase? Mimi and the others hid themselves as best they could, trying not to fall asleep.

Then Mimi heard the voices more clearly. They spoke English. "They are Americans!" Mimi exclaimed in Dutch. Her companions showed no sign of comprehension. So she repeated it in French. "*Ils sont americaines!*" Then Mimi shouted in English, "Over here! Over here!"

The American soldiers ran toward the sound of Mimi's voice, carrying flashlights. "What the hell?" said a sergeant, who was first on the scene. At five feet tall, Mimi was so emaciated that the soldiers thought at first that she was a child.

"We are prisoners from Buchenwald," Mimi whispered in English before she collapsed to the ground. "Please help us."

The soldier lifted Mimi like a feather and carried her to his jeep. He gave her water from his canteen.

Mimi took a sip. "Can I have more?"

"Have all you want," said the American.

Mimi drank deeply, then vomited. "Sorry." She wiped her mouth with the back of her hand. "We don't usually get so much water." The other prisoners arrived, and Mimi told them in French that they were safe.

"Are you French?" asked the American.

Mimi shook her head. "Dutch. But I have a cousin in France who will be glad to see me."

The Germans had surrendered, and the leaves had started to turn in the Voorschoten neighborhood when Kees stopped by the cottage where Hetty still lived. She answered the door blank-eyed. Kees held out a bottle of whiskey, but Hetty only turned and lumbered wearily to her bedroom and an open suitcase on the bed.

"What do we have to celebrate?" she called out listlessly, eyeing a photo of her brother on the nightstand. "Can you believe I don't even have a photo of Karl?" she lamented. "Such a simple thing, but we never had time."

Kees followed, two glasses of whiskey in hand. "How about—" He furrowed his brow, pretending to think deeply. "How about we celebrate that we fought evil and won?"

She took the proffered whiskey. "Maybe we should celebrate how much I drink and smoke now," she said ironically, swallowing the contents of her glass in one gulp.

Kees brightened when he saw the open luggage on her bed. "So are you coming with me to visit Mimi after all?"

Hetty shook her head. "I leave tomorrow for that school in Switzerland I told you about," said Hetty, folding clothes into her suitcase.

"Right," said Kees, pausing to remember. "Chatelard? The British boarding school."

Hetty nodded. "It will be hard enough to teach French to fourth graders when I can barely look after myself." She sat forlornly on the bed. "I'm too broken to help Mimi right now."

"Take your time," said Kees, putting his arm around her. "I'll say hello to Mimi for you."

Hetty reached in a drawer and extracted a blood-stained blouse. "I don't remember why I kept this." She threw the bloody garment in the trash, ending her connection to Jasper, the dog whose blood adorned her garment.

"We both have memories we'd sooner forget." Kees brightened. "Here's something to cheer you up. Your friends from Czechoslovakia, Daniel and Hanna, are alive. They ended up in a Swiss refugee camp."

"I'll celebrate that," said Hetty, perking up. "Yacov won't be an orphan."

Hetty started to reach for her whiskey, when suddenly the front door burst open and in the next instant Hetty dove for the floor, breaking a lamp that had survived the war. Breathing hard, she looked up—straight into the worried face of Aldon.

"Oh, it's you." She reached a trembling hand out to touch the boy's cheek. Aldon gave Hetty an embarrassed smile as Kees helped her up.

"It's OK, Hetty. It's OK," Kees crooned to her softly.

"You're bleeding." Aldon said, touching a finger that was cut by her shattered lamp. He handed Hetty a handkerchief, and she wrapped her finger in it. Kees smiled encouragingly at Aldon over her head.

"I like your house," said Aldon brightly. He plopped down in a stuffed chair as though he'd lived there all his life.

"How did you get here?" Hetty asked, still shaken up.

"I took the train to Leiden and hitched a ride from the station with one of your neighbors," said Aldon.

"I wish I could see more of you," said Hetty, casting a dismayed gaze at the broken lamp.

"Hetty's determined to teach French to British kids in Switzerland," said Kees, bringing a broom from the kitchen to clean up the shattered glass. "She leaves tomorrow."

"Since she's leaving, can we live here?" Aldon asked excitedly, his head turning right and left to inspect the room before he turned his attention back to Hetty. "Kees is going to adopt me. Can you believe it?"

"What?" Hetty exclaimed, scurrying to Aldon for a hug. "That's great news!"

"He freeloaded off me for so long that we decided to make it official," said Kees, his face aglow. "I put in the paperwork last week."

"Even more to celebrate." Hetty refilled her glass and raised it for a toast. "Will it feel good to have a home again, Aldon?"

"I have to find a pretty woman for Kees to marry first," said Aldon with his dimpled smile. "When Kees is my father and we live in this house, I'll still need a mother, don't you think?"

"Absolutely," Hetty laughed. "Kees will be a good catch for some lucky woman."

"Leave the wife-hunting to me, Aldon," said Kees, joining the laughter.

The train lurched as it left the station, startling the baby awake. "Shhh." Mieke tried to quiet the infant in her lap. "Mommy's here." But the baby continued to fuss.

"I am glad you're able to visit Chatelard," said Hetty. "I've actually enjoyed my fourth graders these past two years. Such a beautiful setting for a school."

Mieke squeezed her friend's hand. "Did you hear about the judgments entered against collaborators?" asked Mieke, rocking the baby gently with no success. "Your father's friend Reiner received a long jail sentence."

"Here, let me try." Hetty adjusted herself to accept the hand-off of

Mieke's son. "Reiner should have hanged," said Hetty, soothing the infant against her shoulder. "Some say that nearly three-quarters of Dutch Jews who lived here when the war began were dead when it ended. Reiner helped kill them by giving Dutch population records to the Germans."

Hetty stared coldly out the window of the train while she hummed a lullaby to sooth herself as much as the baby. "My father deserved to be punished too—for turning me in to the Germans if nothing else. He just denied it and got off scot-free."

Finally, Mieke's son fell asleep.

"You're a natural, Hetty," said Mieke, taking the sleeping baby in her arms. "What was that song?"

"Sussje sang it to me the day my brother died." Hetty smiled sadly at her friend.

Mieke peered out the window as the train pulled into Bern, the last stop before Chatelard School. "Do you miss the resistance?"

"It's just something I did once."

"But it was such an adventure," said Mieke. "I wish I had your courage."

"Not an adventure," Hetty reflected. "When I first joined, my biggest fear was dying. Then I learned that there are worse things than dying, and they kept happening to me over and over."

Both women sat quietly, watching the baby sleep.

Outside Hetty's window, a young man wearing a beret emerged from the waiting area with a small suitcase in his hand. "The train is already moving," said Hetty, clutching Mieke's hand. "You don't suppose he'll try to board?"

"It's sort of thrilling, don't you think?" said Mieke as the man trotted alongside the train as it picked up speed. "He's handsome too." Mieke's eyes twinkled at Hetty.

Hetty fixed her gaze outside, where the man sprinted to match the pace of the moving train. Her heart did a flip when he leaped onto the boarding step, clutching the vertical handrail with one hand, while holding his suitcase in the other.

"He could have been crushed if he'd slipped." Mieke spread her hand over her heart, wincing at the thought.

"He's not from Europe, that's for sure," Hetty chuckled.

"Wait, he's coming our way," Mieke giggled.

Hetty moved across the aisle to an unoccupied bench. The man removed his hat and sat next to her, extending his hand with a warm smile. "Hi, I'm Walter."

Smiling for the first time in weeks, she shook his hand.

"Hetty."

AUTHOR'S
POSTSCRIPT

THIS NOVEL WAS INSPIRED BY the life of Hetty Kraus (1920–1994), a Leiden University student who served in the Dutch resistance. In 1947 Hetty married Walter, the handsome stranger she met on the train. The next year they had a daughter, Jacinta, whom I married in 1972. Together, Jacinta and I assembled the stories told by her mother about her service in the Dutch resistance. The novel is entirely fiction, created from my own imagination, but Hetty's stories are its soul.

One of the accounts that inspired me is a narrative written by my mother-in-law about her 1982 reunion with a resistance friend who spent time in the camps. With minor edits, I share excerpts of it here.

The Americans found Mimi and a few dazed survivors hidden in those beechwoods, from which Buchenwald got its name. Our homeland, Holland, was still in German hands, so she was sent back to France, to her relatives at Plaisance, to recuperate. She never regained her health, and she never left Plaisance again.

Mimi had turned inward, with only her husband for company. He remained a lifelong invalid after three years in a death camp. They learned to forgive and forget together.

After the war ended for me, I escaped to the ends of the world, always choosing high open places to live so I could see the enemy coming and flee in time to new high places.

I'd learned during the war that man is the murderous animal, he pursues and kills for fun. While everyone around me was imprisoned or killed during those three last endless years of war, they never caught me; but then, I was always on the wing, always in flight. I've never stopped running since and have never found the time to forgive.

Mimi had written prior to my visit in 1982: "You'll find the gate locked. We have become modern too. These days burglars come in moving vans to clean out a castle in a few hours. Just stop at the gatekeeper's lodge and honk your horn."

This gave me time to admire the splendid pikes and spikes of the Plaisance gate, which I barely noticed on my first visit.

Madeleine, the gatekeeper, hadn't changed at all. When I was twenty-three, she had seemed very old—like sixty maybe?

"Madeleine, enchanted to see you; still opening these heavy doors, *hein?*"

"It keeps me young, Madame."

"How old are you now, Madeleine?"

"Next year I'll be a hundred years old," she answered proudly.

So she had been sixty then! How well I remembered the

ten-foot-high hedges that kept the castle hidden from the road. Then I saw Plaisance, smiling mistress of the sun, returning her lover's gaze, glowing under his caress.

It was good to see the courtyard with the pigeon tower again. It was Mimi's courtyard now, for she inhabited the servant quarters at Plaisance.

The pigeon tower still held the courtyard under its protection. It was learning to live with a swing set, a bone of contention between Mimi, doting grandmother, and Francois, lord of the castle, who called it "my cousin's abomination."

God, she looked old in that green morning light. She had been such a lovely girl. Now the tragic beauty of the Delphic Sibyl looked through her eyes, the wisdom and resignation of one who had seen millennia of evil.

"Mimi, how long did it take you to accept evil as normal?"

"Not long," she answered. "In my first camp in Saarbrucken, we were housed next to a penal camp for men. Their punishment was to crawl on hands and knees, always."

She looked at me through those beautiful green eyes. Her hair was streaked with gray now. "You know how Germans use the word 'Schweinehund,' pig dog? In that camp the prisoners had to act like dogs; they could never walk upright again, never speak again, only bark. They had to sit up and beg for their food and then slobber it from troughs. They were whipped twice a day and slept in kennels two feet high."

Her face wore an intense sadness while she related these things to me. "The Germans would goose step around them and laugh. When you see real pigs and real geese, they are so beautiful and innocent," she sighed. "It's good that you came. I have never spoken of this before, not even to Peter."

Peter, her husband, had died six years earlier, after thirty years of marriage. They had one child, a daughter. And now she has grandchildren!

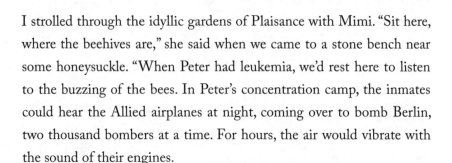

I strolled through the idyllic gardens of Plaisance with Mimi. "Sit here, where the beehives are," she said when we came to a stone bench near some honeysuckle. "When Peter had leukemia, we'd rest here to listen to the buzzing of the bees. In Peter's concentration camp, the inmates could hear the Allied airplanes at night, coming over to bomb Berlin, two thousand bombers at a time. For hours, the air would vibrate with the sound of their engines.

"Like the buzzing of these bees, only immensely louder. Peter told me about the joy they felt, thinking of all the Germans who were going to die that night. It was their hatred that kept those prisoners alive. Peter would say, 'If only I could still hate like that maybe I could stay alive now.'

"But he was too old to hate," said Mimi with a sigh. "The leukemia had made him transparent and as emaciated as when I saw him for the first time on the freedom train that took us back to France."

While we walked up the winding path toward the castle, I asked, "What did you and Peter love most about Plaisance?"

She stretched her arms wide, "It was the solitude," she said. "In camp you were never alone. In our barracks five hundred women slept in two-tiered rows of bunks, four in each twin-sized bunk, and every-one had diarrhea.

"You had to run the length of this castle and cross the drive and where you see the white front door of my house, that's how far away the bathhouse was. It had forty washbasins and twenty toilets for two thousand women!

"Oh, the bliss of a heated house to come home to, where you sleep alone, and go to the bathroom alone. A house that doesn't smell bad, cool in summer and warm in winter, all this and our pigeon tower too."

"Did you love the food and wine when you came back?"

Mimi pondered. "Not really. I had stopped caring about food."

It was the honesty that made us feel good.

The next day we went to a nearby village. "Look at all that merchandise in the street," said Mimi. "It's safe, untouched. In camp everything got stolen."

It was true. There is no honor among thieves, and without honor life loses its value.

"Those schoolboys in our local market look at that jewelry store just for fun," said Mimi. "But in camp girls their age snatched the one piece of bread a day from old women too weak to defend themselves. Moments later young women would rip the only pair of shoes off those same girls' feet. Stealing becomes a vicious circle in the camps."

"Let's buy chocolates for my grandchildren," said Mimi. "They are coming tomorrow. Don't those bonbons look charming? This time of year, candy stores make them in the shape of acorns to celebrate fall. We'll buy some snails too, they're almost the last of the season," she added.

I asked, "Do your grandchildren like snails?"

Mimi laughed. "Are you kidding, snails are much too expensive for kids."

While we turned into the driveway, she spoke. "I just remembered," said Mimi as my rental car took us into the driveway. "My daughter wants you to take a picture of me and her children tomorrow, and they want to be taken on the front steps of the castle. Would you?"

Who wouldn't want to take young France against a background of old France? They made a charming tableau vivant against the typical Henri Quatre wall of masonry panels encased in brick.

The kids and their parents came almost every weekend. All Paris apartment dwellers hunger for the countryside and how lucky can you get if you have a grand-mère who lives there? The girls, eager to be photographed, said they hoped I was *une feministe americaine* and asked if I would take their picture, just this once, without their brothers.

I remember the frost hit early that year when I visited. One morning the upper lake had frozen over. As I sat with my friend, I noticed she looked frail and sick.

"I hate the cold," she shivered as we sipped our tea by the fire in the old stone fireplace that was once used by servants when they lived here.

"When winter came to the camp, people started to die in droves. I woke up one day and the girl next to me was dead. The other two upper-tier bunkmates, who slept on the outside, were gone. I was all alone with the dead girl, on the inside. I had to roll over her to get out. She was frozen stiff!"

We continued to chat as I stoked the fire to keep a steady source of heat going.

"People just gave up," said Mimi, taking another sip of her tea. "First, they stopped washing, saying the water was too cold. That was pure nonsense, of course. You could never wash more than your face and hands anyway. But washing meant having pride. Those who stopped soon fell apart."

While we were talking, I noticed there remained some open water in the lower lake at Plaisance on the windy side of the island, where the statue of Pan stood.

An old swan had moved in on the lake, a beautiful creature, sturdy and proud.

"Mimi did you ever feel like giving up?"

"No," she replied. "I knew my mother wanted me to stay alive. You and I and the swan are the strong ones. You know that living is largely an act of will."

"Yes." I knew. "And it didn't always mean you liked living that much after all."

Mimi's face suddenly glowed when she remembered when she was rescued. "Oh, I remember when we were hiding in the woods and we heard those lovely American voices, and we knew we were free. Those gorgeous soldiers took us with them. Imagine, I rode back to liberty in a jeep!

"You know what made me happiest that day? It was the horror and the pity in those Americans' eyes when they saw us."

Walking away from the lake toward the house, Mimi continued. "We had become burnt-out skeletons. In German eyes we had seen only disdain and disgust. In American eyes we saw the greatest tribute of all: the gift of pity."

Driving home from the village the next day, we saw the pigeon tower from afar. Mimi said, "I'm glad you're an American now. They are generous people. Maybe you too will learn to forgive one day. But even if you never will, I'm glad you came to stay with me, to walk and talk in freedom. To share with me what still makes life so good: a fire, nice food, a friend. All this and heaven too."

RESOURCES

FOR THOSE INTERESTED IN READING more on the subject of this novel, here are a few literary sources that I found useful as background: *Soldier of Orange* by Erik Hazelhof, *All the Frequent Troubles of Our Days* by Rebecca Donner, *A Woman of No Importance* by Sonia Purnell, *The Nightingale* by Kristin Hannah, *Three Ordinary Girls* by Tim Brady, *A Bridge Too Far* by Cornelius Ryan, *The Hare with the Amber Eyes* by Edmond de Waal, *The Second World Wars* by Victor Davis Hanson, *The Second World War* by John Keegan, *The Rise and Fall of the Third Reich* by William Shirer, and *Inside the Third Reich* by Albert Speer.

I visited too many online sources to list here. The most helpful was a collection of personal accounts about the resistance, helping downed pilots, hiding Jews, and more: "WWII Netherlands Escape Lines," Bruce Bolinger, https://wwii-netherlands-escape-lines.com.

Other online sources include:

- Emily Retter, "Jewish woman, 98, relives her daring secret life infiltrating Nazi headquarters," *Mirror* (online), September 25, 2020, https://www.mirror.co.uk/news/uk-news/jewish-woman-98-relives-daring-22744278.

- "The Amsterdam General Strike of February 1941," The National WWII Museum, April 10, 2018, https://www.nationalww2museum.org/war/articles/amsterdam-general-strike-february-1941.

- "Dutch Escape Lines," WW2 Escape Lines Memorial Society, https://ww2escapelines.co.uk/escape-lines/northern-europe/dutch-escape-lines/.

- Jan Bos, "Battle of Nijmegen Bridge: Taking the Crossings Over the Waal," Warfare History Network, https://warfarehistorynetwork.com/battle-of-nijmegen-bridge-taking-the-crossings-over-the-waal/.

- "Leiden Classics: Leiden University's First Women Students," Universiteit Leiden, February 18, 2014, https://www.universiteitleiden.nl/en/news/2014/02/leiden-classics-leiden-university%E2%80%99s-first-women-students.

- "The Netherlands," United States Holocaust Museum, https://encyclopedia.ushmm.org/content/en/article/the-netherlands.

- Becky Little, "This Teenager Killed Nazis with Her Sister During WWII," History, updated February 22, 2021, https://www.history.com/news/dutch-resistance-teenager-killed-nazis-freddie-oversteegen.

- Alish Lalor, "The Hunger Winter: The Dutch Famine of 1944-45," DutchReview, February 10, 2022, https://dutchreview.com/culture/the-hunger-winter-the-dutch-famine-of-1944-45/.

- Allert M.A. Goossens, "Friday, 10 May 1940—Invasion," War over Holland, updated December 17, 2021, http://www.waroverholland.nl/index.php?page=10-may.

- Matthijs Kronemeijer and Darren Teshima, "A Founding Myth for the Netherlands: The Second World War and the Victimization of Dutch Jews," Humanity in Action, https://humanityinaction.org/knowledge_detail/a-founding-myth-for-the-netherlands-the-second-world-war-and-the-victimization-of-dutch-jews/.

- "Anti-Jewish Measures in The Netherlands and Belgium between 1940 and 1944," Facing History and Ourselves, https://www.facinghistory.org/resource-library/text/anti-jewish-measures-netherlands-and-belgium-between-1940-and-1944.

- Manfred Gerstenfeld, "Wartime and Postwar Dutch Attitudes Toward the Jews: Myth and Truth," Jerusalem Letter, August 15, 1999, https://www.jcpa.org/jl/vp412.htm.

- "'Resistance' Cache Uncovered in the Netherlands," Key Military, April 30, 2020, https://www.keymilitary.com/article/resistance-cache-uncovered-netherlands.

ACKNOWLEDGMENTS

Shortly after Hetty died, a close friend of hers came to our house to deliver an essay that Hetty had written about her brother Jan's role in the resistance. This essay, which Hetty had directed us to see posthumously, inspired my wife and me to explore Hetty's other writings to find the clues she had left behind about her life during the Nazi occupation, and there were many. These writings, plus the stories that Hetty told during the twenty-seven years that I knew her, form the core of *The Lioness of Leiden*.

I could not have written this novel without the tireless efforts of my wife, Jacinta, who helped me remember the details of her mother's stories, which were usually told over a glass of wine when no one was taking notes. Jacinta also sorted through Hetty's writings to find hidden gems that expanded her mother's oral history. Her patience and support were essential as we derived plot lines from what we knew about Hetty's experiences.

I am also grateful for the steadfast support of our children: Kimberly,

Todd, and Brittany; also my son-in-law Nate, who has been a perfect addition to our family.

Jacinta and I visited with the people who inspired the characters of Mimi, Mieke, and Arie, and I am grateful for the time we spent together.

I am also indebted to the wonderful guides we hired locally when we visited Leiden and The Hague. A guide provided by the administration of Leiden University was of significant assistance in developing the story of Professors Meijers and Cleveringa. And we were inspired by the Dutch Resistance Museum in Amsterdam, which has an excellent collection of artifacts from the war.

This novel would not have been possible without the enthusiastic assistance of several writing professionals. A huge shoutout to my developmental editor, Julie Gray, who taught me a master course on writing fiction. Julie was also enormously helpful with the subject matter as she pursues her own journey to introduce a Czech holocaust survivor to the world. I recommend her book, *The True Adventures of Gidon Lev*.

Also, I owe much to everyone at Greenleaf Book Group, especially the editing team—Lee, Diana, Anne, and Melinda—Neil for the cover art, and Dan and Brian for managing everything. I could not have done this without them.

Thank you, Valda, for getting me started on the right path.

Finally, I am grateful for the love and support of my many friends who read my manuscript from its earliest versions. Will, Phil, Carle, John, Jen, Jeud, Bill, Randy, Jimmy, Al, Denise, and Kelly's dad. I love all of you. Thank you.

ABOUT THE AUTHOR

ROBERT LOEWEN was born in Bakersfield, grew up in the San Francisco Bay Area, and raised his three children in Laguna Beach.

A 1970 graduate of Pomona College, Robert served two years in the United States Army, including a tour in Vietnam. His 1972 marriage linked him to Hetty Kraus, his mother-in-law, who told fascinating stories about her experiences in the Dutch resistance during World War II.

After a year serving as a law clerk to Justice Byron White at the United States Supreme Court, Robert returned to California in 1977, where he built a successful litigation practice at an international law firm. Known for his persuasive legal briefs, he has always been a natural storyteller who yearned to write fiction.

Now retired, Robert has published his debut novel, a fictional history of Hetty's life in the Dutch resistance.